The
TELL-TALE
HOMICIDE

The TELL-TALE HOMICIDE

A Rare Books Cozy Mystery

DAPHNE SILVER

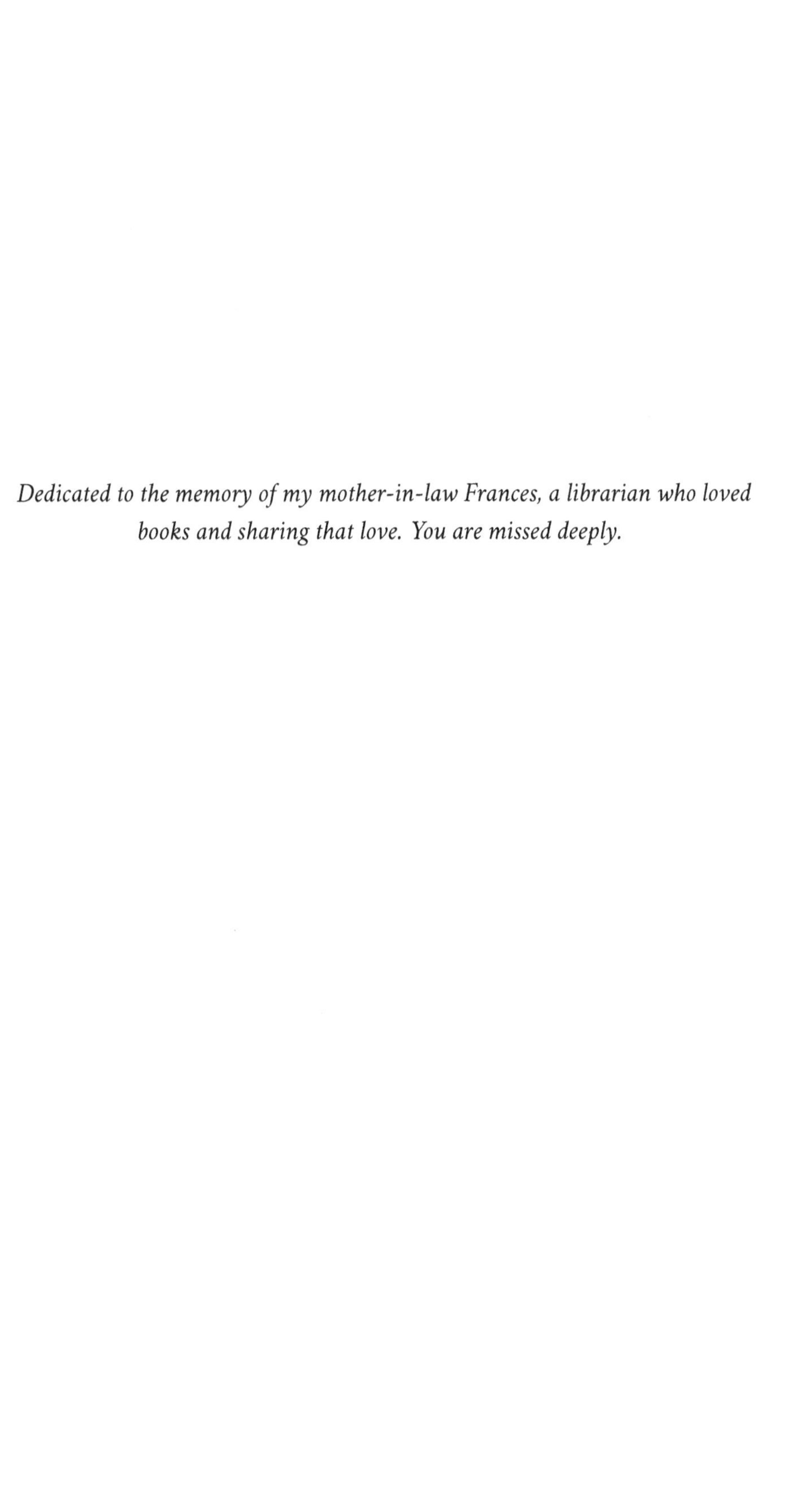

Dedicated to the memory of my mother-in-law Frances, a librarian who loved books and sharing that love. You are missed deeply.

Praise for The Tell-Tale Homicide

"*The Tell-Tale Homicide* by Daphne Silver is as warm and entertaining as a summer vacation on Chesapeake Bay. With Poe references and bloomin' puns galore, librarian-turned-sleuth Juniper Blume's keen research skills and encyclopedic knowledge help decipher the mystery and save the day!"—Olivia Blacke, author of the Record Shop and Brooklyn Murder Cozy Mysteries Series

"Award-winning author Daphne Silver uses her expertise in Maryland history and lore to once again bring a literary-laced murder mystery to life. This time, our intrepid librarian Juniper discovers a rare books mystery relating to Edgar Allan Poe, a one-time Baltimore resident. As twisty and mysterious as Poe himself, this tale will draw you in!"—Rosalie Spielman, award-winning author of the Hometown Mysteries

"Juniper Blume continues to blossom in this page-turning new mystery. I love a mystery with a side of Poe and missing rare books. Silver seamlessly blends in a bit of Maryland history in *The Tell-Tale Homicide*."—Sherry Harris, Agatha Award-nominated author of the Sarah Winston Garage Sale and Chloe Jackson Sea Glass Saloon mysteries

"Daphne Silver does it again! Put off all chores and engagements once you open this book because there is no way you are getting anything else done. Between the wonderfully twisty mystery and the characters you'd love to tag along with, this book will grab you and not let you go until the very last page!"—Misty Simon, author of The Sunny Side Up Mysteries

"After enjoying Daphne Silver's award-winning *Crime and Parchment*, I was eager to return to Rose Mallow on the Chesapeake Bay—where small-town charm is accompanied by long-brewing resentment, protests and politics, and…murder.

"In *The Tell-Tale Homicide*, Silver crafts a new mystery, blending my favorite returning characters with fresh faces that add depth to the tale, each carrying secrets that kept me guessing. I loved tagging along with Juniper as she searched for solutions to the town's problems, risking her job, her complicated relationships with family and friends, and possibly, her life."—Cathy Wiley, Derringer finalist and author of the Fatal Food Festival Mysteries

Chapter One

My four-year-old niece Violet crashed into me in the hallway of the Wildflower Inn in Rose Mallow, Maryland. She was coated in white powder with thick clumps of something red smudged across one cheek. A ghostly trail of footprints followed behind her, as did my dog, Clover. He eagerly licked at the floor before darting over to us.

"Are you okay?" I ran a finger across her cheek to check the unknown substance. Sure enough, it was as I suspected: strawberry jam.

She smiled proudly and held up a spatula. "I'm helping Mommy."

"Oh?"

"Come on, Auntie Juniper."

"Sweetie, I'm running late for my new job. Plus, I'm already dressed," I said, not wanting to coat my retro dress in flour and jam. Violet ignored my protests. She grabbed my hand with her sticky fingers and led me to the back kitchen. I debated arguing further, but my curiosity won out. Not to mention my stomach rumbling. I'd figured I'd skip breakfast to save time, but that was before I caught the scents wafting down the hallway.

The kitchen resembled a crime scene. Flour splattered the walls, floors, and my normally fastidious sister, Azalea. A small mountain of cracked eggshells towered over their bowl on the countertop beside several empty milk containers. There were trays of decadently delicious-smelling food everywhere. Violet climbed up onto her booster seat and dug into a plate of something that smelled far better than it looked. Clover sat at her feet, waiting for Violet to inevitably drop crumbs. He didn't have to wait long.

"Don't you need to leave?" Azalea asked.

"Well, yeah, but I think I can manage…" I checked the clock on the kitchen wall. "Uh, maybe two minutes?" That was pushing things. I shouldn't be late on my first day. Being the new boss, I probably should have arrived early. Set a good example. I shook my head. What do they say about best-laid plans? Besides, my stomach put up a noisy battle.

"How'd you sleep?" she asked.

"Beautifully. That bed is spectacular. And there's actually room on those antique nightstands for all five books I'm reading." I was staying at my sister's boutique inn until I found a place of my own.

"Five?" she repeated.

"I started with one, but it created rabbit holes." When I could see she didn't understand me, I explained further, "I read a book about Edgar Allan Poe in Baltimore, which made me wonder about the city at the time he was living there in the 1830s, so I grabbed a couple of books on Maryland in the early nineteenth century. Meanwhile, I was curious about what other authors were doing at the same time as Poe, so I'd picked up a piece on that."

"Not rabbit holes. You have shiny bird syndrome," Azalea said with a laugh.

"What?"

"You're like a magpie with research, Juniper. I mean, I get it. There's so much out there to explore. But you jump from item to item. Will you ever finish any of these books?"

"Eventually," I said. "That's why I get most of my books from the library. Forces me to finish them in a timely manner. And to not spend millions of dollars." I recognized I had a reading problem, but with these guardrails, I could keep it under control. Usually anyway.

"I love reading too, but not like that. Give me a great, cozy mystery I can escape into. I don't really want my reading pile to resemble that of someone researching their dissertation," she said, shaking her head.

"Oh, really?" I pointed to the stack of opened cookbooks on the kitchen table. Looking down, at least two had fallen to the floor.

She sighed. "Point taken."

"So, what's going on?" I asked.

"Try this," Azalea said, before stuffing a forkful of food into my mouth.

The taste was familiar, but not something I'd had in years. It had a crepe-like exterior with a decadent creamy cheese inside, intermixed with fresh strawberry jam. "Now, be honest, Juniper. What do you think?"

"Oh my goodness, this is heaven. Is it a blintz?" I asked after swallowing.

Azalea nodded. "I'm recreating Nana Z's recipe. But it's not quite right." She shook her head and twirled around to get a forkful of blintz from another tray. There must have been nearly a dozen trays of blintzes around the room. The sink and countertops overflowed with dirty bowls and pans.

"Not quite right? This might be the most amazing thing I've ever had," I said.

She shook her head. "But it's not *hers*. Something's missing. I can't remember." I heard the disappointment in her voice. Our grandmother Zinnia Blume—or Nana Z as we called her—passed away a few years ago, and blintzes had been one of her signature dishes. Like any Jewish *bubbe*, she also made an amazing sweet noodle kugel and the best latkes at Chanukah. I missed her greatly, and I knew my sister shared in my grief.

Azalea had recently converted our grandmother's century-old Queen-Anne-style mansion into the boutique Wildflower Inn. She had painstakingly restored the building while updating it to make luxurious guest rooms, as I could attest. My sister maintained Nana Z's generous garden, overflowing with a colorful riot of anemones, cosmos, and even the start of chrysanthemums now that it was September. The hydrangeas were lush right now, but of course, the best flowers were the zinnias, planted in Nana Z's honor. They provided such brilliant colors: shocking magenta, crisp oranges, and dreamy purples interspersed with bright yellows and warm pinks. Nana Z loved them as much as she would have loved how my sister had renovated the house. Our grandmother's memory influenced everything Azalea did.

I felt somewhat guilty not doing more to honor Nana Z's legacy myself, but at least I was here. For years after she died, I had avoided returning to Rose Mallow, still stricken with grief. However, an incident earlier in the summer had brought me back. Azalea's estranged husband had supposedly found part of an ancient Celtic manuscript in a local cemetery, but he disappeared, and I discovered a body instead. I eventually located him and the killer.

As stressful as it had been, coming back had reunited me with my sister and niece. Plus, returning gave me a new job. Today was my first time overseeing the creation of a new museum from the Calverton family's private collection.

I wasn't sure it was the best move for me. I had never been in charge of staff or a collection before, but I certainly wasn't one to turn down a challenge, especially if it gave me an excuse to be with Azalea and Violet.

Checking the clock, I needed to leave. About ten minutes ago.

I put a hand on Azalea's shoulder. "You'll figure it out. Nana Z would have loved your blintzes." I started for the door when a thought crossed my mind. "How long have you been up to make all these?"

She shrugged. "Oh, not too long. Maybe since four?"

"Four in the morning?"

"I guess so. Not sure," she said with a yawn.

"Why? Testing out a new breakfast for inn guests?" I danced my eyebrows, hoping to offer myself up as a guinea pig for additional taste testing. Checking at the table, Violet certainly approved, and given the globs she dropped on the floor, so did Clover.

"Well, maybe, but that's not the main reason. It's for the Rose Mallow Labor Day Festival. I'm entering the blintzes in the cooking competition. Nana Z won so many times. I'd like to honor her," she said. As kids, Azalea and I used to spend our summers with Nana Z here in Rose Mallow, on the west coast of the Chesapeake Bay in southern Maryland. Held over a long weekend, the Rose Mallow Labor Day Festival had always been a highlight, even if it meant the end of summer before returning to school and our parents in Baltimore afterwards.

"You honor her every day."

"Thank you." She sighed. "But I also had trouble sleeping to begin with."

"Something the matter?" I asked.

She looked as if she didn't want to say anything, so I kept my mouth shut and waited. Eventually, she broke down. "It's Rory."

"Rory?" I was surprised she mentioned her estranged husband. At least they had been less estranged lately. The two had a falling out as Azalea became more involved with the Wildflower Inn, but after he was hurt earlier in the summer, they realized how much they still cared about each other.

"He wants to go on a date."

"That sounds good," I said.

She twisted a dishrag in her hands. "I can't decide. Maybe I should wait a little longer."

"You can do that too."

"But maybe I should try out a date," she said. "Then we can see if we're ready to take another step…and then, maybe…." She started breathing heavily.

I walked over to her, worried she was going to hyperventilate. "Azalea, you're only talking about a single date. That's it. You don't have to think about anything further than that."

"Plus, there's John," she said in a quieter voice. John Torres was a Deputy on the police force. While he and Azalea had never officially gone out, they had made plenty of googly eyes at each other.

"Don't overthink this," I said. "Decide if you want to go on a single date with Rory. Don't think about anything else. Can you do that for me?" I put both hands on her shoulders.

Azalea nodded. "Thanks, Juniper." It was unusual to have my older sister seeking advice from me, but I didn't mind.

She then inspected my outfit. "Oh, but I'm an idiot."

"An idiot?" I repeated.

She waved at me. "I should have said something earlier. Look at you, Juniper. Her dress fits you perfectly." She smiled at the sea-foam green 1940s swing dress I'd found in Nana Z's wardrobe. I'd paired it with an ivory cardigan, thick pearls, and a silver brooch with a B for our last name, Blume. Instead of vintage shoes, I went with a pair of glittery Mary Jane-style Fluevogs, a favorite modern brand of mine. The clunky shoes evoked a retro librarian vibe with a touch of adventure.

"You don't think I look lost in it?" I asked. Both Azalea and I were fairly petite, barely reaching five feet. Although I was a few years younger at twenty-eight, we looked almost identical except for our hair. I sported a slanted bob, while she kept hers longer and wavier, reaching past her shoulders. Phyrne Fisher, the glamorous 1920s private detective star of

Kerry Greenwood's mystery series, inspired my look.

"Are you kidding? You look like a million dollars."

I blushed. "Thanks. That means a lot. I'm feeling pretty nervous."

"Sure, I can imagine. First day at a new job jitters. But I still don't really understand what you're going to be doing?"

"I'm working for the Calverton Foundation."

"How's that different from the Calverton family?" Azalea made a face as she talked. The Calverton family had been in the area for centuries. They were rich and powerful. Like most people in Rose Mallow, Azalea wasn't a big fan of them. I understood her apprehension. The family was aloof and rarely mingled with the townspeople. They ran most of the major businesses, including the bank that managed Azalea's house restoration loans. I'd seen earlier in the summer that her finances weren't doing great, which was another reason I'd returned. I wanted to help however I could.

"The family created the foundation to manage their charitable operations. That includes developing a new museum based on their extensive archives and collections."

"And you're going to run that museum?"

I nodded. "Creating it from the ground up. I'm both excited and overwhelmed." I tapped my fingers on the kitchen table. "I'm not even thirty. Honestly, I'm not sure I can manage this type of project."

"You'll do an amazing job. You left the Library of Congress for this position. You're an expert rare books librarian, and you know how organizations like these operate. Plus, you've got a good head on your shoulders." She put her hands on both my shoulders in reassurance before lifting them quickly. "Oh no. Did I mess up your dress?" Since there wasn't a mirror in the kitchen, I twirled around for Azalea while she inspected my outfit. She breathed a sigh of relief. "You look great."

"That's good. I better get going. You'll be okay with Clover today?" My dog looked up at me when I said his name, but didn't leave Violet's side.

"Pretty sure he's Violet's best friend," she said with a laugh. "And I'm also pretty sure he's ready to help me clean the entire kitchen. Did you want to take some blintzes with you for lunch?"

"Leo's treating me today to celebrate." My cheeks burned slightly.

"Is he?" Azalea's shoulders danced. "So you're dating?"

"I'm not dating my boss. This is a business lunch to welcome me onboard. That's all," I said. At thirty, Leo Calverton was the oldest of the Calverton siblings. The museum was his passion project, filled with items and books from his ancestors. While the museum would focus on their artifacts, he also funded current archaeological digs across the globe, like many of his grandparents had. His biggest dream was to discover a lost cultural treasure and share it with the world.

Unfortunately, he hadn't much success yet, so making this museum successful was important to him. And to me. That he'd entrusted me with this project was both amazing and nerve-wracking. I wanted to do a good job for him, his family, and all of Rose Mallow. I took a deep breath and focused back on Azalea.

"Uh-huh," said Azalea. She obviously didn't believe that I wasn't seeing Leo. I made a face. It was bad enough that he and I had already been on a date once before. I didn't want people to think that he was the only reason I'd gotten the job, even if I sometimes wondered that myself. Between the negative local opinion of the Calverton family and the potential accusations of nepotism, I worried I hadn't gotten myself in over my head entirely. But I'd seen the collection, which deserved to be shared with the public. Being part of that meant a lot to me.

I glanced at my vintage watch, which had also been Nana Z's. The beauty was white gold with an Art Déco-styled design. "I need to get going. I don't want to be late."

"See you tonight. Good luck, Juniper!"

Chapter Two

The Calverton Estate was massive. More than a single office, the estate comprised a college-like campus of rock-hewn buildings. Each building housed a different headquarters for the family's various projects, including the Calverton Bank. They called the umbrella company Calverton Industries. Everything was Calverton this and Calverton that. They needed some more originality. I suspected the museum would be more of the same. Maybe I could push back and suggest something more unique.

Somewhere inside the complex was the family's grand home, but I hadn't seen that yet. My new office was inside the archives and collections building, all the way out near the golf club at the back of the campus. I drove towards the gates in my 1965 Karmann Ghia convertible. Painted robin's egg blue, I'd nicknamed my precious roadster "KG." As I drove closer, I noticed a sizable group of people in front of the gate. However, they were off to each side, as if watching a parade. Were they here to welcome me on my first day?

As I came closer, I saw they carried signs with sayings like "Go Away!" and "No Port Chesapeake!" My heart dropped into my stomach. The group was protesting the Calverton family's efforts to replace historic Rose Mallow with a high-end development called Port Chesapeake. I wasn't a fan of the idea either, which I thought would destroy the charm and character of the town, but I hoped to affect change from within the foundation.

I'd originally planned on parking inside the complex, but with the protest so close to the gates, I didn't see how that was possible. Instead, I parked in the back corner of the guest parking lot outside the gates, as far from the group as possible.

I wondered if I could somehow slip inside without being noticed. I waited for other people to show up, but no one did. I checked my watch. I was horribly late. I'd have to go in now through the frenzy.

I pulled my petite self up as large as I could muster. As I walked up, someone thrust a sign into my hands, but I pushed it back and shook my head. I didn't want trouble, but the protester must have realized I wasn't part of their group. He was a large, burly man, maybe in his late fifties. Even though it was a scorching morning, he sported a heavy tweed jacket, opened over his wide belly with suspenders holding up his dark pants. He chomped on an unlit cigar and eyed me curiously.

"You part of the Calvertons?" he hollered.

"I want to get to work." I held up my hands in mock surrender.

"Whatcha do here?" he asked in a growl around the cigar. He glared at me. I tried to meet his stare, studying his icy blue eyes and a constellation of freckles peppering below. He'd missed a few days shaving, and his reddish-brown hairline had receded considerably.

"Librarian." It was my default answer. I didn't bother explaining about opening a museum.

"Librarian? Huh. You work with all those old books they have?"

"That's right." I silently cursed how unsteady my voice sounded.

"Ever been to Boardwalk Books?"

That answer shook me.

"Not since I was a teenager," I replied. Boardwalk Books was, as the name suggested, a used bookstore on Rose Mallow's boardwalk, overlooking the Chesapeake Bay. I used to go all the time when I spent summers here in high school. "Is it still open?"

He scoffed. "Barely. No thanks to the Calvertons. I've seen their plans for the town. They want to replace all the boardwalk businesses with high-end nonsense. Turn their noses up at a used bookstore." He studied me, as if I were a quiz. Then he asked, "What's a librarian doing with the Calvertons?" He drew out the family name as if it were a sneer.

"Working with their special collections. It's my first day." I wasn't sure if sharing that would garner sympathy. I wanted to get around him, but his gigantic frame blocked my way.

"Girl like you shouldn't work with scoundrels like them. Hiding away all their expensive books like misers hoarding gold."

"They're opening a museum to share with everyone," I replied.

His eyes grew wide, but then they squinted into thin rows. He wagged a finger in my face. "You better learn that the Calvertons do nothing just to 'share with everyone.' Unselfishness isn't something they understand."

I didn't know how to reply. He shook his head. "You work for the Calvertons. You remember that you're not any better than they are."

"Hey, wait, that's not fair…"

"She's one of them," he shouted. Suddenly, people surrounded me. Voices blended together. I wasn't sure what they were saying, although I could tell it wasn't good.

Someone threw something bright red and powdery at me. I sneezed several times. I worried about the stuff destroying my grandmother's dress.

People chanted. This time, they chanted in unison, and I could easily understand. "Rose Mallow, Rose Mallow, Never Cheap and Never Shallow!"

I couldn't tell how many people were in the group, but it felt like dozens, maybe more. I thought I recognized a few faces, but I had been away from the town for so long that I couldn't be sure.

The crowd converged upon me. I rarely felt claustrophobic, but everyone surrounding me made everything inside me tight and on edge. I wasn't sure how many there were closing in. I heard my heart beating.

Someone yelled at me for being a "Calverton con." My breathing quickened, and my body tensed. As people crowded around me, I felt hot and sweaty.

Someone else grabbed at the pearls around my neck. I couldn't see them, but I screamed out to let go. I clutched the necklace hard, not wanting to lose Nana Z's necklace. It was ironic, given she would have been the first to lead such a protest. She had been deeply proud of her adopted town and had a strong social activist drive. But I didn't have time to ponder the irony now. I needed to escape.

Chapter Three

Someone grabbed me by the arm and ushered me through the gauntlet of hecklers. When we reached the other side of the mob, I saw my escort was a man a few years younger than me. Maybe twenty-four? A guard joined us, taking my other arm, and led us through the gate. I wondered where he had been a few feet ago. Had he not realized I worked here? I shook my head and smoothed down my dress. I touched my neck and was relieved to find my necklace had survived unscathed.

Once we reached the other side, the guard disappeared back to his post.

"You okay?" the young man asked.

"Fine, I think. You?"

He shrugged. "Could've been worse. There was one day, they'd lit a small fire, and I thought it'd get out of control. The authorities came for that one, and at least they haven't tried that again."

"Why didn't the guard do anything?" I asked.

The young man shrugged. "From what I've heard, as long as the protesters stay back some distance and don't touch anyone, there's not much anyone can do."

"But they grabbed my necklace." I was ready to march back to the guard and give him a piece of my mind. Not that I wanted to go anywhere back near the crowd.

"Maybe you were off the property?"

"Doesn't the parking lot count as Calverton property?"

"I don't know. I'm new," he said.

"How long will they be here?" I looked over my shoulder. The protesters were going strong outside the gates. I'd deal with the lack of security later when I didn't need to be back near them. I could complain to Leo when I saw him.

He smiled. "Oh, that I know. They're gone before 10 am. They harass anyone coming in. I haven't seen them in the evening. And they're not here every day. Once a week."

I wiped again at my dress and at my hair. Whatever they had tossed on me was small and dark red, like dust, but it had a strong smell. The scent was familiar but so overwhelming that all I could do was sneeze again.

"Rose Bay," he said.

"What?"

"They threw Rose Bay seasoning on us," he replied. I noticed he also wiped the spice off his polo shirt and khaki pants. He waved his glasses around, clearing the specks off.

"What is Rose Bay?" I asked.

"My mom told me about it. She's a baker. Couple years ago, the Calverton family tried to get into the spice business. They made their own version of Old Bay seasoning and called it Rose Bay. Never took off, but I guess there's still some around."

"That's weird."

He shrugged. "Yeah. The protesters say it's about the Calvertons ripping off Maryland values."

"Guess it's better than paint." At least it was nothing a shower and a dry cleaner would take care of. "But I suppose it makes some sense for a statement like that." I paused and thought about the use of the spice as an element of protest. I knew a lot about history, especially Jewish Maryland history, given my love of books and my family's background. "Did you know a German Jewish refugee who escaped Nazi Germany created Old Bay?"

He adjusted his glasses. "I didn't know that. Incredible."

"Gustav Brunn had been a spice maker in Germany. When he came to Maryland, he couldn't keep a job because of antisemitism, so he opened his own business: the Baltimore Spice Company." I hoped I sounded more impressive than rambling. Many people shut up when they're anxious, but I talked more. Talking felt like opening a release valve on a pent-up steampipe.

"And he created Old Bay as part of the Baltimore Spice Company?"

I nodded.

"Then you must be Juniper Blume," he said.

"How'd you figure that out?"

"I heard my new boss was a walking encyclopedia of history, especially about Maryland." He thrust out a hand, which I shook happily. His description touched me. "I'm Eric Gutierrez, your new collections technician."

"Eric, it's a pleasure to meet you," I replied. "How long have you been with the Calverton Foundation?"

"A few weeks."

"There you are!" The voice came from behind us. I turned on my toes to see Leo Calverton, my new boss. My stomach flip-flopped at the sight of him. Although only a couple of years older than me, his dark hair featured a single brilliant stroke of silver. He wore a well-tailored suit that fit nicely to his sculpted body. I held my breath, trying to stop noticing how handsome he was.

He's your boss, I reminded myself.

"Mr. Calverton," Eric squeaked. I bit back a giggle at his obvious nervousness. The men were likely less than a decade's difference in age, but I doubted that mattered much to my young and enthusiastic staffer. When you're new, talking with your supervisor's billionaire boss can be intimidating.

Leo tapped his bottom lip before snapping his fingers. "Eric, right?"

"Yes! That's right. Eric Gutierrez." He looked shocked that Leo knew his name.

"Gutierrez? Are you related to Maria Gutierrez? Who has that amazing panaderia on the boardwalk?"

I didn't think it was possible for Eric to look even more surprised, but he did. "Yes, that's my mother's place. You've been to our family's panaderia?"

My stomach grumbled. Hearing about his mother's bakery made me wish I had eaten more than a few bites of my sister's blintzes earlier. I had seen the Mexican bakery a few times, but I'd yet to go inside. I needed to fix that soon.

Leo nodded. "I often end my morning runs at La Artesa. So many amazing pan dulce. I can't resist her gluten-free sopapillas. And I like how she drips them with agave for me." As a vegan who couldn't eat wheat, I knew Leo must have appreciated the extra effort. The way his eyes twinkled as he talked, I imagined the sopapillas must have tasted amazing.

Eric beamed with pride. "She's an incredible baker. I wish I was as talented, but I spent more time with my head in a book than in the kitchen."

I nodded, understanding exactly what he meant. My sister was the cook and baker between the two of us. I loved old cookbooks, but I couldn't make anything edible from them.

"And you're working with Juniper?" Leo asked.

"Yes, sir. I mean, yes, Mr. Calverton," Eric replied.

"Please, call me Leo."

"Thank you, sir."

I couldn't help laughing. I waved my hand in front of my face as an apology. "Eric, I promise, Leo's a good guy. He doesn't need to be treated special."

"Don't tell him that," said Leo with a wink.

"No way. I'm not lying to my staff on day one."

"What about day two?" he asked.

"No promises," I replied.

The three of us walked across the campus to the archives and collections building. It wasn't far, but I didn't look forward to doing it in the rain or snow come fall and winter. Being early September, it was hot, and the humidity was overwhelming. Summers in the Mid-Atlantic could be brutal.

"Quite the perfume you're wearing," Leo said with a small chuckle.

I was confused for a moment, since I hadn't worn any, but then he brushed away some errant Rose Bay from my upper arm.

"Thanks. Your cologne is becoming too," I replied, as I spotted the same burnt red-orange spice across his shoulders. "I got hit with the Rose Bay bombs at the protests."

"Did you get whammied in the protest, too?" Eric asked Leo. "I thought you lived here at the big house. Or had some secret entrance. I'd heard there was an underground tunnel. Or..."

Leo shook his head. "I'm not Batman. I have a small place nearby and come through the front gate, same as everyone else."

"What does the foundation board think about the protest?" I asked.

Leo shrugged. "Honestly, I think they hope if they play ostrich and put their heads in the sand, it'll somehow magically go away."

"I don't think that's going to happen," Eric said.

"Neither do I. But is there anything we can do to change their minds?" I asked.

"I don't know. They don't like to be wrong," Leo replied.

I nodded. "We need to think creatively. There's got to be some way that reminds everyone how important your family has been to the community. And maybe that way can also remind your family how important the community has been to them."

Leo smiled. "I knew there was a reason I hired you. Let me know when you come up with a plan, and I'll make sure it gets green-lit."

My cheeks flushed from his praise, and I gulped a little, noticing his dimples. Why did my boss have to be so attractive? I steadied myself. I was going to be a professional. I didn't want people thinking the only reason I had this job was because of Leo. They needed to know that I could do it.

"Here we are," said Leo as we walked into the archives and collections offices. I felt the stress instantly lift from my shoulders. The library was my happy place. Beyond a small foyer was a sizable reading room, filled with long wooden tables, comfortable chairs, and individual reading lights. Bookshelves lined the walls, filled to the brim with leather-bound volumes. There was a narrow iron staircase leading to the library's mezzanine level. At one end of the wall was a large window, looking over the expanse of the Calverton Golf Course. The glass was tinted with a UV filter to protect the books and was durable enough so that it wouldn't break from any errant golf balls.

The only thing missing was people. I didn't see a staff person anywhere.

"Where's everyone?" I asked.

"Everyone?" Eric repeated. "Florence is probably in the storage area. She gets here early. But until you came, it's only been the two of us." He headed to a workstation in the back and sat down at a computer.

"Just the two of them?" I looked over at Leo. He shrugged. "There are three of us for the entire collection?" I'd seen the size of the collections storage previously. The care and maintenance of the books and items alone needed more staff, let alone what we'd require to start a new museum. "Aren't there plans for reaching a dozen full-time staff?"

Leo looked down at his shoes. They looked like expensive Italian leather. "Yep, plans. You'll get to build your own department. Eventually."

"Eventually?" How on earth would we maintain the current collections and open a museum to the public with such a small staff? I knew there were many small museums out there. Rose Mallow's own historical society came to mind. However, I didn't imagine most of them had collections that could fill multiple department stores.

"I'm working on convincing the board. It takes time. Now that you're here, it'll help," Leo replied.

"Convincing the board? The foundation board?" I sounded like a parrot.

Leo shrugged. His cheeks warmed. "Not everyone is ready to share the collections widely. Some think they're a waste of time and energy."

"But they invested so much into this building," I said. "And I've seen the storage. It's state-of-the-art."

He nodded. "That all was thanks to my grandmother. She made this possible." He pointed to the bronze letters adorning the mezzanine level that read "The Dorothea Calverton Archives and Collections."

"Can she help us now?" I asked.

Leo grimaced. "No, she can't."

I put a hand to my mouth. "Oh, no, did she…pass away?"

He shook his head. "No, she's taken a 'sabbatical' from our family."

"What does that mean?" Eric asked.

"It means she's upset with how my parents are running Calverton Industries. She's holed up at her own place. Right as we were about to launch this project." He sat in a chair at one of the reading tables and slumped back. I joined him. Eric stood behind me. Leo didn't seem to mind, so I didn't tell him to leave. "I have to apologize, Juniper."

"For what?"

"My grandma was the champion of the museum. Honestly, no one else in the family wants much part of it. They don't want to invest in keeping 'old stuff,' and they certainly don't want to share it with the public. They're a secretive group," he explained.

"But now your grandmother has backed out?" I asked.

He nodded. "Until things improve, she's cut off additional funding. And my money is tied up in other projects, including an archaeological dig we're starting this fall in England. But even if I had access to most of my funds, it wouldn't be anywhere near enough to give what this place requires." He put his hands out in apology. I didn't understand all of his finances, but from what I had gathered, he was given an annual stipend, with most of it allocated to particular charities and projects. Even though he was thirty, his family's money was still governed by his parents. At least he talked so openly with us. I glanced over at Eric, who seemed unaware of how far his jaw had dropped.

Leo continued, "That means we have this magnificent building for the collection, but few staff and even fewer advocates to get this idea off the ground. I'm doing what I can to drum up support, but I don't have her gravitas."

I nodded, thinking about my Nana Z and how much she meant to the community. I wished she were here. She would have been able to rally support easily. I wished I had half the charm and energy she had. I missed her.

"Honestly, I think my parents are holding up my funding because they're upset at her being upset." He rolled his eyes. "Family politics."

"Probably gets worse when you add money into the mix."

He nodded. "So much needless melodrama."

"So, no museum?" I looked back at Eric, whose eyes grew wide behind his glasses. I hoped he wasn't afraid he was about to be fired, although I couldn't help thinking it. Hearing that everything might fall apart wasn't exactly what I had expected. I had imagined so many other nightmare scenarios of being a terrible manager, but not the protest or this.

"There will be a museum, but it might not be what I had originally envisioned. Or what I had promised you. It might be a much smaller place. At least to begin with. I'm sorry, Juniper. I'll understand if you want to go back to the Library of Congress," he said. "I may not have a lot of weight in my family on this project, but I know how to pull some strings in D.C."

I thought about this for a moment. "Smaller might not be such a bad thing. Maybe we could do a pop-up exhibit somewhere. Perhaps that could garner some interest and build support?"

Leo smiled. Deep dimples appeared on the sides of his mouth. My heart skipped a beat. "That's something I really admire about you."

"What?" I asked.

"Your ability to pivot. You're always coming up with new plans, and you're eternally optimistic. I need that. Thank you."

I felt my cheeks flush. I hoped I didn't look like a teenager with a crush, even if that's exactly how I felt. "We'll figure it out, Leo. We'll make it work. Won't we, Eric?"

"Yes, ma'am," he said with surprising enthusiasm.

"Juniper works."

"For whatever it's worth, I'm on your side… Leo." Eric looked uncertain at saying the name, but Leo smiled and nodded appreciatively.

A little alarm went off on his fancy smartwatch. "Okay, well, I need to head off to another meeting. Yay," Leo said. He twirled a finger in the air sarcastically.

"Have fun."

"And I have to apologize," he said.

"For what?"

"I know we were supposed to have lunch today, but my schedule changed last minute, so it'll need to be postponed until tomorrow."

I tried hiding the hurt feelings. It's not like I couldn't manage waiting a single day to catch up with the boss I was definitely not dating. Instead, I mustered up, "No worries. Tomorrow sounds good."

Chapter Four

Not long after Leo left, a young woman waltzed in, carrying a small paper bag. Was this Florence? I put a hand out to greet her, but she blasted past me. My hand remained stuck out into space for a few awkward moments. I plastered a fake smile on, hoping I didn't appear too foolish.

"Eric, you forgot your lunch," she said, thrusting the paper bag at him. She shook her head, but she was smiling.

"Again?" Eric replied sheepishly.

"Again." She handed it to him and gave him a quick peck on the cheek.

I coughed a little too loudly on purpose.

"Brandy, meet my new boss, Juniper Blume. Juniper, this is my girlfriend, Brandy Rivers." She twirled around with a big smile and shook my hand.

"Eric has been very excited about you joining the library," she said. Although I placed Brandy and Eric as being a few years younger than me, Brandy projected a conviction that belied her young age. I fought the tinge of jealousy swirling inside me, as I wished I could boast such a confident attitude.

"I'm excited too. Do you also work for the Calvertons?"

"Me? Work with the Calvertons?" She made a sour face. Eric stared at his feet. "No, I'm with the Rose Mallow Public Library. We may not have all the resources that the Calvertons have, but it's a great library."

"Another book lover," I replied, ignoring her slight at her boyfriend's workplace. As I was discovering, it wasn't exactly an uncommon thought around here. Still, I felt my shoulders lift, and my smile grow a little wider.

It'd been ages since I'd last visited the library here, and I looked forward to getting a new library card. The Calvertons' collection wasn't exactly the kind where you could take home the books. Most places frowned on people borrowing antique books to potentially rip, tear, or stain, let alone lose or destroy.

She nodded. "The library's what brought us together." She and Eric shared a knowing smile.

"Were you in library school together?"

"No," she replied with a giggle. She nudged Eric with her elbow. "Remember?"

He shook his head but was smiling. "Of course I do. There was a fundraiser for the Public Library, and part of it was this competition to see who could carry the tallest stack of books. It came down to Brandy and me—"

"And I won!" she interrupted with a big grin. Eric nodded, looking proud of his girlfriend.

"Nice," I replied. "Librarians are stronger than most people realize."

"Exactly," she said. "I could have taken two or three more books."

"Maybe I'll join in next time," I said. Most people discounted my upper body strength because of my petite stature, but I was used to hauling boxes of large leather-bound books. Not to mention carting around my personal collection. I hadn't even officially moved out of my D.C. townhouse yet, but I'd still brought two suitcases filled with nothing but books with me to the Wildflower Inn. I couldn't part with them.

Brandy nodded. "It'll be good to have some *actual* competition next year. Well, assuming I'm still around here."

"You're moving?"

"Brandy has often talked about seeing the rest of the world. I have promised her that when I save up enough, I'll take her to my parents' hometown in Mexico," said Eric.

"All those stories in the library make you curious to see life beyond Rose Mallow," she said.

I nodded, thinking about my own travel history. I had spent a few years traveling to as many countries as I could. It meant a lot of odd jobs and cheap hostels, but exploring different cultures had been eye-opening. Those experiences drew me to librarian work. I could open any book and travel as often as I wanted.

I was about to say something else, but a bellowing voice interrupted us.

"Eric, do you have that inventory for… Oh, it's *you*. Finally," said an older woman appearing from the back doors, carrying a bundle of stapled papers. She wore all black except for a bright red scarf around her neck. It matched her red earrings. Brandy and Eric's smiles vanished. Were they standing straighter, too? It took little detective work to gather who the additional person was.

"Florence, it's a pleasure to meet you." I extended a hand to her. She sniffed the air first, but eventually took it. Her handshake was limp, cold, and brief. Out of the corner of my eye, I spotted Brandy waving goodbye as she disappeared out of the room, leaving Eric and me with my other employee.

"Ms. Dowd, thank you very much. And we normally begin promptly at nine," Florence replied.

"Well, next time, I'll tell Leo Calverton to hurry." The words slipped out before I could stop them, but I didn't appreciate her acting like she was my supervisor.

Her left eyebrow shot up, but she didn't reply. Instead, she looked at me hard before her gaze traveled down to my shoulders. Instinctively, I started rubbing my arms. Sure enough, tiny reddish flakes of Rose Bay had continued to coat my cardigan.

"If you want to avoid the protesters, arrive before them. They're normally here by eight," she said with a look I couldn't decipher. Was she being helpful or reinforcing the idea I was late? I assumed the former.

"Thank you. I'll adjust my schedule. Now, what were you saying about an inventory?" I asked.

She sighed and waved the stapled papers in the air as if I had asked for an enormous favor. "Eric, aren't you working on the inventory?"

"Yes, I'm about to work on that," Eric replied as he raced across the room to get started on his day.

"No running in the reading room," said Florence. She reminded me of a miserable Sunday school teacher. I half expected her to pull out a ruler and start smacking tables with it.

Eric slowed his pace but continued forcefully to a book cart. Likely left over from yesterday. With only two people working, it probably didn't seem like a big deal to leave projects out in the reading room, but it wasn't a smart practice. I'd have to talk to them about it, but I wanted to get a better feel of current procedures and expectations first.

He pulled a file folder off the top of the archival boxes and brought it back to us. He handed it to Florence, who flipped through the papers inside, adding her stapled copy. I would need to review those staples to make sure they weren't corrosive. I preferred using stainless steel paper clips to keep materials together. Especially since they didn't puncture anything either. But one fight at a time.

"Thank you. That'll be all," she said.

Eric didn't move. He bit on his lips and wiggled on his feet.

"Was there something you wanted to say?" I asked.

"Well…"

"Stand up straight and spit it out," Florence said.

"You see…" He looked at a loss for words. His eyes stared upwards as if he might pull down the phrases he wanted from the reading room ceiling.

"What is it?" I asked, using my gentlest voice.

"Uh…"

Florence shook her head. "I don't have time for this. Either start talking, or I'm leaving." She took a step towards the doors to the back area.

"There are books missing," Eric said in a rush.

Chapter Five

"What?" Florence and I replied at the same time.

"I don't know how big the problem is, but there are several books gone," he said.

"Well, things sometimes happen. When was the last inventory completed?" I asked. I knew of many organizations with substantial collections that spread out their inventories or simply did spot checks. Some smaller places often lacked staff to conduct one at all. The Calverton Foundation's collection seemed to combine the two issues into one enormous problem. There was a massive collection with a gorgeous reading room and storage, but we needed many more staff for proper management. I remembered that Eric had only recently started, which meant that Florence had likely been the only one taking care of everything.

"Let me see," Florence said. She pulled out a pair of foldable reading glasses. "This collection was last inventoried… Only last summer. I conducted the inventory personally. There were no books missing then."

"How many are gone now?" I asked Eric.

He shrugged. "I don't know. Maybe four? I haven't finished yet, so I'm not sure of the scope."

While it sadly wasn't unusual for libraries to lose books over the years, it was surprising to hear if they had been inventoried so recently. "What books have disappeared?"

"I don't know all of them off the top of my head, but I remember there are some first-edition Edgar Allan Poe's missing," he said.

"Do you know which one of his?" I asked.

"*The Tell-Tale Heart, The Cask of Amontillado,* and *Tales* are all I can remember," he said. "I really love Poe's books."

"Okay, let's find out how many books are affected." I turned to Florence. "Even if you conducted an inventory recently, you've obviously been understaffed. It would be far too easy for any books to be misplaced…"

"Misplaced!" Florence said with a huff.

I shook my head. "I didn't imply that you misplaced them. But anyone here could waltz in and pick up a book. You can't be everywhere at once." I remembered when Leo first showed me the extensive collections earlier that summer. During my tour, we ran into his smarmy younger brother Cecil and his girlfriend du jour, searching for a quiet place for a rendezvous. They'd decided that the collections were a perfect spot. I shuddered at the memory. None of us had seen Florence that visit, so it showed how easily others could access the space unsupervised.

She still looked itching for a fight. "I run a tight ship, Miss Blume. It is more likely that our young Mr. Gutierrez needs more adequate training on inventorying procedures."

I glanced at Eric. He shrugged and said, "I always welcome more training, but come on, Juniper's right. We don't have enough staff for this place."

All we got was a "Harrumph" from Florence.

"Florence…" I said.

"Ms. Dowd," she replied. I wanted to roll my eyes but decided that was more teenager than boss-like. I wanted her respect, not to further her indignation.

"Ms. Dowd, why don't you and Eric discuss the inventory more in-depth? I'm sure there's a lot on your plate, but I want to know if these books really are missing and how many others are gone too. Will you oversee the project?"

She took a long moment to respond. I almost expected her to turn me down, but she said, "Yes, of course. I'll get to the heart of the matter. You can expect a report within the week."

"Thank you, Ms. Dowd," I replied. "Okay, now, with all this talk of the collections, I'd really like to get a comprehensive tour of them. See what we're working with." Although I'd been through them once with Leo, I needed to become more familiar with everything if I was expected to oversee the program.

"Certainly," she said. "Follow me."

Florence Dowd and I slipped into the maze of administrative offices behind the reading room. Again, I found the building remarkably expansive for having such few staff. How many would this place need? Maybe dozens? More? My chest burned. I had never overseen anyone, let alone a potentially huge staff. Two people I could manage, but what if it were hundreds?

"And over here is your office," she said. I hadn't been listening. The traditional corner office with glass panes and a view over the golf course. We kept moving.

"This is the loading dock and down to the collections," she continued. We left the offices for the large spaces where the delivery of materials happened. A large overhead door touched the floor. Empty pallets waited. "Keep up, Ms. Blume!"

I turned and saw Florence had entered a stairwell. An elevator also stood nearby, but I joined her on the stairs, heading down into the belly of the building.

If the reading room, offices, and loading dock had been labyrinth-like, they had nothing on the collections storage area. A circuitous hallway connected seemingly endless rooms, filled with gleaming white shelves, holding the eclectic collection generated by generations of Calvertons. At least each door had a large number outside, so there felt like some sense of order. But even so, it felt easy to disappear down here.

I followed Florence inside one of the rooms. "These are primarily the collections of Dorothea Calverton," she said, waving her hands around.

"She's the one the building is named after," I said.

"Correct. Her career involved significant travels across the world, so she brought back materials from every continent."

I surveyed the shelves. While I couldn't peer inside the archival document cases, there were objects carefully laid out on crisp, acid-free paper. I expected artifacts from different cultures, but to my surprise, I found that most items were spycraft: a tiny camera worn by pigeons during World War

I, a shoe with a false bottom containing a radio transmitter, and even an enigma machine that created codes during World War II.

Florence must have noticed me examining the unusual collection, because she commented, "Dorothea Calverton collected a wide assortment of materials. This is only one component. Not surprising to see so much in the way of intelligence items, given the family's multi-national reach. It's not just governments concerned about espionage."

"I see."

"If only she'd allow us to house her personal collection..." Florence's voice wavered.

"We don't have her personal collection?"

She huffed. "We have the cultural material the Calverton family collected over the centuries, but she retains their personal archives: letters, diaries, and so on."

"Interesting. So we only have what they want the public to have access to."

"So it would appear, but determining the nature of the collections is above my pay grade," she replied with a barely concealed sneer. "Come along."

We spent over an hour touring the collections. By the end, I felt a strange twist of being invigorated and drained. Although the objects were fascinating and eclectic, before long, everything blurred together. As did the rest of the afternoon. I ended the day feeling completely exhausted and hoping that my sister wouldn't mind if I taste tested more of her blintzes from bed.

Chapter Six

The next day, I got up earlier, but Azalea was already hard at work in the kitchen. I snatched a few of her blintzes as I headed to work. Some protesters had already arrived, but it was a smaller group. Although their stares remained hard, no one accosted me this time. As I entered the gates, I looked back, spotting the cigar-munching guy from yesterday arriving. I hurried along, not wanting to deal with him again.

As promised, Leo showed up at the library to invite me to lunch. However, I soon learned that he didn't mean a private meal for only the two of us. "The top brass on the foundation board have put together a nice welcome party. Your team should come as well."

I sighed, but knew I couldn't object. I thought Florence might scoff at the suggestion, but she was eager to attend. As was Eric, even if he appeared more nervous at the idea.

"Who are the board members?" Eric asked.

Leo replied, "Mainly, they're staff from different Calverton Industry businesses."

"Are you the only family member on it?" I asked.

"Officially, there are several of us on it, but I'm the only one who actually goes to meetings," he said, not bothering to suppress his frustration.

"How many people are on the foundation board?" Florence asked. I was surprised but pleased she expressed an interest.

Leo thought for a moment. "I'm not sure. We have about a dozen who come frequently. I'll have to check the by-laws to see how big it can be."

We all headed to the restaurant at the Calverton Golf Club for what I hoped would be a quick meal.

Unfortunately, it lasted over two hours. With all the foundation board members who attended, I barely had time to talk with Leo. One particularly obnoxious board member wrapped his arm around my waist without asking before carting me off to meet a cavalcade of people I wouldn't remember.

After shaking myself off from that greasy encounter, I slipped away to the bar to get a glass of ginger ale. The last thing I wanted to do was drink anything questionable during business hours during my first week. However, that didn't seem to stop anyone else. I noticed a couple of board members nearby with large glasses of something colorful. One woman had a deep pink drink, while the other woman's glass was a vivid orange. I could smell the alcohol even from a few feet away. They were involved in conversation and didn't realize I was behind them.

"She looks like she's a teenager," one woman said to the other. She had the deep pink drink.

"I don't think she'll last the year," replied the other with the vivid orange cocktail.

A dreadful feeling swirled in my stomach. I suspected who they were discussing so indelicately.

"Guess it depends on how long Leo keeps her around. I know the family wants him married, but I can't imagine they'd approve of a poor townie like her."

"She's not even local. Her sister has some little motel in the area or something. I heard it's deep underwater, though. Martha will know."

I wondered who Martha might be, but I didn't interrupt their gossip. Both anger and curiosity swept through me while listening to their chatter. I let curiosity win for the time being.

"I can't understand what he sees in her," said the pink cocktail woman.

"She's sort of pretty, I guess. If you go for that *Amelie* look. But that was, like, thirty years ago," replied the orange drink lady.

"Did you see what she wore today? Some strange costume. Not exactly screaming professional."

The orange drink lady laughed and nodded. "Well, maybe Leo has some sort of interest in weird librarians. Everyone has a thing, right?"

They laughed again and clinked their drinks.

Tired of being degraded behind my back, I summoned up my courage and gave a loud "Excuse me" as I pushed through them. It took everything I had not to look back. I hoped they were stunned into silence, but their gossiping reminded me more of the popular mean girls back in high school, who would have laughed at their victim if overheard.

I found a quiet corner of the Golf Club. I sat at a two-top near a large window that, like the reading room, overlooked the golf course, although from a different angle. As I gazed at the scenery, I nursed my ginger ale.

"What are you doing over here?" asked Leo.

"Hiding," I answered truthfully.

Leo laughed. "It can be overwhelming."

I nodded. "Good food, at least. Lots of vegetarian options." Although I wasn't a vegan like he was, I still avoided meat products. I appreciated the spread the staff had put together.

"And it looks like your team is having an enjoyable time." He nodded towards them. I looked over and saw that both Eric and Florence had each engaged in robust conversation with various board members. To my surprise, both were all smiles.

"I'm guessing they don't get many opportunities like this to talk with the leadership," I said. I wondered how many of the so-called "leaders" were as toxic as the mean girls I overheard. It was probably best to keep my staff at a distance from them until I could find out more.

"Probably not. How's it going?"

I shrugged. I wanted to recount my pities at being sucked into a protest with Rose Bay tossed on me, discovering my staff was only two people (and how one of them seemed upset she didn't have my job), and overhearing board members gossip untrue assumptions about me, but I didn't think it'd help anything to put that all on Leo. Instead, I went with the bland "A lot to take in."

Leo smiled and patted my hand. A surge of energy ran up my body, and goose pimples flecked across my arm. I shivered uncontrollably.

"Are you cold?" he asked. "They keep it pretty chilly here." He started taking off his jacket.

I waved him away. "No, I'm fine." I didn't want to tell him how his small touch could produce such a powerful impact on me. Somehow, I'd convince myself to stop liking my boss. Eventually.

"Well, at least it can't get any worse," he said.

"Famous last words," I replied, before taking another sip of ginger ale.

* * *

I left before everyone else, wanting to familiarize myself with the procedures Florence had written up and look through the collection's database. I reassured Eric and Florence to stay as long as they wanted at the party. Leo offered to join me, but I hadn't had a moment to myself all day, so I suggested catching up later.

An indoor glass hallway connected the club to the archives building, but I opted for a leisurely stroll outside. The sun was heavy, but after growing up with the Chesapeake summer, I didn't mind the heat.

"Busy working?"

I looked up to encounter a woman I didn't recognize. She was in her late fifties, tall, and wore a pinstriped suit. She carried a portfolio in one hand and her phone in the other. Everything about her screamed the jet-setting corporate type.

"Heading back to the archives and collections building," I said.

"Ah, you must be the new girl. Juniper something." She waved a finger around as if hooking my last name from the air.

"Juniper Blume," I replied, trying not to sound ticked off at her condescending tone.

"Right, right, Leo's pet project." She tsked and shook her head. Her silvery hair was pulled back into a crisp French twist.

"And you are?" I asked.

"Martha Dresdale."

The name sounded familiar, but I couldn't place it. She looked at me expectantly and then sighed heavily when I obviously blanked on her identity.

"Head of Calverton Bank," she added. "And chair of the Calverton Foundation board."

"Oh."

"'Oh' is right," she said. "Apologies that I missed your little shindig at the Golf Club, but I had important things to tend to."

My face flushed. Even Florence's chilly reception hadn't been so dismissive. The museum—and myself, by extension—were obviously nothing to this woman. I assumed she had been an obstacle Leo must have encountered in getting this project moving.

"Don't you need to run along? Play with those old things?" Her fingers flexed as she spoke, as if disgusted by the idea of anything antique.

"I have work to do," I said. "I'll let Leo know we met."

"You have his ear, do you?" She sounded more interested than a moment ago.

"I do. The museum is an important project to him and the Calverton legacy," I said.

She scoffed. "Is that all you have of him?"

I bit back the urge to shake her. How dare she be so rude to me? Then I remembered the women at the bar. Everything was suddenly clear. The higher-ups obviously saw me as nothing but Leo's pet. It reflected how they didn't have respect for the museum either. Given the billions that the entirety of Calverton Industries brought in, I couldn't understand why they didn't see that this place was important. I wasn't sure why they felt that way about maintaining the family's world-class collection as a way to honor their legacy, but their attitudes were apparent.

The swirl in the pit of my stomach returned, but it was outmatched by the anger coursing like lightning shooting through my limbs. Did these people not understand what they had in their collections? Did they not respect what a privilege it was to be given their trust and care?

"Don't you need to run along? Play with your little bank?" I asked.

Martha looked surprised at my mocking tone. Her perfectly lined right eyebrow arched high into her forehead. A forehead that looked remarkably devoid of wrinkles. Then she smiled. "Well, now, the new girl has some backbone. Okay then."

Was this all a game to her? I didn't care. I decided that I'd had enough and started walking away. I couldn't resist looking back over my shoulder, where she stood, continuing to size me up.

Maybe Florence should have been named director of the upcoming museum. I could have hidden back in the stacks with all the books and away from this high school drama. For all my anger, I couldn't help wondering if these people were right. A thought floated in the back of my head, wondering if I really was qualified for this position. Given the board's obviously cavalier attitude and lack of belief in me, I suspected I'd be fired before the week was out.

Then what would I do to help Azalea and the Wildflower Inn? No matter what Leo had said, I couldn't exactly slink back to the Library of Congress, and there wasn't a great call for rare book experts in southern Maryland. I sighed and wondered what horrible thing would happen next.

Feeling a bit overwhelmed, I took an extended walk around the campus. I told myself I was simply familiarizing myself with the place, but honestly, I was questioning my decision to work here. The protesters had a valid point. Could I really do much to change the way the family worked with the community? Who was I to enact change?

After ten minutes, I finally headed back to the reading room. Inside, I was shocked to find a protester, asleep at a table, with an opened book next to him. Although I couldn't see his face, I recognized his tweed coat and burly form. This was the guy who had stopped me from entering and interrogated me about working here.

I shuddered upon seeing him. If he'd made it here, was he back to do something to the collections or to me? How did he make it past the security guards?

He didn't wake up as I drew near. The cigar he'd been chomping on had apparently fallen out of his mouth and now laid upon the table, half of the ashy end on the opened book. Seeing it upon an old book made my stomach curl, while it took everything I had not to race over and throw the offending item at my sleeping invader.

I crept closer, uncertain what would happen if I startled him awake. To my surprise, the book was opened to the first page of *The Gold Bug* in the collection of *Tales* by Edgar Allan Poe. I could tell it was an old copy, based on the font, binding, and look of the paper. Could this be our missing book? The 1845 first edition? In addition to the chomped cigar, I noticed the open pages were marred with dirt and leaves. What had he done to this poor book? Gardened with it? I wanted to snatch it away and hold it tight in reassurance that the book would be safe now.

Then I noticed a piece of paper beside him and the book. Unlike the old book, this looked like regular printer paper, although a bit crumpled as if it had been folded and unfolded multiple times. I spotted a few handwritten rows, but the letters were strange and not easy to read. At first I thought the note might be in another language, but it wasn't anything I recognized. The rows consisted of a mix of letters, numbers, and glyphs—small pictures and symbols—without any spaces. The handwriting had started out neatly, but as the rows progressed, it became loopier and more erratic. A pencil had rolled down the table, so I wondered if he had been creating the strange note when he fell asleep.

Mad at his arrogance, I felt no shame at snapping a quick photo of the strange note. I knew it wasn't mine, but I couldn't help being curious about the strange writing.

I breathed deeply and scrounged up all the courage I had left. That he was asleep on the table—my table in my library, I reminded myself—increased my anger. My face flushed, and my fists tightened. How dare he sneak in here, with his cigar and mistreated book, and fall asleep on my table?

My first instinct was to yell at him for somehow making it inside, but as I studied him, I realized he wasn't asleep at all. He was slumped onto the table with his arms dangling. His face appeared clammy with an unpleasant dew across the skin.

I was pretty sure he was dead.

Chapter Seven

I reached out and gently shook his arm. He didn't react. I checked for a pulse but couldn't find anything. His hands were dirty. I tried tilting his head back slightly, looking and feeling for breaths, but nothing happened. I tried calling the authorities, only to discover that I couldn't get a signal in the reading room.

"He needs help!" I yelled, but I was alone with him. I searched for a landline phone in a near-blind panic. I raced around the room until I found a desk set on the other side. I tried dialing 911, but it didn't work. I couldn't get an outside line.

"Help!" I called out, but again, no one responded. Feeling a flurry of panic bubbling in my stomach, I pressed buttons at random, hoping something would happen.

"Calverton Industries, how may I direct your call?" a no-nonsense female voice replied.

"There's a man. In the reading room," I said, struggling to make a coherent sentence.

"Reading room?"

"Yes, in the collections building."

"Hold on. I'll connect you with claims and collections," she replied.

"What? No!" I tried interrupting her, but the call had already been transferred. I didn't even know for sure which button I'd pressed to get to the operator.

"Calverton Industries, accounts receivable," said a male voice.

"I need 911," I yelled at the phone.

"Then why are you calling me?" he asked, sounding annoyed.

"I don't know how to get a line out. I'm in the reading room. In the collections and archives building. There's a man here," I said.

"What? Slow down. What are you going on about?"

"I think he's dead," I said. Tears welled in my eyes.

"Dead? A dead man? Where?"

I repeated my location again.

"I'll transfer you to security," he said.

"Wait, please. I'm brand new. I don't know..." But there was silence. I waited as moments passed. It felt like forever.

"Calverton Industries. Security," said a gruff male voice.

"There's a man dead," I said.

"Is this a prank?" the voice replied.

"No, no, he's dead. In the collections and archives building. Please, help me."

"Sandra, is that you?" he asked.

This was a comedy of errors. A very dark one. Tears streamed down my cheeks, and my knees nearly buckled beneath me.

"No, this is real. Please. I need help. He's a protester."

That caught the security person's attention, and his tone changed completely. "Wait, you've got a dead protester *inside* the library?"

I nodded, even though he couldn't see me. "Hurry, please."

"On our way."

* * *

After the police cordoned off the scene, the foundation board called an emergency meeting to discuss what had happened. They wanted me there as well, but I found myself paralyzed in the foyer, terrified to enter the conference room. I felt like the biblical Daniel about to face the den of lions.

Leo found me there and led me to a bench in the hallway. He bought me a water bottle from a nearby vending machine. I didn't immediately drink it but put the cold bottle against my neck to cool down.

"Who was he?" I asked Leo. I stared at the conference room door. There were only a few minutes before the meeting was about to begin. I moved the water bottle to the inside of my left wrist. I swear I could feel my pulse beating through the bottle.

"Big Al Cooley. Owns Boardwalk Books. Secondhand place," he replied. "I was there almost every week as a teenager. Big sci-fi and adventure reader."

I remembered how many times I'd gone in there as a teen, visiting Nana Z for the summer. However, I'd been all about the mysteries, stocking up on Agatha Christie and Elizabeth George. I wondered if Leo and I had ever been there at the same time.

I had vague memories of a curmudgeonly owner, but we had rarely interacted beyond my paying for my books. He was simply a faceless grown-up to my self-absorbed teen self. More than the person, however, I remembered the smell of the store, a strange mix of almonds and vanilla. Even now, I found that aroma comforting and calming.

After school, I traveled the world, searching for something that I couldn't describe. I visited so many libraries and bookstores on my journeys. Each had its own take on that fragrance, but none had been exactly the same. I never realized how much I associated that scent with a sense of home. How bizarre that such a meaningful memory could be connected to someone who had been so awful to me this morning.

"He was at the protests. I'm pretty sure he's the one who tossed Rose Bay on me," I told him. Leo wrapped an arm around my shoulder. I wanted to sink into him, but I fought the urge and slumped his arm off. A look of disappointment flashed across his face, but he hid it with a vague smile.

"Time to face the Wizard," I said, feeling like Dorothy in the *Wizard of Oz*.

"You're not wrong. This board is…" He seemed to be searching for the right word. "Passionate?"

"What is that a euphemism for?"

"You'll see."

I gripped the water bottle tight as Leo opened the door, revealing a battle in progress. Board members clashed loudly with each other. People pointed fingers, yelled at one another, and stomped their feet. They seemed less like grown adults than toddlers. I'd seen board meetings get out of control before, but nothing like this.

"We never should have let the protests happen," said someone. I thought I had met him at the lunch, but the faces became a blur.

"Yeah, you were too coddling to the community," said a man next to him. This guy, I remembered. He was the one who put an unwelcome arm around my waist. I shuddered.

"Teddy is right. We should have served them all with trespassing claims," another replied.

About a dozen people stood around a long conference table. I followed Leo to some empty seats at the back.

"Nice way to start a new job" said Martha, staring down the table at me. When she spoke, everyone else suddenly quieted and turned to look at me. A few hours ago, they were toasting me and the new museum project in the Golf Club. Now, I felt the weight of their eyes baring deep into my soul. I wanted to shrivel up and crawl away. Instead, I tugged at the label of my water bottle, pulling less than an inch off. The chill had dissipated, and condensation pooled below it on the conference table.

"Weren't you involved with that last murder?" a woman asked. People murmured around me, remembering the death at the nearby Tidewater Cemetery that I'd ended up investigating. Not exactly the kind of experience one put on a resume.

"Juniper wasn't involved with any of this," Leo said with a defiant tone. He looked like a tiger, pent up in a cage, ready to attack. I patted his arm, willing him to quiet down. As much as I was feeling sorry for myself, I at least knew how to stand my ground.

"A protester died in *her* library," Martha replied. "How is she not involved?"

"It's not *her* library. It's *our* library." Leo stretched his hands wide to indicate the whole room.

"Come off it," said the unwelcome arm guy. I thought someone called him Teddy, but I wasn't sure. "This was your grandmother's idea. Then she abandoned the project to us. And now we're all wrapped up in this mess."

"It was an unfortunate incident," I said, sounding more confident than I felt.

"Unfortunate incident?" Martha said with a vicious laugh. "That's the type of language *I* use." She shook her head. I couldn't be sure, but I thought she was amused.

"Oh, come on, Martha. No gallows humor now," said the man beside her.

"But what are we going to do about this? We already had such bad press from the protests. And now one of them is dead, inside our building. It doesn't look good," added Teddy.

"You're right," said Martha. "All of you are. This tragedy isn't helping our existing problems."

"Stocks are tumbling," said a woman.

Martha sighed. "I'll fix this. I've gotten us through tricky times in the past."

"Tricky times," I muttered, thinking of how she remarked about me using a polite euphemism a few moments ago. I went back to tugging at the water bottle label.

"What was that?" Martha asked.

"Nothing." I let go of the bottle, afraid that if I kept touching it, I'd be inclined to toss it at Martha. I wasn't normally so petulant, but she managed to get under my skin.

"I didn't think so," she said. Her voice drilled lasers into my soul.

"What are you going to do, Martha?" Leo asked. He sounded cautious and concerned. He still reminded me of a giant cat, waiting for the right opportunity to pounce.

Martha ignored his question. Her gaze remained locked on me. "What can you tell me about finding Mr….Cooley, was it?"

"Leave her out of this," Leo ordered.

Martha didn't stop staring at me.

"There's not a lot to tell," I replied. My voice almost cracked as I talked. I felt like a kid caught doing something wrong. That wasn't fair to Big Al, though. My stomach turned somersaults.

"Really?" She didn't sound like she believed me. "You get verbally assaulted by a protester on your way into your first day of work here, only to later find him dead. And you can say with a straight face that 'there's not a lot to tell'?"

I opened my mouth to respond, but Leo rushed in before me. "Sounds like you have all the facts, Martha. Why are you zeroing in on Juniper? She has nothing to do with this." I tapped his arm, but he ignored me, continuing on, "Juniper is a consummate professional in the museum and libraries field. She understands a collection like ours and how creating a museum can help smooth over these divisive relations with the community. That she has been through another… what was your phrase, 'tricky time,' is honestly an asset to us. She was steadfast then and will be again now."

My cheeks burned red. I didn't need Leo saving me. I didn't need anyone doing that for me. I could show them I was capable all by myself. "I don't know if you're insinuating anything," I said to Martha, "but it should be clear that I wasn't involved. Then or now."

"Well, if you weren't involved in Mr. Cooley's passing, then where were you while he died?" Martha asked.

"That's what I'd like to know too," said another voice. One I recognized. My heart dropped lower than my stomach. I'm pretty sure it suddenly puddled on the floor.

At the door was Detective Laskhmi Gupta. Like always, she wore a well-tailored lamp black suit, this time matched with a baby blue blouse and several strands of thin gold beads around her neck. Her long, dark hair was pulled back in a chignon. Not a single strand flew out of place.

"I was on a walk," I said, hearing how meek my voice became.

"A walk. That's a good idea. Why don't we take one together? To chit chat."

"Does she need a lawyer?" Leo asked.

Detective Gupta put her hands up in supplication. "I have a few questions. Nothing else. No hidden cards up my sleeves."

"You should get a lawyer. There are several in here," Leo said to me. He motioned around the room, and multiple people raised their hands.

I shook my head. After watching these grown toddlers battle each other, I would never consider any of them for representation. But getting a lawyer seemed a bit overboard. I certainly didn't have anything to do with Big Al

Cooley's death. And I'd do almost anything to get out of this room at the moment, even go chat with Detective Gupta. "No, I'll be fine," I said. "There's nothing to worry about."

I hoped I was right.

He protested, as did the many lawyers in a Greek chorus, but I ignored them and walked out of the room. I was happy to leave there. Detective Gupta followed. We had met earlier that summer when I found the body in the nearby Tidewater Cemetery. We weren't exactly friends, but we respected each other. Or I hoped we did.

We walked along the pedestrian path through the campus. Short native fringe trees and eastern redbuds lined the pathways. Behind the buildings, far taller trees like persimmons, black gums, and oaks towered above us. I found a bench for the two of us, out of the way of everyone, and sat down. Detective Gupta joined me.

"How are you holding up?" she asked.

I shrugged. "It's been a long day. And it's only mid-afternoon." Even beneath the canopy of a willow oak, the summer heat was exhausting. I wish I'd brought that water bottle.

She nodded and said, "I hear you just started here."

I suspected she wanted a blow-by-blow of everything, so I supplied it to her. She listened attentively, taking the occasional note as I went over as many details as I could recall.

"Where did you go after lunch?" she asked.

I told her about running into Martha Dresdale. "After that, I needed a chance to calm down, so I wandered the campus a bit."

"And no one else came into the library while you were away?" she asked.

I shrugged. "I don't know. But there wasn't anyone else inside when I returned."

"And you'd never seen Mr. Cooley before?" she asked.

"No. Not that I'm aware of. Maybe when I was a teenager visiting his store, but I don't remember him all that well. Leo said he owns that used bookstore, Boardwalk Books."

"Any idea why he was in the reading room?"

"Not a clue. The book beside him matched the title of a Poe book missing from our inventory. I don't know if it's the same one. Maybe he was returning it?" I tried to sound optimistic, but my suggestion felt weak.

"Do you know how he got the book?"

"I honestly don't know anything. Maybe someone brought the book to his store, and he realized it was ours, so he brought it to us?" I didn't believe my words any more than Detective Gupta probably did. I couldn't imagine an ardent protester returning a stolen book to us.

"We'll look into all the possibilities," she said vaguely.

"Did you see the weird message?" I debated about showing her the photos I'd taken, but I didn't want to risk her taking my phone and destroying the images. If I could figure out what that message meant, maybe it would explain more about what had happened.

"You mean the note on the table?" she asked.

I tried to pull up the image in my memory. I could visualize the paper and scrawl, but I couldn't remember the exact order of letters, numbers, and symbols. Eric had called me a walking encyclopedia, but truth be told, I did not have an eidetic memory—what was commonly known as a photographic memory. I was simply nerdy. "Yeah, it looked like it was in a secret code."

"We'll have our best people look at it," she replied. "Unless you know what it means?"

"Not a clue." I did have one idea. There was a man I'd met at the historical society while I investigated my last mystery. If I recalled correctly, he was retired from some intelligence agency. Perhaps he could help out? My staff and I needed to go there for research anyway. Another thought tugged at my brain. "Wait, the book was opened to *The Gold Bug…*"

"I don't know what that is."

"It's a short story by Edgar Allan Poe."

"I've never heard of that one." She leaned closer to me. "*The Tell-Tale Heart* is my favorite. So creepy." She shuddered but smiled. I appreciated her sharing. Every librarian loves hearing about people's favorite stories. *The Tell-Tale Heart* was one of my favorite Poe stories, too. I agreed that it was indeed a creepy story.

"*The Gold Bug* used to be very popular, but it's a problematic story, so it's not read as often as it used to be," I explained.

"Problematic? How?"

"Well, to be honest, Poe's depiction of an African-American man in the story is pretty racist," I said. "Maybe not surprising given that the story was first written in 1843. The book of *Tales* it's included in was published only two years later."

"And you think that has something to do with Mr. Cooley?" she asked.

"I don't know. Maybe? But I brought up *The Gold Bug* for a different reason."

"Oh?"

"The plot is all about deciphering a secret message to find buried treasure," I said.

That stopped Detective Gupta in her tracks. I could practically see the wheels turning in her mind, but she didn't tell me what she was thinking. I would never admit it, but I was jealous of her strong poker face. I knew that every emotion I felt waltzed openly across mine. It was hard enough trying to control the swell of feelings I'd experienced today, let alone keep a calm or stoic expression, no matter how much I wished I could.

"Well, thank you, Ms. Blume," she said. Instead of saying anything else, she stood up and walked away. I'd been dismissed.

"Wait," I shouted, holding up a hand. Detective Gupta turned and paused, looking at me expectantly. "Do you know how he got in? Have you gone through the security tapes?"

Detective Gupta laughed. "I can't snap my fingers and have everything examined like magic, Juniper."

"Right. But do you have any idea how he died?" The words rattled around in my head. I didn't want to make a habit of finding people dead. My stomach twisted inside of me.

Her face softened. "We're at the beginning of the investigation."

"Maybe he had a heart attack," I suggested. Gupta shrugged. I didn't like her shrug. My mind was already spinning, so somehow, her casual response suggested to me that it wasn't a heart attack. "A stroke?"

"It's not up to me to determine the cause of death. I'm here because things are suspicious."

"Suspicious?" I repeated.

She looked at me like I was five years old. "A protester shows up dead in your library with one of your missing books." She paused and corrected herself, saying, "Suspected missing books. No matter how he died, I'd mark that as suspicious. Wouldn't you?"

"Yeah, that's true. What happens next?"

"Honestly, if I were you, I'd go home. It's going to take time to comb through the collections building. And if the medical examiner decides it wasn't a heart attack or stroke or something like that, well, it'll be longer before you can go back in."

"How long?"

"As long as it takes," she said. "Go home, Juniper. And I don't want to hear you're investigating this time, okay?"

I nodded, firmly believing at the time that I could stay out of trouble.

Chapter Eight

I drove my Karmann Ghia back to the Wildflower Inn. When I went inside, I was surprised to see the place looked immaculate compared to yet another round of cooking messes this morning. I couldn't believe that was only a few hours ago. It felt like weeks had passed.

"Hey, you're back early," said Azalea, coming up to the front desk. She laughed and said, "What, did you find another body?"

I couldn't bring myself to say anything. Azalea watched me seize up, and her eyes lit up with concern. She darted around the front desk and wrapped me in a hug.

"Oh, no. I'm so sorry, Juniper," she said. I collapsed into her. All the feelings I'd struggled to hold together all day suddenly gushed out of me, and I started crying into her shoulder. When my knees gave out, I fell to the floor. She gently came down with me, ensuring I didn't hurt myself. We stayed that way for a few minutes before I finally pulled away and turned down the waterworks.

"Can you stand?" she asked with concern. I nodded and carefully stood up. My legs were like jelly, but I stayed upright. She took my hand and led me down the hallway to the kitchen. The mess of flour and jam was gone. She led me to the table and magically produced a plate of cookies. They were likely for my niece or guests coming soon, but I couldn't resist eating one. Chocolate chip and hot out of the oven. The gooey mess felt like a hug from inside.

Azalea started a pot of tea. She joined me and took a cookie for herself. We sat in silence, eating the cookies until the kettle went off, and she jumped up to get me a mug. She didn't even bother asking what kind of tea I liked, automatically knowing we both loved Darjeeling black tea. She even added plenty of honey for me. I was so relieved to have her with me.

I let the heat of the tea warm my face. The smell of the tea and the taste of the cookie reinvigorated me. Once the tea cooled, I sipped on it, finding it to be the perfect mix of a rich, musky taste matched with the sweetness of the honey.

After a few minutes, Azalea asked quietly, "Do you want to talk about it?"

I nodded. She allowed me to ease into the conversation. I told her everything that had happened.

"Big Al Cooley? Of Boardwalk Books?" she asked with surprise. "I shop there frequently. They have a great selection of kids' books for Violet. But what was he doing in your library?"

"I don't know how he got in there," I said.

"And he had a book stolen from you?"

I shrugged. "I think so. The title matched, but I haven't been able to confirm it. Have you heard of *The Gold Bug* by Edgar Allan Poe?"

She shook her head.

"It's about a secret message."

"A secret message? What kind of secret message?" She leaned in closer across the kitchen table.

"One that led to a pirate's treasure," I replied.

Her eyes got big. "Do you think Big Al was looking for the story's treasure?"

I tried not to laugh. "No, it's a story. And besides, it takes place way down south on an island off the coast of Georgia."

Her shoulders slumped. "Oh well. So why was he there?"

"I do not know. He was at the protest. I think he was the one who tossed this Rose Bay on me." I pointed to the small red flecks still infecting Nana Z's dress. I suddenly felt the deep need to take a shower, but it could wait. I should finish my tea first.

"That protest has been going on for a while."

"You knew about the protest?" I asked in surprise. She hadn't warned me about it, and I didn't understand why.

"I didn't realize you didn't."

"How would I have known? It would have been good to have a heads up."

"Sorry." Her eyes averted my gaze. There was some awkward silence, before she continued, saying, "Look, I support you turning their collection into a new museum, but honestly, it is hard when I'm not okay with some, well, most of the rest of the Calverton family's many businesses."

"I only took this job to help you and the Wildflower Inn out."

Azalea looked like I'd slapped her across the face. "That's the only reason?"

"Well, no, that was a poor choice of words…"

"No one asked you to take the job." She stood up. Her face was as red as a tomato. "All I ever asked was to see you more often. To not miss your niece's birthdays. Things like that. We're going to be fine." She stood taller and squared her shoulders. Her nose lifted into the air. I sighed. My sister could have all the pride she wanted, but it didn't change the truth. She was struggling to keep the inn. If I could keep her from losing our grandmother's house, then I was going to do whatever it took, including taking jobs at questionable organizations.

"Azalea, I've seen the loan notices. I know that Calverton Bank is coming after you. I don't want you to lose the Wildflower," I said.

"I won't lose the Wildflower." She crossed her arms and stared at me as if she dared me to defy her statement. Given what I'd seen, she was wrong, but I knew it wasn't worth arguing. She was determined, and mountains would move, and oceans would drain before she backed down. I appreciated the sentiment, but I'd still help her. I had given up my job at the Library of Congress for this. In her eyes, I'd obviously made a deal with the devil, and she refused to accept that, even if it was for a good reason.

I put up my hands in defeat. "I'm sorry."

"You don't need to feel sorry. For me or for Violet. I've got this under control. I don't need your or anyone else's help. And I certainly didn't ask you to go work for the enemy."

"The enemy?" I repeated. That seemed harsh.

"You know how the Calvertons are trying to change Rose Mallow? They want to strip it of all its history and character and make it into a luxury blandness that no one around here could afford if they wanted to. Their bank and their Port Chesapeake development arm are going to destroy everything we've worked so hard to make special," she said. "I would have been at that protest myself, but I figured it'd make your first day awkward."

"Do you want me to quit?" I asked. If I'd known she felt that strongly about the Calvertons, I would have found some other way to assist. Although, as soon as I thought that, I wondered if it was actually true. As much as I kept telling myself the job was to help my sister, honestly, I wanted it too. Sharing their collection with the world was one way I could help the organization change and make things better. From what I'd seen, the collection was worth the work.

She sighed. "No, don't be so melodramatic."

"Melodramatic? But you're the one getting angry," I replied.

"Of course, I'm getting angry. I should be angry. You should be, too. The only reason that bank is coming after me is because they want to take down the Wildflower Inn. I will not let them," she replied. I'd never heard such defiance in her voice. I was both impressed and unnerved.

"I don't think the bank wants to personally attack you," I replied.

She rolled her eyes. "I know that. But it's part of the Calvertons' big vision, and obviously, the Wildflower Inn isn't part of it. I won't let them have it."

"Where will you find the money?"

She sighed. "I'll figure something out. We can sell Nana Z's jewelry and clothes. I'll drain my retirement fund if I have to. Even Violet's college fund. There's not much in it yet, but all of that should equal something."

"Don't say that. I can sell my townhouse in D.C." When Nana Z passed away, she had given her house to both of us. Azalea had bought me out of my half to create the Wildflower Inn, and I had used the funds to purchase my townhome in Washington, D.C. Once I sold it, I hoped to give the money back to Azalea to get her out of debt, but everything had happened so fast that I hadn't had a chance yet to start the process. "Or I can return to D.C. Maybe get my old job back at the Library of Congress? Then, at least, I wouldn't work for them anymore."

Azalea shook her head. Her face was more pink than red, although not all the way back to our normally pale skin color. "No, you're not to blame. You're working for their foundation, right? The part of them that seeks to do some good?"

I nodded.

"Then do some good." She wagged a finger in my face.

* * *

After a long shower, I settled down in the inn's library to read a book. There weren't any guests that evening—besides me—so I figured I might have a quiet night to rest and relax after such a long day. Violet and my dog Clover were running after each other, but it wasn't enough to interrupt my reading plans on the comfy chaise lounge.

"Uh, Juniper?" Azalea appeared in the room. She had a look on her face I rarely saw. My fiercely independent sister wanted something. From me.

Furthermore, she was dressed up. My normally prim and proper sister was wearing a tight black dress with actual high heels. Not kitten heels but at least three inches high. Her hair was styled into a loose updo with romantic strands framing her face. She'd even put makeup on.

"Yeah?"

"I'm sorry about earlier. I got a bit riled up," she said.

That was one way to phrase it. But I knew what she was feeling. I was excited by my work, but it was hard for me to work for the Calverton family for the same reasons she had laid out. Was I doing more good trying to change things from the inside, or should I find some other way to make a difference with them?

"Don't worry about it. I understood. I'm sorry, too," I said.

"Thank goodness. Because I got a call that Rory is suddenly free tonight," she said. I hadn't expected that. Rory was my brother-in-law. Well, nearly ex-brother-in-law. When I first came back to Rose Mallow, Azalea and her high school sweetheart, Rory, had been going through divorce proceedings. However, after he was kidnapped, they realized how much they still cared for each other.

"So you decided to go for that date?" I remembered how unsure she had sounded about giving even a single date a try.

She nodded. Her face lit up like a teenager. I swear I heard her even giggle. Were we having an *Invasion of the Body Snatchers* moment? My sister never giggled, even when she was a teenager. "He still has a long road of recovery from what happened to him, but he's been okayed to go out, as long as it's low-key."

"Is the divorce off?"

"Not off officially. On hiatus. Like you said, try a date. I told him I needed to take things slow."

"Sure, that makes sense." I figured that's why he wasn't back living here. At least not yet. I hoped things would improve between them. "What about Deputy Torres?" Last time I was here, he and my sister made ridiculous googly eyes at each other, but I wasn't sure if anything had progressed. I didn't think my sister would get involved with someone else while separated, but I also knew that emotions sometimes made people make poor choices. I couldn't help thinking about how much energy I was putting into fighting off my feelings for Leo.

She gnawed on her lower lip. "I'm not sure. I really like John. He's so different from Rory. He's driven and serious, where Rory was always playful. John's been in law enforcement since he finished high school, while Rory has bounced from job to job. Working at the car dealership has been his most stable position, and he's been there less than a year. But I figured I owed it to Rory and Violet to try this first."

"What about you?"

A fireworks display of emotions exploded across Azalea's face. It settled into a wistful expression. She nodded. "Yeah, to me, too. We have a lot to sort out, but it's worth trying. I think John understands. I hope he does."

"If he doesn't, then he's not worth even considering. Like you said, you have Violet. Rory's her dad. That changes everything."

"Speaking of Violet, if it's not too much of a bother…" She paused and looked at her feet.

"Of course!" I offered before she could finish her request.

Her shoulders dropped. "Thank goodness. I didn't know where to find a babysitter this last minute."

I smiled. "I would have been mad if you hadn't asked. Where are you two going?"

"To the Indigo Room. With his recovery, we haven't had many chances to go anywhere, so he wants to take me somewhere special for dinner. With the nice weather, he got a table looking right out on the Chesapeake Bay." Azalea seemed to have stars in her eyes. I'd been to the Indigo Room once before on my one and only date with Leo. It was a beautiful restaurant at the southern end of the boardwalk's commercial district. After that, the boardwalk continued south, separating historic houses like ours from the water. It ended in Redbud Park.

"That sounds lovely," I said, getting up from the chaise lounge. I snapped my fingers. "But you need something."

"What?" She looked slightly alarmed.

I pulled out Nana Z's pearl necklace. Her eyes misted as I walked over and placed it around her neck.

"Thank you. This is perfect." She caressed the pearls gently.

"Of course. You look stunning, Azalea."

"I won't be out too late, I promise."

I waved her worries away. "Take your time. Enjoy yourselves."

"Thank you, Juniper. I really appreciate this."

I walked over to her and gave her a quick hug. "You've done so much for me. This is the least I can do for you. Good luck with Rory."

Chapter Nine

I was the one who needed luck. Trying to be the cool aunt, I let my four-year-old niece stay up later than her usual bedtime and gave her as many cookies as she wanted. The combination of tired plus wired on sugar turned out to be a bad decision. While Violet was normally a delightful kid, I had unintentionally unleashed chaos.

My dog Clover sniffed out Violet's crayons and raced around the house with them in his mouth. My niece must have thought this was a great game because she pulled out more crayons and ran from both of us. That was fine, if a bit tiring, until Violet drew their race on one of the library walls. I had been chasing after Clover, so I missed the first few stick figures she added.

"Oh no, your mom is going to kill me," I said, but Violet laughed. It was only then that I noticed that she had grabbed several tubes of Azalea's lipstick. Not only had she drawn on the walls with them, but on herself as well. Smears of red and pink coated her face.

I focused on cleaning her up and tried giving her a bath. Clover jumped in as well, and soon, the bathroom was drenched. Bubbles were everywhere. I reminded myself that it wasn't a big deal, but I hated the idea of Azalea returning to find the house like this.

"Okay, it's time to get out," I said to Violet.

"No!" She splashed water on me. What happened to my sweet little niece?

"Clover?" I asked for help, but my young dog was happy to stay in the water with his new best friend. I wondered how hygienic it was for them to take a bath together. What if I had unwittingly exposed Violet to some unknown doggy germs?

I reached over to get the drain, but Violet popped it closed again. She sat back in the tub, crossing her little arms, and stared defiantly at me. I tried picking her up, but she wiggled out of my grip.

"It's time to get out, Vi. Time for bed," I said.

I instantly regretted saying the "bed" word. A wail like a Greek harpy belted out of Violet. "No bed! No bed!" She splashed and splashed, probably leaving more water outside the tub than in it.

How did Azalea handle this? I didn't want to call her and interrupt her date with Rory. Knowing my sister, she'd come home immediately, worried that she'd burdened me with too much. She'd probably never let me babysit again. I needed another solution.

I couldn't contact Rory for the same reason. I thought about reaching out to his aunt Harmony, but when I checked my watch, I knew it'd be prime time at her café.

Keisha! Azalea's teenaged assistant, Keisha Douglass, had babysat Violet many times. She probably had a good idea.

"Pick up, pick up," I said in a quiet prayer to the phone. However, the call went straight to voicemail. I left a detailed message, but the phone cut me off. I thought about calling again when Keisha texted me. She was on a camping trip in Western Maryland with her family and spotty coverage. Not wanting to disrupt her trip, I texted back, wishing her a great time.

Who else did I know nearby? I needed some friends here. Although I'd grown up coming to Rose Mallow in the summers, I didn't have much in the way of friends left. The only other person I could think of to reach out to was Leo. I stared at my phone for a minute, debating whether to reach out to him. Then I looked back at my little niece and dog. I tried again to pick her up, but she shimmied out of my hands. Clover wasn't any better. He danced around, making it hard for me to get a good grip on either of them.

Yeah, I needed help.

I texted Leo, "Do you know how to work with kids? I can't get my niece out of the bath."

Less than a minute later, Leo replied with a laugh-cry emoji. "Raised my sibs. Need me to come over?"

I sucked in my breath. Having him come by seemed like a big ask, especially now that he was my boss and not just my friend.

"Don't want to be difficult..."

A few seconds later, he responded, "On my way."

"Anything to try in the meantime?"

Shrug emoji. "When in doubt, offer a bribe."

It seemed worth testing.

"Come on, Vi. If you get out of the bath, I'll...uh...give you a cookie," I said. While Violet seemed uninterested in my treat suggestion, Clover jumped around at the magic word. He climbed up onto the bath's edge and barked happily. It was a stark contrast to Violet, who sulked behind him. I figured she was still upset at the mention of 'bed.'

I tried once again to pick my niece up, but she flailed as I got hold of her arms. I held them by her sides, but Clover decided it was a game and tickled my arms with kisses.

The next few seconds were a blur of moving limbs, slippery soap, and a jumping dog. I somehow ended up falling into the bath. At least that was one way to get rid of any remaining Rose Bay off me my shower may have missed. I'd changed out of my grandmother's dress earlier, but it still wasn't comfortable getting my sweats drenched.

After my pratfall inside, Clover licked the bubbles off my face. Violet changed from disturbed to delighted to have me join them. She tried to have me play with her bath toys, spilling yellow boats full of water on me.

Part of me wanted to yell or cry, but mainly, I laughed at how ridiculous it all was. When I started laughing, Violet joined in. I took advantage of the moment and scooped her up, placing her outside of the bath. Clover jumped out as well and shook his wet fur everywhere.

* * *

I had finally put my niece and Clover to bed when the doorbell rang. I looked down at my wet clothes and worried about my drenched hair, but there wasn't time to fix anything.

"You asked Leo to come here," I reminded myself. I sighed and trekked downstairs, hoping I wasn't leaving too big of a puddle trail behind me.

"Hey Juniper…" Leo's voice trailed off as he took in my soaked self. He carried a couple of pizza boxes in his hands. "Are you okay?"

I waved him in. "Yeah, fine. A little more humiliated than anything else. Thanks for coming over. And for the pizza. You can put those in the kitchen, down the hall. I'm going to get changed."

He nodded and headed off while I finally tackled a change of clothes and pulled my hair back in a headband. When I came back down, I found him waiting in the kitchen.

"Guess you didn't need my help after all," he said.

"I should have called sooner. I didn't know what to do."

"How old is she?" he asked.

"Four."

"Ah, yeah. I remember that age well. Being the oldest of five siblings…"

"Five?" I repeated in disbelief.

He shrugged. "Yeah, five Calvertons. I'd like to think it's because my parents loved kids, but honestly, knowing them, I suspect they were ensuring someone would live up to the so-called Calverton legacy. They were rarely around. We were raised by an army of nannies. And when I got old enough, I was expected to help as well. That was besides keeping straight As and about a million different extracurricular activities. Not that my parents attended any of them. But as a Calverton, I was expected to always excel."

"Jeez, that sounds horrible." I pulled out plates for the pizza. I'd been surprised Leo had gotten them being vegan and gluten-free, but one was a red pizza with plenty of vegetables on a gluten-free crust. I tried a slice and found it delicious. It'd been sprinkled with a cashew crema that was much more decadent and creamier than I had expected.

I found a bottle of wine and cracked it open. I didn't normally drink, but after this day, I poured glasses for both of us.

"It was what it was." He sounded resigned. I noticed he hadn't touched any food yet, although he had already dug into the wine. Without thinking, I patted his hand on the table. He took it in his. For a moment, I enjoyed our hands locked together, but then I shook mine loose. He stared at the spot where our hands connected, but neither of us said anything.

"How are things with your parents now?" I asked.

He inhaled deeply. "They are…I'm not sure there's a good word to describe our relationship. They're very stoic. Stiff upper lip and all that jazz." He downed the rest of his glass. I'd left the bottle of wine on the table, so he refilled it.

"Are they still involved with the businesses?" I tried pushing a slice of the vegan pizza towards Leo. He didn't seem to notice. Instead, I followed his gaze out the back bay window to the gardens, carriage house, and the Chesapeake Bay beyond.

"My parents are technically retired, but they remain involved," Leo said. "Rarely with the day-to-day now. They're more likely to be wining and dining senators and heads of state. I think they're somewhere in Europe right now. Probably meeting with various prime ministers. I'd call them lobbyists, but they'd never agree to that term. Knowing them, they'd probably say they were ambassadors or something snobby like that."

I thought about my parents. They both taught at Johns Hopkins University in Baltimore, but when they weren't teaching, they played in a Klezmer band. I wondered if Leo had ever heard Klezmer with its traditional East European Jewish styles. Their band toured most summers, which is why Azalea and I always came here. As far I knew, they had never played for heads of states but a circuit of festivals, summer camps, and synagogues. Unfortunately, neither Azalea nor I had inherited their abilities, but we had grown up with a love for music thanks to them. I nearly laughed, considering the differences in how Leo and I were raised, but I bit it back, seeing how forlorn he appeared.

"And your parents are both like that?" I asked.

He nodded. "Everything's a competition between them. How it is with my siblings and me. I try not to play their ridiculous games, but it's hard not to get sucked in."

"Why do you stay?" I asked. After today, I wasn't sure if I should stay, but I tried telling myself that finding another body was a horrible fluke. At least everything else I'd gone through today had paled to that discovery.

He laughed dryly. "I've tried to break away. Do my own thing." He shook his head. He drank some more. "Look, once a Calverton, always a Calverton." He didn't say more, but as much as his expression was neutral, I couldn't help but see a deep sadness in his eyes. I wondered what I'd gotten myself into taking the job with the upstart museum. It'd only been my first week, and already I felt pulled into a strange, upside-down world. As I tried another slice of pizza, I hoped I wouldn't feel as stuck as Leo did now.

He shook his head and turned in his seat to face me. He looked concerned. "But I'm going on about me when it's been you who's had a horrific day. How are you doing?"

"Less wet," I said with a laugh. Leo made a face. I knew he wanted me to talk about it, but I felt talked out. "Look, all I'd like to do is forget about today. At least for the rest of the night. Eat pizza with a good friend." I raised a slice of pizza as if I was giving a toast. I had not touched my wine, but I noticed Leo filling his glass up again. Was this his third glass? I wished he would eat something.

A quick expression darted across his face. I figured the word "friend" stung. Maybe it wasn't a good idea having Leo here. I'd survived putting Violet and Clover to bed. I could put on some bad TV and eat pizza on my own. It wouldn't be any different from all those nights in my townhouse back in D.C.

"Is that all I am, a friend?" Leo asked with a touch of sadness.

I gulped. "That's all we can be. I'm your subordinate."

He cringed at the word. "You're more than my *subordinate*. You're the director."

I sighed. "Maybe. But it'd be a bad idea. You know it would be. People would think you only hired me because of our relationship. And what would happen if we broke up?"

"You're right. I let this wine get to me. I'm sorry about that." He pushed the still-filled glass away from him. He'd only had two glasses, so that wasn't horrible, was it?

"Slice of pizza?" I asked.

"Probably a good idea." He reached out to grab one, but then paused. "Wait, you have a point."

I debated asking which point I'd made, but I waited while he sorted out his thoughts. While he did, he finally grabbed a slice of pizza. He ate slowly, while staring upwards, obviously thinking.

"It might not be a good idea for me to be here," he said after finishing.

"What do you mean?" I asked. "You're here as a friend."

"Yeah, true, but you pointed out that some people think I only hired you because we'd dated." He grabbed one more slice.

"We went on one date," I said.

He shrugged. "But others don't know that. And what if people saw me here now? At your inn?" He pointed the half-eaten slice at me for emphasis.

"My sister's inn," I said, as if that made a difference. Even as I spoke, my stomach dropped. His tone was leading to something bad.

He ignored me and continued, "They wouldn't know we were only friends."

He was right. If someone saw Leo come into my family's inn, that probably wouldn't be great optics. Rose Mallow was a small town. It wouldn't take much for word to get around.

"I hadn't considered that." I thought about the mean girls board members gossiping at the club earlier and could only imagine what they'd say if they knew he was here alone with me right now.

"It might be best if we didn't see each other outside of work," he said.

"What?" This wasn't going how I wanted. Not that I knew what I wanted, but it wasn't this.

"I get it. You're worried about ethics. And you're right to be." He sounded resigned.

"I don't want to make things worse for the museum," I replied. Protests and a mysterious death were bad enough before adding in an inappropriate relationship. Any of those scandals could destroy the project, let alone all of them combined.

He nodded. "I shouldn't have come over when you texted."

I didn't want to admit it aloud, but he was right. I should never have texted him.

A thought popped into my head. If he and the board had done their due diligence, hiring me based on my abilities and background after considering other candidates, then the perception might look less awful. "Leo, did you interview anyone else for this job? Run a nationwide search?"

He didn't respond.

Unfortunately, that answered my question.

I'd already felt uncertain if I was up for the work. Besides my ambivalence at working for the Calverton family, I knew I was young and had never had this type of leadership role before. I wasn't sure I was up for the job. If people thought the only reason I had it was because of Leo, that was going to undermine everything I was attempting to achieve.

And if I lost the job, then how would I help Azalea keep the Wildflower Inn? Even if I sold my townhouse, I'd need the money if I didn't have a salary. Where would I go next? It wasn't like there were lots of rare book librarian positions here. Or anywhere. I would be stuck. I'd given up a lot to take this position—my job at the Library of Congress, my life in D.C.—but I'd lose even more if I couldn't keep it.

"Oh," was all I could say.

"I'm sorry for making things uncomfortable," he said.

"It's not your fault."

"Well, I am your boss. I should know better."

"It's been a long day for both of us. Our emotions got the better of us," I said.

"I promise not to make that mistake again. I'll see you at work." He stood up. Part of me wanted to forget everything and ask him to stay, but I didn't.

He disappeared down the hallway. I heard the front door open and close. Only then did I finally get up. Everything felt fast and slow at the same time. I followed him, but his black Tesla was already gone.

Even though we hadn't been dating, I felt like we'd broken up. I returned to the kitchen and polished off way too much of the pizza.

Chapter Ten

The next day, our office was closed for the investigation. I had an inkling of an idea that I wanted to explore, so I called my team about where to meet up.

"Today, we're heading to the public library and historical society," I said over the phone, sitting with my feet draped over the side of a damask upholstered wing chair.

"Why?" asked Florence with caution.

"I want to get a better sense of how the Calvertons connect with Rose Mallow's history," I replied. As I spoke, I stared out the back window across the wide expanse of the glistening Chesapeake Bay. Several ospreys flew across the bright blue sky. I guessed they were searching for breakfast in the waters.

"Cool," said Eric.

"What does that have to do with running archives?" Florence asked.

"If we're going to open a museum about American history, I'd like to know more about the family's history. Since they've been here for hundreds of years, where better to start than Rose Mallow?" I pictured the protesters and thought about what the Calvertons intended to do with the town. If I was right, the answer to these issues lay in the past. And maybe so did the solution.

"So, what do you want us to look for?" Eric asked.

"I'm not sure yet. But I want to get a good sense of what the family has done here since they started," I said.

"Okay." He sounded uncertain. Eric was younger than me, and I guessed he didn't feel confident about doing this research yet. As much as I wanted to help him, I had other plans. I was going to split up the team, taking Florence with me. If we could research together, then maybe I could better understand why she was such a sourpuss.

"Eric, why don't you head to the library? I bet Brandy can get you started," I suggested.

"Great!" His voice immediately perked up. I figured working with his girlfriend would relieve his hesitation.

"Florence, you're with me. We're heading to the historical society."

"I can work from here. I can access several databases from my computer at home." Unlike Eric, she was confident in her pronouncement.

I closed my eyes and pinched my temples. "No, you're with me. We'll do database work, too, but today is all about going into the field. You know the value of connecting with real historic documents, many of which are not digitized and accessible elsewhere." When she didn't respond, I decided that was as best of an agreement as I was going to get.

I didn't add that I had an additional reason for wanting to go to the historical society. I'd met volunteer Harold Graham there while researching my last mystery. He had retired from some sort of work in intelligence, although not surprisingly, I didn't know the specifics. I hoped he'd be there today and could give me some guidance with the secret code.

Examining Dorothea Calverton's collection of espionage items popped into my head. With Rose Mallow as small as it was, I wondered if he knew her, but then again, she was the matriarch of an enormous billionaire family, and he volunteered at the historical society. Even geography couldn't transcend some divides.

"Okay, we'll meet up at the Purple Oyster at lunch to share what we've found. My treat," I said.

"Awesome," said Eric.

Florence said nothing, which I accepted as tacit approval.

* * *

Florence waited outside the historical society when I arrived. She again wore all black, but with a bright Hermes scarf tied around her neck. She sported simple but large pearl earrings and a matching pearl ring, both of which looked at least fifty years old. Her accents popped vividly against her black ensemble. I enjoyed her fashion sense. Maybe we could connect over our love of vintage clothing? Personally, I'd gone full-on Audrey Hepburn with a white and blue striped boatneck blouse, navy blue pedal pushers, and oversized tortoiseshell sunglasses.

The historical society was housed in a historic brick church dating back several centuries. The place was modest, but I appreciated how the church had been reused instead of being knocked down or left to slowly fall apart.

"I didn't get to speak to you much yesterday," I said as I walked up to Florence. She considered me with hooded eyes and a guarded expression. "Hearing about Mr. Cooley being found in our library had to be a shock for you. How are you holding up?"

Her eyes shifted several times, looking everywhere but at me. Finally, she met my gaze and replied simply, "I'm fine." I didn't know her well enough to determine if she was lying, but then I noticed her right thumb digging into her left palm. Fine she was obviously not, but given the icy reception she'd given me so far, I doubted I'd get much more from her.

Even if I'd wanted to ask more, I couldn't, because Florence ducked inside the building. She didn't even bother to hold the door open for me. I shrugged and sighed before heading in.

Not much had changed since the last time I visited the historical society earlier in the summer. Housed in an old church, the interior was a single, whitewashed room. While all the pews and church furniture had been removed, there were still stained-glass windows featuring stories about different saints. I wandered past the tabletop town display in the middle of the room to the desk in the back, below the old altar. An older, bald man sat behind the desk, reading a book on spies in World War II. I recognized him from the last time I was here, while researching another local historic document.

"Harold! It's good to see you again," I said.

"Ah, I remember you. You're drier than the last time," he said with a chuckle. I nodded, remembering getting caught in the rain before coming in that day. Today was humid and hot, but there hadn't been a cloud in the sky this morning.

"Mr. Graham," said Florence. Her arms were wrapped tight around her middle, and her voice had the same hard tinge that she used when she spoke to me. Was there anyone that she liked, or did she naturally sound that way?

"Ms. Dowd," Harold replied with the same detached tone. I noticed he didn't look directly at her when he spoke. That caught me off guard. The two obviously knew each other, but from that brief exchange, I gathered there was no love lost between them.

He twisted back to face me and asked what brought us in. I explained our project of researching Calverton history in Rose Mallow, and he nodded. Before long, Harold brought over several file folders filled with historic documents for us to review. He also handed us copies of finding aids. "These finding aids will provide you with detailed summaries of each collection our historical society has," Harold explained.

"I know what a finding aid is," said Florence with an icy tone.

"Thank you," I said, ignoring her rudeness.

"I've given you several focusing on various members of the Calverton family, along with the individual businesses they had run in town over the years," he said to me.

I perused the many files he'd provided. Regardless of how anyone felt about them, they had been linked to Rose Mallow since its creation in the 17th century.

As I sorted through everything, Harold crooked his finger at me. I followed him to the desk. He whispered, "So I heard you found Big Al yesterday. Sorry to hear that. Are you doing okay?"

"As well as can be. Did you know him?"

"Fairly well. He'd call me whenever he got a shipment of thrillers into the store. I can't stop reading the ones about covert military operations."

I glanced back at Florence, but she seemed content, thumbing through the files. She was taking notes on a large pad of paper with a pencil.

Turning back to Harold, I asked, "Did you ever see any historic or rare books at his store?" I thought about the missing Poe book he had and the other ones we still hadn't located.

Harold shrugged. "Can't say I had paid much attention to those. Any in mind?"

"Oh, like something by Poe?"

His face opened up, and he smiled like a child getting a birthday cake. He snapped his fingers. "Now, Edgar Allan Poe is someone I pay attention to. I'm a bit of a Poe-natic myself, you know?"

"A what?"

"Poe-natic. Fanatic about Poe. Have you been to his grave in Baltimore? I used to go every January to celebrate his birthday. Always hoped to catch sight of the Poe Toaster," he said.

That sounded familiar, but I couldn't place the term. "The Poe Toaster?"

"For years—decades, really—a caped, masked gentleman left a rose and a bottle of cognac on Poe's grave on his birthday. No one ever knew the toaster's identity. Then, one day, a few years ago, he stopped, never to return. That made me sad when I heard, but honestly, I'm glad we never saw under his mask," Harold replied. I loved the romance of the story, which was as mysterious as any of Poe's tales.

"Fascinating," I said. "I wish I'd seen that. I've been to the small house museum near there, but that was years ago. Amazing to see the tiny attic space where he lived and wrote in Baltimore."

"I've been there many, many times. And to the museum about him in Richmond. Actually, spent a summer doing a tour of Poe sites up and down the East Coast several years ago. Poe was a big inspiration to me."

"Are you a writer?" I asked.

Harold laughed. "Me? No." He waved his hands as if to wipe away my suggestion. "But I did work for years for a so-called 'undisclosed government agency.'" He winked at me. I figured he meant the National Security Agency, which was also known as the NSA or "No-Such-Agency." However, he could have easily meant the CIA, FBI, or any number of departments within the Department of Defense. This was still the D.C. region, so none of this was particularly surprising around here.

"I loved Poe's riddles and wordplay," Harold said. "He always did something unexpected in his stories. And the reader was part of the game. We had to figure out the truth. I think that really inspired me to do the work I did."

"Like in *The Gold Bug?*" I chanced.

He nodded. "Exactly. Lots of people think he may have used secret messages in other tales and poems. Some even think his death was subterfuge. The ultimate riddle."

"You think he faked his death?" I had heard lots of theories about the mysterious way Poe died. He'd been found delirious on a Baltimore street in 1849. No one knew why he was in the city, as he hadn't been living there at the time. Poe was taken to a nearby hospital, where he went in and out of consciousness before eventually succumbing to whatever sparked the incident in the first place. Last I checked, there'd been nearly a dozen different theories about how he'd died, but I'd never heard someone suggest that he didn't.

Harold shrugged. "I don't know, but I was taught to keep an open mind and explore every rabbit hole."

"So what do you think happened?"

He was about to answer when Florence coughed loudly. I had gotten so wrapped up in chatting with him that I'd forgotten that she was there. I turned on my heels to face her.

"Excuse me for interrupting your little chit-chat, but we're supposed to meet Eric shortly," she said.

I checked my watch. She wasn't wrong, but we still had a few minutes. I decided to see if I could engage her in the conversation. "Do you have any thoughts about how Poe died?"

Florence looked at me with a strange expression. She blinked several times. "I can't say that I've ever thought about it."

"Are you a Poe fan? Or a Poe-natic?" I asked, employing Harold's word.

She shuddered and replied, "No, I find his work unnerving."

I changed topics. "Did you find anything interesting in your research?"

"*I* found plenty," she said with a self-satisfied smirk. I had to close my eyes before rolling them. She brought over her notepad and proudly displayed page after page of notes. I took a closer look. She'd made three columns: one titled years, another saying Rose Mallow, and the third for the Calvertons. She then noted the dates when interesting things happened, from the town being founded and the family arriving to their opening their first storefront and beyond. She listed different primary sources for each and made suggestions on where to look for more information.

"This is good stuff," I said, meaning it.

She nodded briefly. Florence had filled several pages with information. She was a quick but thorough researcher. I was impressed. This could work for the kernel of an idea I had.

"Thank you, Florence. Very nice work," I said. Then I turned to Harold. "I look forward to returning. I'm sure there's more research we can do. Thank you for your help."

However, as we left the historical society, I couldn't help but wonder about Harold's deep love for Edgar Allan Poe. Could his "Poe-natiscism" have been so great that he might have stolen our books, or worse, killed Big Al? He hadn't shared much about his work history, but it wasn't above the possibility that he'd been trained to do uncouth things for the government. Sure, he was older, but he was in good shape. I bit my tongue to keep the shudder at bay. I really hoped we hadn't spent the morning with a killer.

Chapter Eleven

Eric waved brightly at us as we came up to the Purple Oyster Coffee Shop. Labeling the place a coffee shop was an understatement as it sold a variety of foods, including the best scones I'd ever enjoyed. The shop was a whirlwind of purples and oranges, dotted with artwork by local artists. There was a generous interior, including a stage for open mic nights, along with a patio where dogs were allowed. They also made amazing dog biscuits. Clover was a big fan. Located at one end of the boardwalk, the place overlooked the Chesapeake Bay with spectacular views of the water.

We waited in a long line to order our food from the counter. I spotted the owner, Harmony, at a register. A modern-day hippy, her frizzy red hair was pulled up into a messy bun. She wore her trademark peasant shirts embroidered with little flowers. Recently, we learned that Harmony was my brother-in-law Rory's biological aunt. He had been staying with her while he and Azalea figured out their relationship.

I got into her line, figuring it'd be a nice surprise. Eric and Florence stood ahead of me, and I told them to get whatever they wanted, reminding them that I'd pay. When it was my turn to order, however, Harmony looked at me hard, blinked twice, and dropped the customer-service smile from her face.

"Everything okay?" I asked.

She looked between me and the people in line behind me, obviously deciding something. She must have settled on a decision because she leaned across the counter to talk to me.

"Look, Juniper, you're a nice enough gal, but I'm not crazy about you working for those Calverton folks," she said in a loud whisper. A few people in line watched us curiously.

I was shaken. I knew Harmony didn't care for the Calverton family, but I hadn't expected her to call me out like this. Not here.

"Harm, let me explain…"

"You know how they're planning to change all our stores and restaurants to those awful high-end chains? How they want to strip the town of everything that makes it Rose Mallow?" Harmony's voice rose. She never held back on the things she was passionate about. I'd seen her close the restaurant abruptly because of a strong emotion. People stared at us. I shrunk into myself as she spoke.

"Well, yeah, but I—"

She shook her head. "I'm not kicking you out, Juniper, but take my advice. It might be best if you eat somewhere else for a bit."

I opened my mouth to say something, but no words came out. I could feel the others staring at me, undoubtedly judging me as another "Calverton con" like the protesters had. Feeling defeated, I nodded, paid for Florence and Eric's meals, and excused myself from the line. I half expected the others to start clapping at my dismissal, but their silent stares were just as loud.

I spotted Florence and Eric at a table. Eric waved at me. They were obviously unaware of the dressing-down I'd received from Harmony. I gathered that no one here knew that they worked for the Calvertons. I briefly wondered how many other people in the Purple Oyster did as well. They ran large enterprises, so it seemed unlikely that there wouldn't be a lot of Rose Mallions working for them. However, unlike them, I didn't have the luxury of being anonymous. At least not here.

"It's a beautiful day," I said. "Why don't we eat outside?"

"Outside?" Florence repeated with a sneer. "It's over ninety degrees out."

"I'm sure it'll be comfortable in the shade."

Their orders were called, and they picked them up.

"Where's your lunch?" Eric asked.

"Oh, uh, I'm not hungry," I replied. Naturally, my stomach took that moment to growl loudly. I tried to ignore it. Eric made a brief confused face before returning to his regular smile.

There were plenty of picnic tables available since no one else wanted to hang out in the stinging heat of the midday September sun. However, nothing with shade. Just as frustrating was the series of no-see-'ums hovering around. These tiny little gnats hung out in nearly invisible flying hives, irritating anyone who stumbled upon them. Florence kept up a low-level hum, which, given the pitch, I gathered reflected her annoyance. Eric seemed game to stay outside, and while I appreciated his enthusiasm, it didn't seem fair to torment either of them.

"Yeah, this is pretty unpleasant," I said. "You know, we could always take our lunch to my sister's place. It's down the boardwalk a little. Do you know the Wildflower Inn?"

Eric took a hand over his eyes and gazed down the boardwalk. After the series of stores and restaurants, the southern part of the walk served as a fence line between Rose Mallow's historic area and the Chesapeake Bay. That extended a few miles before ending in Redbud Park at the southern tip of town.

"Okay?" he said, although I could tell the excitement in his voice was wavering. "Why can't we eat inside? There were seats available."

"Well…" I couldn't think of what to say. Even though Florence and Eric also worked for the Calvertons, I didn't think anyone would bother them. I didn't particularly want to reveal that I was the reason we had been unceremoniously kicked out.

Florence interrupted to say, "I've had enough. I'm not going to march around to every single place in Rose Mallow. Go to the historical society, go to lunch, but go outside in the deathly heat, and now go to your sister's place. I'm putting my foot down."

Eric sighed and said, "I'm sorry, boss, but I don't really want to trek all over either."

Feeling defeated, I nodded. "Look, why don't you two head back in? I have a few things I want to take care of, and we can meet up later to go over everything. Even if the police have cordoned off the collections and archives building, there has to be somewhere available on the estate where three people can talk?"

The two barely waited for me to finish my sentence before disappearing back inside. As they did, my stomach growled again. I headed off looking for food when my phone rang. I didn't recognize the number, but the first three digits suggested it was from the Calvertons.

"Juniper Blume?" a woman asked.

"Yes? Who's this?"

"The board wants to meet with you. Can you be at the main office in thirty minutes?"

"I think so."

"Great." She hung up without having identified herself.

Chapter Twelve

When I arrived, a harried woman with thick Coke-bottle glasses and a bird's nest of white hair ran up to me. She glanced at me, at her watch, and then back to me. She reminded me of the white rabbit from *Alice in Wonderland*. I half expected her to announce that she was running late.

"Juniper Blume?" she asked.

"That's me," I replied.

"Oh, thank goodness. Finally. I wasn't sure..." She paused mid-sentence and looked back and forth again. I followed her gaze, unsure of what had caught her attention. She shook her head and said, "Come with me, please."

I followed my newest escort into one of the rock-hewn buildings. I hadn't been in it before, and the inside was dark with long hallways, lit dimly by sconces. I felt like I was traveling back in time.

"I didn't catch your name," I said.

"Ms. Melt. Patty Melt. And yes, I've heard every joke in the book," she said without a trace of good humor. I nodded as I followed behind her.

"Where are we going, Patty?"

She stopped and turned so suddenly on her heels that I nearly collided with her. She looked at me strangely. "To meet with the board, of course. And please, call me Ms. Melt."

"Of course, Ms. Melt. I knew we were meeting with the board, but I wasn't familiar with this building." I shook my head to stop rambling. "Do you know what they want to discuss with me today?"

She stopped in front of a door and grabbed the knob. "I'm simply the executive assistant. Good luck." She opened the door and stood back for me to enter. Instead of following me in, she shut the door behind me. Why did I feel like I'd been tricked? And trapped?

Inside was a conference room with a long table, surrounded by ten seated people. Everyone was older than me, and most of their suits probably cost more than I had made last year. I couldn't help gulping. I felt like I was in a nightmare, the kind where you're given a pop quiz at school but haven't read the material, and worse, you forgot to wear anything at all.

I spotted Leo. I thought about taking a seat next to him, but he was pointedly looking in every direction except at me. Taking that as a bad sign, I found somewhere else to sit. Unfortunately, I only belatedly realized it was next to the two women who had been gossiping about me at the club yesterday. They looked at me, then at each other, and shared a not-so-secret smile. I tapped my temples, feeling the start of a headache.

"Now that we're all here," said Martha Dresdale. She looked directly at me as she spoke. "I want to discuss how to best respond to yesterday's incident. Well, unless we're going to get interrupted by the detective again." She again stared at me.

"Have you heard anything more from the police?" I asked.

Martha shook her head. "All I've heard is that Big Al Cooley's death is suspicious."

"Do we know how he died yet?"

"Waiting for the medical examiner to make a ruling." She sounded displeased having to wait for anything. I doubted Martha was patient.

"Why was he in your library?" someone asked, turning to me.

"No idea," I replied.

"I heard he stole a book," said one of the gossipy women next to me.

"That hasn't been confirmed," I said to her.

"Can't be a coincidence that he owns that used bookstore on the boardwalk," said her friend. The two nodded at each other as if they had somehow solved the case.

"Maybe someone brought it in, and he was returning it?" I asked. I didn't particularly care for Big Al after my singular interaction with him, but it didn't seem fair to jump to negative conclusions. He may have been gruff and unpleasant, but he was also the victim.

"He was one of those protesters," said a man. His voice dripped with obvious distaste.

"Yeah, that's right. Threw Rose Bay on us," said the woman beside me.

"Maybe he was using the book as an excuse," added her friend. "Like, he was going to get inside and then damage the library."

Her friend jumped on to the idea. "So the book was a ruse."

"Right. Maybe he borrowed it and only now returned it."

"We don't lend books," I said, but no one listened to me.

"Do you think others have books?" asked a man.

"Other who?" I asked.

"Other protesters," he said, using a tone suggesting I was an idiot.

"How many books are missing?" asked Martha.

I didn't realize that everyone knew about the missing books. I dug through the paperwork in my messenger bag. I'd made a copy of the report. "Three books that we know about. All are by Edgar Allan Poe."

"Creepy," said the woman beside me.

"Okay, that settles it," said Martha. Everyone around me was nodding, but I didn't know what she meant. "Juniper, you'll need to look into this."

"Me?"

"Her?" Leo asked, sounding startled.

"Yes, you. You're our resident book expert, are you not? And you," Martha said, turning to Leo, "You're the one who hired her."

"Right, but—" Leo said, but Martha cut him off with a hand.

"Juniper, find out what you can about these missing books. Maybe that can tell us more about what happened to Big Al. And make sure it doesn't happen again. But you'll need to do it quietly. We don't want anyone outside this room to know you're looking into it."

With this many people here, did she really believe her suggestion would stay quiet? I stood up. "What? You can't order me around like this."

Martha closed her eyes briefly and grabbed the bridge of her nose. When she opened them again, I felt as if they bore a hole into my soul. "I heard about your exploits with that old Irish book…"

"The *Book of Kells*," I clarified.

She waved away the words. "Whatever. You did a good job finding out what happened there. And I heard you made good use of Calverton resources to achieve that." She turned to Leo. His face turned a deep shade of red. Was he embarrassed or angry? I felt both. I could only imagine what my face looked like.

"We should let the police do their job," Leo said.

"Of course. That's why you'll focus on the books part, Juniper. Like I said, you're our resident expert, aren't you? Didn't you research books frequently when you worked at the Library of Congress?"

"Well, yes…"

"Great, great. So this shouldn't be hard for you. We'll need some sort of cover story. I don't know. Maybe you can embed yourself with the protester group Big Al was part of. Be a mole or something," she said.

I felt nauseous at the suggestion. The last thing I wanted to do was spy on the protesters on behalf of the Calvertons.

"No way. I'm not allowing that," said Leo.

"Besides, we should have the protesters all arrested. That would stop any more issues," added a man. I looked over. Great, it was Teddy, the guy who had swung his arm around my waist at lunch. He rubbed me the wrong way.

"They're not doing anything illegal," said Leo.

"Perhaps we could protest outside their businesses. See how they like it," suggested someone else.

"We'll get them on social media. Modern smear campaign," added another.

I didn't like any of these ideas. They were beyond poor taste, especially now, given that someone had died. There was no way these suggestions wouldn't end up backfiring in the court of public opinion. They also didn't help us find out anything more about the missing books. As Nana Z used to say, we'd get more love with honey than with stingers. Right about now, I wished I could dive into her *Lekach*, a decadently moist cake with locally made honey and slices of apple from a nearby nursery.

"Juniper, looks like you have something in mind?" asked Martha. Every face at the table again turned to stare at me. I counted over fifty people here. I gulped. Martha smirked. "Nothing? I didn't think so…"

"I was gathering my thoughts," I said. The last thing I was going to have was some brassy bigwig believing she could order me around and put me in my place. I'd had a thought, although I wasn't sure how practical it was. It was the same idea that had me send Eric to the library and take Florence to the historical society this morning. We needed to show the town our sweeter side.

"The Rose Mallow Labor Day Festival is next weekend. Actually, it starts on a Thursday and goes through Labor Day Monday, making it a very long weekend," I paused, making sure everyone was following. No one said a word, so I continued. "Now, it's a pretty tight turnaround, especially with my building currently off-limits, but what if we have a booth with a small exhibit about the town, showing photos and documents of Rose Mallow in its prime."

"How does that help with your search?" Martha asked.

"It gives me a reason to go around town and talk to people. We were already at the historical society and library this morning," I said.

"Isn't the historical society doing something like that?" someone asked.

"No," said Leo. "They're an all-volunteer place. Too tiny to participate."

"Besides," I added, "Our display will also include how the Calverton family has been involved with the town for generations. We lean into feelings of nostalgia and goodwill. Demonstrate some appreciation to the community and how much we need each other. My Nana Z always used to say you'd win more people over with honey than with stingers."

Some heads nodded. "A charm offensive," a person said, and others agreed. I looked at Martha. She wasn't nodding, but she didn't look angry either.

"Can you really have that ready in less than a week and a half?" she asked with more than a glint of challenge in her voice.

"Of course," I said, knowing that it was a completely impractical task. Even if Eric thought I was a walking encyclopedia of history, I wasn't well versed on Rose Mallow's story. Nor did I know what documents we even had available digitally, let alone how quickly we could whip up text and print anything. Creating an exhibit this quickly was a ridiculous suggestion in the best of times. However, I smiled and hoped I projected confidence.

75

Chapter Thirteen

"I think it's a great idea," said another woman. I wondered how I'd missed her before with her bleached pixie cut and dangling earrings. Her hair was in bright contrast to her deep brown skin. Everything about her screamed artistic, trendy, and confident. "My team will get the booth registration squared away, and I can get Juniper scheduled for newspaper and radio interviews."

"Interviews?" I repeated. "Newspaper? Radio?" What had I signed myself up for?

"Look at how darling you are," she said, tapping a long lavender fingernail against her hot pink lips. "I love that totally retro vibe. Especially that *Amelie*-style haircut you're rocking with those super vintage clothes. So adorable. You're a fresh face and a fresh look. Plus, I've been reading up on you."

"You have?" I asked.

She nodded and winked. "I'm Desta. I oversee marketing for Calverton Industries. You're the granddaughter of Zinnia Blume. A local icon. With you returning to town, it gives these great prodigal granddaughter vibes."

"But I only came in the summers as a teen," I replied.

Desta waved my concerns away. "You're family. It's good enough. Plus, your sister's turned that old house into that truly adorable boutique inn. We could plug that in as well."

I did like the idea of drumming up business for the Wildflower Inn.

Martha looked less convinced. "Are you sure, Desta? I know your marketing department works wonders, but she's brand new. She doesn't know us at all."

Desta nodded. "It'll be a challenge, Martha, but I'm always up for one. Besides, a few talking points, a couple of practice seshs, and we'll be golden. Right, Juniper?" She winked at me. It felt like being friends with the coolest girl in high school.

"Oh, yeah, totally." I smiled brightly, hoping no one saw through my obvious lie.

"All right, then, let's get to it. Desta, get everything scheduled. Juniper, I'll be curious to see miracles you can make," said Martha.

"Me too," I whispered. Fortunately, no one appeared to hear me.

I sat in my seat as everyone piled out of the room, wondering what I'd gotten myself into. Our collections building was closed because of a death, I was brand new, and the town hated us. Judging by the protesters, they didn't care that I considered myself different and wanted to change things. To them, I was part of the "Calverton con" crew. And from what I'd seen at the Purple Oyster, the feeling extended well beyond that group.

I should have kept my mouth shut. If I couldn't pull this off, I was going to get fired. Who was I kidding? I was undoubtedly going to be fired anyway. Then, instead of helping Azalea, I would be an additional burden. Maybe I'd even have to move back home to our parents. I shuddered at the consideration.

"You okay?" Leo asked. He sat in the seat next to me. Everyone else was gone.

"I may have bitten off more than I can chew."

He laughed. "What else is new?"

I wanted to be mad, but he had a point.

"Look, I'm sorry. I didn't mean to make you so uncomfortable last night. I shouldn't have pushed you into a relationship you don't want. That wasn't fair. I know you're juggling a lot, and I made it worse," he said.

"What changed your mind?" I asked, thinking of how he wouldn't look at me when I first walked into the room.

He gave such a tiny smile. It felt like he was handing me a hidden treasure. "You did."

"I did?"

"You're not letting anyone get the best of you, Juniper. You're what this company needs. Everyone else can be so toxic, and I think I've become somewhat numb to their antics. But you came in here and suggested something positive," he said.

"It's a town fair booth," I replied.

He laughed. "Engaging with Rose Mallow would be a big step for the Calvertons. I think starting with a booth is a good strategy. Besides, it's not just a booth. You watch Desta. She'll get you on every local media outlet."

I dropped my head into my hands. "What have I signed myself up for?"

He placed a hand on my shoulder. "Nothing you can't handle."

I looked up. "Thanks, Leo."

He nodded. "I've got to go, but I'll see what I can do to help you guys. I'm sure we can pull some materials together. I mean, how hard could this be?"

"It feels like writing an entire thesis the night before it's due." In my head, I checked off the list of things we'd need to accomplish over the next week and change. When I worked at the Library of Congress, I didn't do many small festivals on their behalf, but it was all hands on deck for the annual National Book Festival each summer. I volunteered wherever needed, assisted with the visiting authors, and did a couple demonstrations about caring for historic books people might have at home.

I thought about what needed to happen next. We'd need to finish the timeline that Florence started, focusing on important milestones in the history of Rose Mallow and the Calvertons. That could be turned into some panels, or maybe even some pop-up trade show style displays. If we could locate some historic photos or prints to go with the timeline, that would be good, but since I wasn't sure when I could get into our collections, we'd only have access to anything already scanned and saved in the cloud.

I wondered if Desta would have some swag we could give away. It'd be great to have something to hand out to festival attendees. Plus, it'd be nice to have something for kids to do, like coloring pages or a simple activity. Maybe we could have something announcing the museum somehow, although there weren't a lot of firm details to share yet. I'd have to check with Desta about what news she'd want to push at the booth.

"There you are, boss!" Eric said, pulling me out of my thoughts. "We couldn't find you anywhere."

"Apologies. The board wanted to meet, and I was thinking through some logistics," I replied honestly.

"What kind of logistics?" Florence asked. She and Eric took some of the empty seats at the long table. I explained the plan to create a simple display for a booth at the Rose Mallow Labor Day Festival. "Simple?"

"Well, I know it's a big ask," I said, "But I have full faith we can accomplish it."

"Sounds fun!" Eric replied.

"Sounds unrealistic," said Florence.

I shrugged. "Look, you already have a good starting timeline. And we don't want an overly complex one anyway. Let's highlight some major points of how the Calvertons have always been part of Rose Mallow. We should find some photos to go with it. I'll talk to Desta in marketing about the rest." I explained about the interviews planned for the week.

Florence sat with her arms crossed. Given her grim expression, she didn't appear convinced.

"I can dig some images up," Eric added. I appreciated his enthusiasm. "It'll be good to focus on something besides…well, you know." He waved a hand in the general direction of the collections and archives building.

Without meaning, I turned towards that way. I thought about how the board wanted me to investigate Big Al's death. That meant I'd need to learn more about the missing books. As much as the idea of looking into his death left me feeling queasy, my librarian senses were aflutter at wondering why he had the book next to him.

"Did you learn anything about the missing books at the library this morning?" I asked Eric. His head tottered back and forth on his shoulders like a kid's seesaw.

"Not a lot from Brandy, but I got into our database online and printed out some materials about the books themselves. Then I looked up some information about Edgar Allan Poe." He rifled through a bag and handed me a thick stack of sheets. I thumbed through them but knew I'd have to spend more time digging through them later.

"What did you learn about Poe? Everyone knows his biography," Florence said in a know-it-all voice. I had to close my eyes to keep from rolling them.

"I wanted to see if he'd ever been to Rose Mallow," Eric said.

"And?" she replied.

"No luck. I couldn't find anything about Poe and Rose Mallow. So then I tried to look up about Big Al and Poe," he said.

That was a good idea. If there'd been any articles about Big Al selling books by Poe recently, that could tell us something. Or maybe some other connection I hadn't considered between the two.

"But it was also a bust," Eric said.

My shoulders fell in defeat, but I couldn't let them see my concern. Instead, I patted Eric's arm and said, "Good effort. Research is always full of rabbit holes. But one of them may lead somewhere special. We'll have to keep trying."

Eric nodded, but I spotted Florence rolling her eyes behind his back.

"Okay, it's been another day. We have our assignments. Tomorrow, we'll reconvene to go over the festival project and figure out what else we can learn about the missing books." I smiled, hoping to project confidence. I wasn't sure if the phrase "fake it until you make it" was accurate or not, but I was going to do my best to believe in it.

Chapter Fourteen

Back at the Wildflower Inn, I found Azalea working on another batch of blintzes. At least the kitchen resembled more of a sparkler than the full-on fireworks detonation I'd witnessed previously.

"Taste this," Azalea said, holding up a spoon to my mouth. I happily played guinea pig to whatever concoction she'd made.

"Lemony goodness. This is magical." I wanted to lick the rest of the spoon. I never got to eat lunch, so I hoped she wouldn't mind if I downed a bowlful of the blintz cream cheese filling.

"Okay, but what about this one?" She brought me another spoon. This one was filled with a purplish jam.

"Berry good," I said. She made a face at my pun.

"Can I try?" Violet came into the room, followed by Clover.

"I don't want to ruin your dinner. You can have some later," Azalea said.

Violet's face dropped. "No, now!" Clover danced around in agreement.

Azalea watched her daughter for a moment. I could see the calculations playing out across her face. Then, a mischievous smile spread across my sister's face. Whatever she had decided was devious. "Fine. Try this."

She handed Violet a third spoon. Violet happily took it but spit the filling out. "Ewww. Yuck." The spoon fell to the floor, where Clover had no issue lapping up the remainder.

"What was it?" I asked.

"Care to try for yourself?" she asked, still sporting the same smirky smile. "Maybe?"

Azalea handed me a fresh spoon with filling. With trepidation, I tasted it and immediately made a face. "Oh, is that…"

"Cream cheese with mint?" she supplied.

"Ugh. I hate mint," I said.

"Me too!" added Violet.

Azalea laughed loudly but good-naturedly. "She's definitely your niece. I don't know anyone else who hates mint besides the two of you."

"You know how some people taste soap when they have cilantro?" I asked.

"Yeah, I've heard that," she replied.

"So it's like that for me with mint," I said.

"It tastes like soap?"

"Well, no, but it tastes weird. I guess we have mutant taste buds," I said, wrapping an arm around Violet. She giggled beneath me.

"You're definitely a mutant," said Azalea with a wink.

"Hah. Hah," I replied with mock sarcasm. Azalea responded by flicking a bit of cream cheese at my nose. Violet lost it at that, falling to the floor in laughter. Clover bounced up onto my lap, licking the tasty treat from my face.

Azalea sat back on a kitchen chair and sighed. "Oh, it's so good to feel like this."

"Like what?" I asked, joining her at the table.

"Like family." Her eyes got slightly misty.

"Are you okay?" I put my hand atop hers on the table. She nodded, but her eyes remained moist. "I didn't ask how things went with Rory last night."

She took in a deep breath and looked thoughtful for a moment. "It was nice. Really nice."

Something about the way she spoke bothered me. "That's good, right?"

She turned away from me and looked out the bay windows to the Chesapeake Bay. "Yeah, it is. But…. Oh, this is going to sound silly…"

"What?"

"Have you ever gotten what you wanted and then not been sure it was what you wanted?" She looked up at the ceiling and shook her head.

I laughed dryly. "Yes, I think I understand that pretty well." Taking this job definitely fits that description. I want to work with the collections and open an amazing resource, but I wasn't sure that working with the Calvertons was worth the stress. At least not this Foundation board. I shivered in frustration. And now, with the death and everything else, I was feeling overwhelmed.

"Well, that's how I feel with Rory. I told you that he wants to get back together with me. And I want that too, but… Well, I don't know. It feels too fast."

I nodded. "Then tell him. You need to take your time."

"I don't think he understands. He's ready for everything to go back to the way it was right now. I want us back together, too, but I'm scared that if we move too quickly, then we'll end up making the same mistakes we did before." Azalea gazed over at Violet and Clover playing. "What if we get together only to break up again? I don't want to put Vi through that. Not again."

I wanted to tell my sister that everything would work out perfectly this time, but sadly I'd yet to find a book that predicted the future correctly. Even if I couldn't read into what would happen in the world, I knew how to read her. "You'll figure out what works best for you. All three of you. And I'll support you no matter what you decide."

Her eyes grew cloudy. "Thanks, Juniper. I really appreciate that."

"I missed being there for you before, but I will never do that again," I said.

Suddenly, Violet was chasing after Clover. "Bring that back!"

I looked over and noticed my messenger bag was on the ground, wide open. The contents had spilled all over, including files on the missing paperwork. A shiver went up and down my spine.

"Clover!" I darted after them. I heard him running up the hallway towards the front door. He made a muffled bark. He must have grabbed some of my files in his little mouth.

"Drop it, Clover!" said Violet.

I caught up with them in the lobby. Violet wagged a finger at Clover, commanding him again to drop the thick file folder in his mouth. His little bottom wiggled furiously in the air, while his front half lowered to the floor. I recognized his posture immediately. He thought this was the best game ever. Violet reached for the papers, but he jumped away, running into the library.

"Come back, Clover!" yelled Violet.

"What does he have?" Azalea asked, catching up behind me.

I kept my eyes trained on my young dog. "Important papers. About missing books from the collection. Including the one found with Big Al."

"Oh no. You take the left, I'll take the right. I'll block the entrance to the library," she said. I nodded and headed in. We tried to corner Clover, but he dashed up on the antique fainting couch. Fortunately, he dropped the papers. I went after them while Azalea grabbed Clover. He must have been feeling victorious because he covered her face in kisses.

"Bad puppy!" Violet said.

I shook my head. "He's not bad, Vi. He thought it was fun. Probably means he needs a walk." As I spoke, I flipped through the paperwork. It was soggy and dented in but still readable.

"I think it means we need to take him to the playground," Azalea said.

"Playground! Playground!" Violet chanted.

"As soon as I get the kitchen cleaned up," she said while giving her daughter a sweet bop on the nose.

"I'll be happy to do that," I offered.

Azalea laughed uproariously. "Oh no, that's okay."

"Hey, I'm not *that* horrible at cleaning," I replied, slightly offended.

She bit her lower lip and nodded. "Uh-huh."

I crossed my arms. "I've cleaned my townhouse in D.C. before."

"And how many things got broken along the way?"

I didn't answer. I could manage the delicate work of caring for rare and historic manuscripts, and yet, for everyday cleaning, I was an utter mess. When it came to basic housekeeping, something refused to click. It wasn't even a situation where you break a glass to get out of doing the dishes. Unless the item was leather-bound, I was truly and completely incompetent.

Azalea stood up and headed back towards the kitchen. "It's fine, sis. Get cracking on the case. I know you're on it."

"Is it that obvious?" I asked.

She laughed. "There's a book involved."

I sighed. My sister knew me too well.

* * *

After they left, I returned to the chaise lounge in the library and flipped through my files. Among other printouts, Eric had given me a copy of the finding aid for the collection he'd been inventorying from which the books were missing. Eric had done a good job of giving background about the collection and the Calverton who had assembled it. I skimmed the pages, reading about one of Leo's relatives, Dorothea Calverton. I recognized the name as the same one adorning the library building. Apparently, she was a big Poe fan herself, having collected as many first editions as she could of the literary icon's works. She also had correspondence and other papers connected to Poe. Out of twenty stories in the collection, there were three missing, the ones Eric had mentioned.

As I read through the file, I paused occasionally to search for related items on my phone. I wanted to find out more about Dorothea Calverton and the particular volumes impacted. Maybe I'd find an unexpected connection to our thief and, more importantly, to Big Al's death. I wondered if someone had targeted Poe, or if that book had been convenient for them to access in the moment of the theft? Would they go for more books in the collection, or was this all they wanted?

I rifled through more of what Eric had provided. He'd printed out several pages at the library, including short biographies on Poe and different books they had on file. Somewhere he found a timeline of different places Poe had lived. I noticed he'd only been in Maryland for around a year, starting in 1829. He returned in 1835 to marry his young cousin, Virginia, but the couple moved with her mother to Richmond shortly afterwards. There was no indication he had ever spent time in Rose Mallow instead he had lived in Baltimore. Since Poe never lived in the state again, it was uncertain why he suddenly showed up in Baltimore right before dying unexpectedly in 1849. Poe had been only forty.

I wondered how Big Al might have gotten the book featuring *The Gold*

Bug. I tried looking up information on him, but the databases I accessed mainly provided basic and bland clues about his life. There were a couple newspaper articles about his store, but nothing which gave me an in-depth feeling for the man. However, I found a group messenger board announcing a makeshift memorial for him at his house tomorrow. Maybe I could find out more about him there.

Chapter Fifteen

The next morning, I checked in with my team. We'd found space in some random Calverton building, although I wasn't really sure of the place's normal function or even where exactly on the campus we were. That the police hadn't allowed us back into the collections and archives building worried me. I wasn't sure they'd have done that if Big Al's death had been completely natural.

"Earth to Juniper?" Eric waved a hand in front of my face.

I blinked a few times and shook my head. "Oh, I'm sorry. I was a little distracted."

He smiled in an understanding way. "I think we all are."

"You were saying something about…" I stopped. Eric had been explaining his work to me when I'd spaced out, but I couldn't remember what he had been telling me.

"Yes, about the timeline project. Florence and I made some headway." He glanced over his shoulder to the grumpy librarian behind him. Florence sat in a desk chair with her arms folded across her chest. She was pointedly not looking at me. I was grateful to Eric for his patience in working with her. Maybe she was better with him when I wasn't there?

"That's great news. Anything you want to share?" I asked.

"Not quite." He put a finger up, as if asking for an extra minute. "But by the end of the week, I think we'll have something solid for you to review.

"Okay, that sounds promising."

"What are you going to do?" Florence asked. Her voice dripped with derision. I ignored it, but I couldn't be polite for much longer. How could

I get through to her? With it being only the three of us working here, I couldn't afford to fire her. Especially when she held so much institutional memory. I wondered if that's why she felt could get away with being so rude to my face?

"Well, I'm going to pop by the memorial for Big Al," I said.

Florence sat up, dropping her arms to her sides. She looked alarmed. "You're what?"

"I figured it would be a nice gesture to attend."

"That's…that's…." Florence seemed to struggle for the right word.

"Nice?" Eric offered.

She made a raspberry with her tongue. I was caught off guard by her immature reply. Eric, however, put up a hand to hide his laughter.

"No, that's ludicrous!" Florence cried.

"Why?" I asked, surprised at her response.

Florence breathed in deeply. Her face flushed. "It's…." She obviously struggled to find her words, but I didn't know how to help her. Flustered, she waved both hands in front of her face and stomped off.

I looked at Eric. "Do you know what that was about?"

He shrugged. "Not a clue. Maybe because he was so anti-Calverton? She's worked here a long time and obviously hates the protesters."

"Yeah, I guess so." I didn't know why the answer didn't settle me, but there was something in her response that seemed off, even for her. I couldn't quite put my finger on it. However, it wasn't the moment to frustrate her further. I'd leave things alone and come back to her another time. Besides, if Eric was right, then it was time for me to rebuild some of these burnt bridges. Wasn't that what an executive director should do?

* * *

The memorial wasn't for another hour, so I headed down to the boardwalk. Surprisingly, Boardwalk Books was open. I found that strange, but then again, it was unlikely Big Al wasn't the only person who worked there, so I shouldn't have assumed it would be closed. He'd died at the Calverton Estate, so the police must not have closed off his store. Regardless, I wondered if the place held any clues to our book mystery.

I poked my head inside and felt transported back to my high school summers. I'd spent many hours in this store, deciding which books I could get for my meager allowance. Although the store was narrow, it went deep and jammed with bookshelves. It was easy to get lost in the labyrinth of shelves, overflowing with used paperbacks and dogeared hardback books.

There was a certain scent to this bookstore I couldn't quite place, like softened leather or maybe tobacco. Being a librarian specializing in old books, I often encountered a similar aroma in libraries, but there was something different about being in a used bookstore, filled with loved books, looking for new homes. The scent of aged papers captivated me. If it was ever bottled up into a bottle or lotion, I'd be the first to buy it.

"Juniper?"

I twirled on my heels to encounter a face I recognized. "Nuri Cho? Is that you?"

"Of course it is, you rapscallion," said my old library school roommate.

"Scoundrel," I replied.

"Knave," she said.

"Rogue."

"Imp."

At that, we both burst out laughing. I enveloped her in a hug. Having been petite all my life, there weren't many adults I towered over, but Nuri was one of them. Her frame was curvaceous like a 1950s Hollywood bombshell— "*zaftig,*" as Nana Z might say. Nuri was at least an inch shorter than me. Okay, so towered might have been a strong word, but I'd take it.

We both loved vintage clothes, although from different eras. While I loved all things mid-century, she rocked a 1970s black bomber jacket over a t-shirt emblazoned with the logo of a punk band I didn't recognize. Her black hair was in a shaggy cut with thick purple and blue strands.

"I've missed you," I said earnestly. Midway through school, Nuri had to go back home to somewhere in Pennsylvania. I wasn't sure of the details, but it seemed to be a family matter. If I remembered correctly, Nuri's father was from South Korea, while her mother hailed from Turkey. She'd told me that they'd selected her first name because it was used in both countries.

We lost track of each other. For a while, she used to put up some photos on her social media of various concerts, women she was dating, and, of course, her favorite libraries, but that became less frequent, and I didn't know where she ended up.

"I never expected to find you here," I said.

"Or to find you! In this tiny town?"

"I used to come here every summer. My grandmother owned a house here. Now my sister has turned it into an inn," I explained. I debated whether to mention my new job with the Calvertons. If Nuri worked here, I wasn't sure what she would think of that. She might have felt the same way as Big Al.

"That's so cool. I came here because I didn't have any connections here," she said. "I needed to get away and start fresh. Well, you know how that goes, given all the times you took off for those random adventures. Remember the time you took a last-minute flight to Paris? For one weekend?"

I smiled and sighed. Those had been good times. I'd sometimes look on different websites to find a last-call fare to anywhere in the world. Before I'd found library school, I'd spent a lot of time train-hopping across different continents. Trying to find myself, I suppose. But, eventually, I realized books could take me anywhere at any time. I still loved to travel, although it'd been a while since I'd done something so spontaneous.

"I wish you would have come with me," I said.

Nuri nodded. "I know, but money doesn't grow like my succulents do. Come check these out." She led me to a row of plants basking in the shop's display window. In between the spiky green wonders were various books for sale.

"That's a nice display."

"Thanks. It took a while to convince Big Al to let me play with this window, but while he would never have admitted to it, I spotted him grinning at it a few times."

"I'm very sorry about what happened to him," I replied.

Nuri's face dropped. "He was gruff and rough around the corners, but I'm sorry he's gone. Working here really gave me an opportunity to rekindle my love of books." She reached out and caressed the spines of books packed into a nearby bookshelf.

"Oh, Nuri, I'm so sorry," I replied. We walked between the aisles. Each had a different theme: mystery, cooking, sci-fi, etc. There was a bump-out addition tacked on the back with kids' books and used toys. No one else was in the store.

"Thanks. I don't think it's really hit me yet," she said.

"Are you going to the memorial?" I asked.

She sported a sad smile. "I don't think so. Someone needs to take care of the store. I was Big Al's only regular employee."

It seemed strange that she wouldn't close the store and go, but I didn't push the issue. Instead, I noted sympathy cards and flowers displayed along the countertop. There were so many they nearly obscured the cash register. "Looks like there's a bit of a memorial here."

Nuri nodded. "Yeah, people have been dropping off a lot of stuff. So much food, too. I gave some to Emily."

My face must have shown my confusion, so she explained, "Emily's Big Al's wife. She helps in the store sometimes, but it's been less often as she's dealing with some health issues."

"Did they all get along?" I asked.

Nuri raised an eyebrow. "Why do you ask?"

"Oh, uh…thinking about my family, I guess."

The answer must have sufficed, because she nodded. "Yeah, I don't know. Emily's really nice. She gets along with everyone, but she has a lot of arthritis issues and some other medical things that make it impossible for her to work here anymore. No idea how well she and Big Al got along. I overheard some fights sometimes, but if you've ever met Big Al, you'd know he's prone to get into fights with everyone."

I flashed back to the fight he picked with me. I couldn't help shuddering a little. "Did you ever hear what they were fighting about?"

"Family matters mainly," she said. A confused look crossed her face, as if she couldn't make up her mind. We stood in an awkward silence until she said, "Juniper, can I show you something?"

"Of course."

She led me behind the front counter and lifted a piece of fabric off a locked Plexiglass case. Inside a shelf filled with older books.

"Can you open it up?" I asked.

She shook her head. "Big Al always kept the key on him. I can't find a duplicate anywhere."

I peered into the case at the spines of the leather-bound books inside. Even from here, I could tell these books were something special. If I was right, most of them were first editions.

"Wow, these are…" I couldn't even get the words out. "They're museum pieces."

Nuri nodded. "Yeah, *Alice in Wonderland, Raggedy Ann and Andy, Oliver Twist.* I can go on."

I couldn't help looking back around the rest of the store. I didn't want to be rude, but honestly, Boardwalk Books was a run-down shop filled with well-loved books. It wasn't the kind of place where you expected to find a bunch of expensive books like these.

"I was never allowed to go into this display. Most of the time, I couldn't even take this fabric off it," Nuri said.

"Did people regularly come here to buy these?"

She shrugged. "I never saw anyone buy them."

"Never? Then were these a personal collection of his?"

"No idea. He wouldn't tell me anything about them. I asked a few times, and he would change the topic quickly. I got the impression he didn't want to discuss that they existed. But it gets weirder."

"Oh?"

"His weird behavior about these books made me curious, so I started taking notes. I guess my librarian training kicked in. I cataloged and tracked them." She pulled out a small notebook from a drawer. Inside, she had listed the books and dates in her typically tiny, neat pencil handwriting. "But sometimes, one or more would disappear. In the middle of the day, when no one had come in for them."

"Could Big Al have taken them when you weren't looking?"

She made a face. "I thought that at first, too. But then, one night, after another book disappeared, I reviewed the security tapes. No one came up to the display the entire day. Not Big Al, not Emily, and not anyone else. The book vanished." She waved her hands around like she'd performed a magic trick.

"That's strange."

Nuri nodded. "I looked all around. Above the display case, below it, everywhere. I couldn't find anything."

I didn't understand any better than she did. Why had Big Al been so secretive about these books? How did they disappear, and where did they go? I had a feeling that they were connected to our missing *Tales* book, but I didn't know how that was possible.

She gnawed on her lower lip. "Are you, uh, going to tell the police about this?" She waved her other hand towards the rare books.

"You haven't?"

"Not yet. I'm going to tell them, but I don't want them to think…" She stumbled over her words. I waited as she regrouped. "Look, I don't want to be any part of this. I've had enough going on in my life. Rose Mallow was supposed to be a quiet place I could go to without trouble."

"What are you talking about, Nuri?" I asked, surprised at the sudden urgency in her voice.

She took a sharp intake of breath before lifting her hands and wiping at the air. "Nothing, Juniper, nothing. Forget I said anything." Her elbows dropped to the counter, and she covered her face with her hands. I spotted a ring with a dragon reading a book on one of her fingers. Her nails were painted in a variety of purples.

"Nuri, do you need help?"

She lifted her face, and I spotted a fleeting expression. It looked like terror. Then it slid away, and the same sad smile returned. "No, I'm good. Thanks for coming in. It was good to see you. I'm going to take my lunch break now." She ushered me out of the store, flipped around the "Store Closed" sign, and turned off the lights.

Chapter Sixteen

After leaving Boardwalk Books, I made a quick stop at the Flower Power florists next door to pick up a small bouquet for the memorial.

"Juniper, right?" a voice behind me asked while I decided on which bouquet to select.

I looked up and around, pleased to see Brandy Rivers, Eric's librarian girlfriend. "Hey Brandy, what brings you here?"

She smiled. "My parents own Flower Power. They had an errand to run, so I'm helping out for a little bit. I think they were sorry I didn't go into the family business, but these thumbs are definitely not green." She held up her hands and laughed. Then her expression turned serious. "But, hey, I heard about Big Al. How are you doing?"

I shrugged. "It was shocking, that's for sure. I'm actually here to pick out some flowers to bring to his memorial."

She leaned in closer to me. "Any update on what happened to him?"

"Not yet. I don't think the police know what killed him. Or how he ended up in our library," I said. We wandered the small boutique as we spoke. I picked up three different groups of flowers and put each back. I couldn't make up my mind.

"Yeah, Eric told me all about it. He's pretty weirded out about it all." Brandy must have noticed my indecision because she led me to another display of flowers. She picked up a small but beautiful one with sunflowers and larkspur. I nodded as she handed it to me.

"He hasn't told me how he's feeling," I said.

She nodded as if not surprised. "Eric's definitely a keep his head down and not make a scene type of guy. His family is here legally, but I don't think that worry has ever fully gone away."

"He wasn't born in America?"

She shook her head. "In Mexico. He came over when he was really little. I think his dad got a job at the National Institute of Health. Researching something pharmaceutical, I think?" She shrugged and cocked her head to the side. "I don't know. Like using natural medicine from plants..." She spread her hands out as if showing off the florist's shop.

"NIH? That's all the way up in D.C. How did they end up down here in Rose Mallow?"

We walked over to the cash register. She went to the other side to check me out. "I don't know the whole story. I think his parents divorced, or maybe they didn't fully divorce because of the immigration status thing? Anyway, his mother brought him down here when she opened the panaderia. You'd have to ask him."

"La Artesa, right? Is it open?" I asked.

She shook her head. "Not right now. They're only open early in the mornings. After that, they do most of their business supplying breads and pastries to caterers, restaurants, and other places. They do a lot of business with the Calvertons actually. I wish that family would work with other local businesses. Our flower store wouldn't mind seeing even a drop of their wealth." She shook her head. "You always hope to get a tiny crumb from them."

"They don't support local businesses?" I asked. Maybe Azalea would consider using La Artesa at the Wildflower Inn? Sure, she loved to bake, but how stress relieving would it be if she could unload that task, while also supporting a local place? Maybe we could support Flower Power, too?

Brandy's laugh was sad. "The Calvertons? Why would they want to support us when they want to bulldoze everything here? Doesn't even matter that this wasn't their land to begin with. They use their money and influence to get whatever they want."

Her caustic tone shook me. "Do you not care that they employ your boyfriend?"

She rolled her eyes. "Don't get me wrong, I'm glad that Eric found a job. But it's measly crumbs compared to what they could do. I probably shouldn't say this to his boss, but you should know the truth. The Calvertons will only part with the absolute bare minimum." She crossed her arms and stood defiantly.

"I'm brand new and learning," I replied. "But I believe things can be improved."

She sighed. "Yeah, so does Eric. He claims he can make things better from the inside. I'd rather leave, but I can't simply abandon my job or family. Eric says the same thing. He told me it was a big enough deal when he didn't want to work in his mother's panaderia. He says he couldn't move away from her, too."

Brandy leaned in across the countertop. She looked left and right, as if about to tell me a secret. I leaned in to meet her. A mischievous smile played across her face. I held my breath, wondering what she was about to reveal.

"It's not officially on the menu, but ask them for their Mexican hot chocolate." She shivered in obvious delight. "Earth-shattering, it's so good. It's quite spicy with cayenne and other fiery chili peppers. Amazing stuff."

I couldn't help laughing. Her revelation wasn't what I expected, but I was happy to receive it. "I'll make sure to try it out. Thanks for helping me choose these flowers. They're perfect for the memorial."

* * *

Since La Artesa was closed to the public, I considered popping into the Purple Oyster for some baked goods, but I didn't want to risk Harmony kicking me out again. I briefly considered stopping by the Wildflower Inn, but that seemed like overkill. The flowers would be good enough.

* * *

Big Al lived in a small Cape Cod-style cottage in a northern neighborhood.

As I walked up to the open front door, I nearly collided with Detective Gupta, who was coming out.

"Juniper, fancy meeting you here," she said.

"I'm making a condolence call," I replied.

"Uh-huh. Well, make sure that's all you're doing." She wagged a perfectly manicured finger at me. I put up my hands in mock surrender. "And if you do happen to overhear anything useful, I want to be the first to know."

"Detective Gupta, are you approving of me investigating?" I asked with a laugh.

She rolled her eyes. "No. But if you keep your ears open, you may learn some things I didn't."

A thought crossed my mind. "Wait, you're still investigating?" Detective Gupta paused, seemingly waiting for me to catch up. "Big Al's death…it's not natural, is it?"

She sighed. "I can't disclose anything."

"Was he murdered?" I whispered my question.

"I said I can't disclose anything."

"How was he killed?" My whisper grew louder.

"Juniper, even if I wanted to tell you, which I do not, I don't have the information to share. Nothing is officially ruled," she said.

"My goodness. That means something makes you think it's worth looking into, even before any official results come back."

Detective Gupta put a hand to her forehead. "Look, tell me if you hear anything, okay? But no playing detective, understood?"

"I hear you," I said, hoping my noncommittal statement was acceptable. I knew she wouldn't be happy if she knew my board wanted me to dig into things. Another thought popped into my head. "Do you have any suspects?"

"Juniper!" She sounded exasperated, but I wasn't done.

"People of interest?"

"Juniper." Her voice was harder this time. If I hadn't crossed a line yet, then I was coming dangerously close to it. I needed to work on my internal editor.

"Okay, but tell me this. Am I a person of interest?" I asked.

She looked at me like I'd spoken in Latin. "Why would you think that?"

"I don't know. Because he was in my library with one of our stolen books. Well, assuming it is one of our stolen books. I still have yet to figure out what the secret message means. Any luck on your end?"

A small smile crept across her face. "I can safely say we're not interested in you beyond your rare books expertise. I may have more questions about that. But enough people saw you walking across campus, and we spotted you on several tapes, so we know you weren't in the library when Big Al died."

I felt oddly relieved, even though I knew I wasn't involved.

"Did you find out how he made it inside? Did you see anyone else?"

The detective sighed. "Stick to the books, Juniper. Please."

I thought about what I'd seen in Boardwalk Books. I felt like I should tell Detective Gupta about the rare books display, but I also got the impression that it might make trouble for Nuri. I wanted to dig a little deeper into that before taking it to her.

"Always happy to help with books," I said.

"Good, thanks." She turned and walked away.

Chapter Seventeen

People jammed the small house. Plates piled atop every surface: casseroles, cakes and pastries, charcuterie boards, and fruit displays. I felt like I was at a college house party, except there wasn't any loud music playing, and it was far too light out. Unfortunately, the house was as smoky as many of those parties. I felt ready to gag, but I was there with a purpose, so I needed to see it through.

At first, I thought the smoke came from a large, three-wick candle on one tables, but as I passed closer to it, I realized a far more pleasant scent emanated from the thick candle. Somehow, it smelled like Boardwalk Books with its sweet aroma of aged papers, leather bindings, and old wooden shelves. There were those same undercurrents of vanilla and almonds I had remembered from my teenage years.

I dodged various groups of people I didn't know until I found myself in the living room. A woman in her mid-sixties sat on a worn-out recliner. Next to her was a side table with a portrait from her wedding to Big Al. She also had a thick ashtray, nearly overflowing with cigarette butts, not including the one she nursed on. I must have found the source of the smoky smell. Her mascara had run down her cheeks. It didn't take a detective to realize this must be Emily.

I held out my flowers and walked up to her. My heart began beating harder, and my hands felt clammy. Instead of going dry, my mouth seemed to get wetter, and I worried I might drool. I hadn't realized how nervous I felt until I was almost upon her, when I wished for anything I could turn around and go home.

"Emily Cooley?" I asked.

"Who's asking?" Her voice was raspy. She looked me over, appearing wary of not knowing me.

"I'm Juniper Blume. I wanted to express my condolences on the loss of your husband."

"Juniper Blume?" She paused, as if figuring out if she knew my name or not. "Howdya know Al?"

"Uh…" I wasn't sure how to tell her I was the one who found his body.

"You one of his harpies?"

"Excuse me?" I asked, genuinely confused.

"You one of his harpies? Got some nerve showing up here, Juniper Blume. Is that even your real name?" She punctuated her questions with her cigarette. The smell made my stomach queasy.

"I'm not a harpy," I replied.

She looked me over, as if assessing me. "Nah, you're not a harpy. You're something worse."

"Worse?" I repeated.

Emily looked right at me and said, loud enough for others to hear, "Yeah, worse than a harpy. You're a Calverton con. I saw Al giving you what's for at the compound gates the other day."

I felt every pair of eyes turn and lock on me. The same feelings of fear and dread I had during the protest came rushing back. My heart beat faster, and my breathing grew shallow. I wanted to run away.

"She a Calverton?" someone asked.

"And all she brought were some measly flowers?" another person said.

"Maybe I'll come by another time," I said. "I wanted to express my sympathies." I dropped my flowers into Emily's lap.

"Leave them alone!" someone else said.

I stepped backwards, tripping into a table behind me, and fell on my behind, narrowly missing the table's corner with my head. I slowly stood back up, relieved I hadn't hurt myself until I noticed that I'd knocked over the lit candle, which smelled like the bookstore.

"Oh no!" I yelled and pointed. Someone shoved me aside to put out the candle before it caught anything else on fire. I felt helpless, having almost started a catastrophe.

"Al's candle!" Emily cried. "He made that for me."

"I'm so sorry," I said, feeling helpless.

The person who had saved the candle brought it over to Emily, setting it in front of their wedding photo. She studied it carefully and sighed, appearing relieved that it wasn't hurt.

I needed to get out of here. Coming was obviously a bad idea. I pushed my way through the crowd, which seemed to delight in knocking into me. It felt like being back in a high school hallway, with all the cool kids ganging up on me.

* * *

Thankfully, I made it outside safely. I sat on the front porch, catching my breath. My heart beat a fast tattoo in my chest.

"Wait," said a voice behind me. I wanted to run, but I felt a hand on my arm. The touch was gentle. I turned to find an older man smiling kindly at me. "You're Azalea's sister, aren't you?"

"Yes," I said, but my voice was unsteady.

"And Z's granddaughter?"

"Yes, sir, I'm Juniper Blume," I said, feeling stronger now. He said both names in such a friendly tone.

He laughed. "Oh, none of that ma'am stuff. I'm Jim. Jim Cheevers. Your grandmother and I were good friends. We were both members of the Rose Mallow Artist's Guild."

"Do you paint?" I asked, thinking of my grandmother's watercolors.

"No, I'm all about sculpture. Like getting my hands dirty with clay." He held them up, and although they looked clean to me, they were lined with callouses. His nails were neatly trimmed. His hands looked strong.

"What can I help you with, Mr. Cheevers?" I asked.

His expression turned thoughtful. "Jim, please. Look, now I don't like what the Calvertons are planning for Rose Mallow any more than anyone else here, but I also don't think it helps anything to antagonize young women showing some sympathy."

"I appreciate that."

"Were you the one to find him?" he asked.

I nodded.

"I'm sorry for that. Must not have been easy."

I sighed. "No, it wasn't. He was in the reading room of the library."

Jim shook his head. Then his eyes narrowed in on me. "What was he doing there?"

"I don't know." I thought about telling him about the Poe book, but I stopped, reminding myself that I didn't know Jim. His concern for me could have masked ulterior interests. I shuddered, realizing that I was assuming the worst of everyone.

"You work in their library?" he asked.

"I'm turning their collections into a public museum," I said.

"Well, that sounds like a mighty fine idea."

"I don't think everyone else thinks so." I looked at the door, half afraid the mob might come tumbling out of it.

Jim sat on an Adirondack chair on the porch. I considered joining him in the adjoining one, but I didn't want to linger long. "No, I suppose they wouldn't."

"Were you close with Big Al?" I asked.

He nodded. "I used to babysit him when he was a baby. They didn't call him Big Al back then." He laughed. "He was a scrawny thing. Always getting picked on in school. I'd like to think I'm the one who introduced him to books. He started his own little book club with a bunch of the neighborhood kids."

"That's really nice," I said truthfully.

"It was. Then he hit a growth spurt and really bulked out. Joined the football team and took them to State. But he was big enough that he could read without hiding it. No one was going to pick on a star football player."

Without realizing it, I found myself sitting beside him. I was still worried about the group inside, but I had the sense that Jim had a lot of standing. I listened intently to him continue about Big Al's life.

"That's when he became Big Al. Went to show how large he'd gotten from being so tiny. We all thought he was going places. He had a nice scholarship to college, and I knew he wanted to get out of this backwaters town."

"What happened?"

"His dad got sick. The big C. His mom called Big Al home from college. He ended up taking over the family bookstore," he said.

"Boardwalk Books?"

Jim nodded. "His dad didn't make it. His mom passed soon after. We always said she died of a broken heart. He inherited the store and house and ended up staying here. I don't think he ever got over that. Nobody likes being stuck."

"Why are you telling me all this?" I asked.

He leaned across the armrest and stared at me deep in the eyes. "I knew he was found in your library. Everyone here has been going on about how he managed to get himself inside, but no one knows how he did it. They make him sound like some sort of folk hero."

"Have they said what he planned to do inside there?"

Jim shrugged. "I don't know about that. I hear people talk. Most of them think he was going to spray some graffiti, maybe put up some banners, all with messages against the Port Chesapeake project."

My eyes grew wide. "He was going to vandalize the library?"

He shook his head. "I don't think so. Even after everything that happened to him, Big Al still loved books. I don't think he would have hurt a library."

A wave of relief passed over me. "Do you have a different theory?"

"No. But I know one strange thing."

"What's that?"

"Big Al only joined the group recently. He'd never attended meetings before, even with how long his bookstore has been here. I'd tried to convince him many times to come, but he was always going about 'survival of the fittest' or 'adapting to the times.' I was shocked when he joined so suddenly and so fervently."

I didn't know if what he was saying meant anything, but it obviously did to him. "Do you know what changed his mind?"

Jim sighed. "I wish I did. Something got him riled up. Or someone."

Chapter Eighteen

I'd gotten back into my car when Desta called me. I'd parked KG on the street a couple houses down from Big Al's.

"Where are you?" she asked.

"Heading to the boardwalk. Need to grab some lunch," I answered. I looked back to the house I'd left, thinking about all the food in there. My stomach rumbled. I wondered if I might be better off stopping by the Wildflower to see if Azalea had any more blintzes to try. I could also give Clover a quick walk, although the mid-day heat had really picked up.

"You're late for being interviewed," she said.

"Interviewed?" I repeated. "What? Where?"

She sighed. "Did you not get any of my texts or emails?"

I scrolled through my phone in a rush. "Nothing here."

"Well, get there as soon as you can. Today, you're talking to the local newspaper, *The Chesapeake Chronicle*. Tomorrow, you'll be on the radio, and I'm working on a TV interview for you, too."

"Wait, what? I'm not prepared for any of that," I said.

"Are you driving yet? Get over there. I'll give you talking points along the way," she ordered. I doubted that Desta realized how loud KG could be, especially when first starting up. I put the phone on speaker and threw it onto the front passenger seat.

"…Family company…community oriented…"

I tried driving, listening, and figuring out where I was going, all while ignoring my rumbling stomach. While nothing in Rose Mallow was far, that didn't mean things were always simple to find. I went down a few streets that ended abruptly. Then, I turned the wrong way onto a one-way street. I couldn't understand why Rose Mallow had one-way streets. Only a few thousand people lived here.

After a few more wrong turns, I finally stumbled upon a bland office building with a large, empty parking lot. I spotted a small sign saying "Chesapeake Chronicle" among the long list of tenants.

"Now this is important…" Her voice was breaking up.

"What's important?" I parked in the office lot.

"Luna is…" Whatever she said after that was muddled.

"Luna's what?" However, before I could get an answer, the line went dead. I looked at my phone and realized it was completely out of battery. I must have forgotten to plug it in last night. I shook my head and hoped that I hadn't missed anything crucial.

* * *

The Chesapeake Chronicle took up the third and top floor of the building. It was eerily quiet up there. I didn't see or hear anyone anywhere. An empty receptionist area greeted me, littered with towers of papers, mountains of used teacups, and forts made of newspaper. That wasn't an exaggeration. In the middle of the waiting room was a child-sized structure made of newspapers. It even had old cardboard tubes and sheets cut into triangle flags waving around it. Curious, I crouched down and peered inside, only to fall back on my heels when a small gray face with yellow eyes appeared.

"Well, hello, who are you, beautiful?" I asked the little cat. She meowed sweetly and came out of the fort to check me out. Behind her was a larger black cat who eyed me with caution. I petted the gray cat, who leaned against me and purred. From somewhere, I heard another sound. When I looked up, I spotted an orange cat hanging out amidst several dusty trophies on a high shelf. The trophies proclaimed *The Chesapeake Chronicle* to be a reader's choice and best in journalism. They all dated back twenty or more years.

"Good thing I'm not allergic," I said as I continued to pet the gray cat.

"I see you've met Tabitha," said a voice behind me. Looking over my shoulder, I encountered a very tall, wispy woman wearing a crown of dried flowers in her hair. She sported a long, broomstick burgundy skirt and metallic green eyeshadow. She looked like she belonged at a fairy festival.

I stood, wiped the fur off, and put out my hand. "You must be Luna. I'm so sorry I was late. There was a miscommunication…" My words trailed off as Luna took my hand, flipped it over, and gazed deeply at it.

"Is everything okay?" I asked.

Luna studied my palm with concern. Like Tabitha, the cat, she also sported gray eyes. They grew larger by the moment. "I was going to ask you the same thing. Look here." She traced some lines in my palm. "I've never seen… Oh, wait." She flicked a strand of cat fur from my open hand. Then she laughed. "Never mind, you're fine."

"Thank goodness?"

She led me into a back office. I didn't see anyone else. Well, except for more cats. A white one lounged atop a cluttered table, and another with large brown spots napped in a black faux leather chair behind it.

"How many cats do you have?" I asked. Luna motioned me to sit in a chair in front of the desk. While I had to move a small stack of papers, at least it wasn't occupied by a cat. Luna moved behind the desk and squeezed onto a portion of the chair, sharing it with the brown spotted cat.

"Right now? I think there are…." She counted her fingers. "Seven."

"Seven?"

She smiled sweetly. "Are you looking for a new friend? Five are fosters. Besides *The Chesapeake Chronicle*, I also operate the Rose Mallow Feline Rescue Society."

I placed a wide hand across my chest near my heart. That was truly generous of her to do. "Unfortunately, no. I don't have a place of my own yet. But I have a young rescue dog, Clover."

"Oh, now, where did I put my pen?" Then Luna pulled one out from behind her ear and plopped down again. "Alright, let's finish this interview up."

"Finish up?" I asked. "We hadn't started yet."

Luna laughed, looking at me like I was an oblivious child. "Of course we have. We've taken care of all the important things. You're new to town.

Obviously, you're not yet committed to Rose Mallow if you haven't found a place of your own yet."

"I'm committed to Rose Mallow. My Nana Z…"

Luna waved her hands in front of me, cutting me off. "This isn't about her. Nor is it about your sister and her inn. I'm talking about you. You're not sure about anything yet. You showed up late and haven't mentioned a word about the Calvertons since we started."

"You hadn't asked a question," I said in protest.

"Plus, your aura looks all out of whack." She drew a circle around me in the air. I wanted to argue, saying that hers would be too if she'd found a dead body, but Luna barreled onwards. "No, no, it's not Big Al. There's a lot unsettled with you." She paused and studied me. Then she snapped her fingers. "Oh, it must be Leo Calverton."

"What about Leo Calverton?"

She smiled as if she had a secret. "Look at how pink your cheeks became. It's adorable."

I wasn't sure it was so much blushing as annoyance. "I came here to talk about the work we're doing creating a new museum for the community. And the table we'll have at the Rose Mallow Labor Day Festival."

Luna looked bored. "Yada yada." Then, without warning, she had a camera in her hands. The kind with the bright bulb on top that temporarily blinded me. Where did that come from?

"Wait, I wasn't ready."

She ignored me and said, "Thank you for coming in." She didn't bother standing up but thrust out her free hand. Her other one still held the camera.

"That's it?"

"I'll have the profile in this week's edition. Comes out Thursday."

"But you didn't interview me," I protested again.

She shook her head. "I have what I need." Then, Luna put her head to one side. It reminded me of Clover. She held that position for several awkward seconds, studying me. I felt strangely exposed. "There's a vision connected to you."

"A vision?"

"My family's a touch psychic. Never at the right times, though. Goodness, I've tried so many times to help the sheriff's office, but nothing wanted to work. Very frustrating," she said with a sigh followed by a chuckle.

"What do you see?" I asked. I wasn't sure what I thought of her, especially given her strange actions, but I couldn't help being curious.

She peered deeper at me. "A body. In a gutter."

"Who? Where?" I didn't know what I thought of her vision, but it was alarming enough to concern me.

She pressed into her temples and tightly shut her eyes. "I don't know. I think it's a man, but I'm not certain. He's dressed… strangely."

"Strangely how?"

She opened her eyes and looked at me. "Like you. From another time."

"From the 50s?" I asked, thinking about my outfit.

"Not the 1950s."

"Older?"

She nodded. "Maybe the 1850s. No, a smidge older than that, actually. I think he's asleep there. Or sick."

"Where is he? Who is he?"

She closed her eyes again. "I don't know. I think there's a bar nearby, but I'm not certain." She opened her eyes and exhaled deeply. "That's all I have."

I wanted to dismiss her as being off, but there was something about what she said that triggered a thought in me. I couldn't quite put it together. Fortunately, being a librarian, I had a good idea of where to go next. When in doubt, go research.

Chapter Nineteen

After the incredibly strange interview, I stopped for a quick bite before making a stop at the local public library. Luna's vision got me thinking about another death, one that happened many years ago—all the way back in 1849. A man in strange clothing had been found unconscious outside of a bar in Baltimore.

Edgar Allan Poe.

I dug through my Rolodex of memories. From what I remembered, Poe was taken to a nearby hospital, where he went in and out of consciousness. He never explained how he showed up in Baltimore or what had happened to him.

Instead, he died a few weeks later. A death as mysterious as any of his stories.

If I was right, then I needed to dig more into him to find my next step. I found an open computer and searched the catalogue for the library's books on Edgar Allan Poe. Amazingly, every single book had been checked out recently. To be fair, I reminded myself that Poe was always popular. It was undoubtedly just a coincidence. Maybe someone was doing a paper on him for school or something, although I didn't think the schools around here started until after Labor Day this weekend.

I went up to the desk to ask a librarian, "Is Brandy here?"

The older gentleman didn't even look up from his computer. He simply shook his head no.

"I saw that all the Poe books have been checked out. Can you tell me who all borrowed them?" I knew what his answer would likely be—another hard no, but I figured it couldn't hurt to check. Maybe things were more lenient in smaller towns.

He glanced my way briefly and then returned to his screen. Again, he shook his head no.

"Thanks," I said with more than a touch of sarcasm.

As I began walking away, I heard the librarian cough. When I turned around, he had pushed a sheet of paper towards me on the desk. I wondered if he'd decided to give me something useful after all. When I picked it up, I saw it was a customer service satisfaction survey.

I left the paper on the desk and turned away. As I was about to leave, I nearly ran smack into Brandy.

"Oof, are you okay?" I asked.

"Fine, fine," she said, although her voice indicated she was anything but fine. Then she looked up and saw it was me. "Oh, hey, Eric's boss. Good to see you again."

"Juniper," I said with an outstretched hand.

She shook my hand with a solid grip. She hadn't been kidding when she said she was strong. I wouldn't want to go up against her in arm wrestling.

"Juniper, it's good to see you again. What brings you to the library?" she asked. "Need something you can't find in yours?" She laughed at her library joke.

"Actually, yes, I do."

She paused, obviously not expecting my answer.

"I was looking for some materials on Poe."

"Edgar Allan Poe," she said with a swoon. "He's one of my absolute faves."

"Me too."

"What are you looking for?" Brandy led me to an information desk and pivoted a computer screen around for both of us to look at.

"Well, see, everything's been checked out. Everything he wrote, everything about his life, everything."

She shrugged. "Well, that's not surprising. Between school projects…"

"It's the summer," I said, having wondered the same thing.

She waved my concerns away. "Summer school then. And, of course, everyone is really curious about what happened with Big Al."

I wondered if everyone knew about the missing book. I debated how to best bring it up. If it wasn't well known, then I didn't want to add to the rumor mill or worse, mess with Detective Gupta's investigation. But this was Brandy, a fellow librarian. Plus, she was Eric's girlfriend. He had probably already told her.

"Did you know Big Al well?" I asked.

"We were collegial. He may have sold books, while I share them for free, but we both want people to have access to them. And neither of us was crazy about the Calvertons," she said.

"Did you go to the protests?" I asked.

She shook her head. "Too much drama. Besides with Eric working there, I thought it'd be weird if I participated."

"I know that business people like Big Al didn't like the Calvertons. Your parents own Flower Power. Is that why you don't care for them?" I asked.

She shrugged. "Partially. The Rivers have been in Rose Mallow for generations. There's always been some rivalry between our families. But that's stuff people like my dad care about. I'd rather get out of this tiny town."

I wanted to stay on the topic of Big Al, so I pivoted my questions back to him.

"Did you and Big Al get along?" I asked.

Her head cocked to the side. "Why do you ask? Did you hear that we didn't?"

"No, not that, but I barely knew him, and yet he died in my library."

"That must have been difficult. How did the memorial go?"

I shook my head, not wanting to discuss it. "The flowers were beautiful. Thank you for those."

"Anytime."

"Did you two ever talk about books together?" I asked. She straightened up when I asked the question, and her nostrils flared slightly.

"Like I said, we were…collegial." She spaced the words out carefully. I didn't understand why she seemed so on alert.

"Okay, so you discussed books," I said casually, but even that seemed to startle Brandy. Her eyes narrowed into me.

"What do you mean we 'discussed' books?" Her voice took on a harder tone. I found the change of attitude to be confusing.

"Librarian and bookseller...." Based on her response, I felt like everything I said dug a deeper hole instead of coming out of it. "Did you two ever talk about Poe?"

She didn't answer at first. She regarded me carefully. I felt like I was under a microscope, being studied. "Why do you ask?" Her words were very slow and cautious.

I probably should have shut up then, but instead, I kept going, believing I could talk my way from confusion to clarity. "Did you hear about the book he was found with?" When she didn't reply, I tried again. "The Poe book?"

She leaned closer to me. I could feel her breath on my face. "What are you asking?"

"He was found with a book from Poe. That's why I came here—to see if I could figure out if there was a connection between Poe and Big Al's death. That's why I asked to see if you knew who had checked out all the books?"

"Wait, what?" She leaned back. "You think whoever checked out the books on Poe might have been involved with Big Al's death?"

"Maybe? I don't know, but I figured it was a thread to follow, at least. And maybe if he had told you something about Poe, maybe you'd have a lead we could go after, too."

Brandy paused again, obviously considering everything I'd said. Then, to my surprise, she laughed. She brayed like a mule, dropping her hands to her knees. Her laughter was so strong and loud that the older male librarian I talked to earlier actually shushed her. She tried controlling herself, but another wave of laughter tore across her. She even wiped her eyes.

"Are you okay?"

She waved at me and finally caught her breath. "When you asked about me being collegial with Big Al, you wanted to know if he had mentioned anything about Poe to me? Anything at all?"

"Pretty much."

"That's it? That's your big lead?"

I straightened up, feeling defensive. "Well, it was an idea. I figured it was worth exploring."

"Sure, sure." She didn't sound like she agreed. If anything, her simple words suggested she thought I was an idiot. I didn't appreciate the implication, but what could I do? Explain that I came here because a so-called reporter had a vision of Poe in a gutter? When I thought about it, she was right. It was silly. Except that I didn't feel much like laughing, too. Instead, I wanted to hightail it out of this library and return to mine.

Chapter Twenty

Back at the Calverton Estate, I found my team hard at work. They were spread out across a conference room with papers scattered across the table. I still didn't feel like much of a leader to them, but it felt good to see them working hard on the project I'd assigned.

"Did you find anything useful?" I asked.

"Did we ever!" replied Eric. His genuine enthusiasm was appreciated after such a long day. I thought about what Brandy told me about his background, especially about being concerned about his immigration status. Was there anything to be worried about? I made a mental note to look at his employee file to see what that said. That would relax the nagging thought at the back of my brain.

"Look at this, Juniper," Eric continued. "Rose Mallow wouldn't exist without the Calverton family. Well, I mean, it might have existed, but it wouldn't have been much. The family has been a major supporter of the local community." He pushed towards me printouts of *Chesapeake Chronicle* articles from over the years. One had a big photo of the Little League team going to a championship game. The team all wore jerseys embroidered with the Calverton logo. Another featured a photo spread from an annual gala benefiting various nonprofits in the area. A third showed one of Leo's grandparents cutting a ribbon in front of a business on the boardwalk.

"These are great, Eric. Do we have the rights to use any of these images?" I asked. Copyright law was a big deal for librarians and archivists. It was bad enough that the board thought I should investigate Big Al's death. It wouldn't help restore the brand name if I got us into intellectual property hot water while I was at it.

He smiled. "Not only do we have the rights, but apparently, we own the entire *Chesapeake Chronicle* archives. Donated about twenty years ago. The agreement gave us permission to use things however we need."

I nodded. "Well, okay, that's good. Then, we should be able to get some really nice images for the displays. Any chance these are already digitized?"

Across the table, Florence laughed. "Digitized? Who would have had time to do that? Until a few weeks ago, I was the only person working in the collections full-time. We'd get some interns or temp work, but there weren't enough people to handle a project like that."

I sighed. As much as Florence bothered me, I knew she was right about not having enough people for the size of the job. If Leo and the family really wanted a museum, we were going to need to hire more staff soon. I knew Leo had told me about things being stalled and allowing me to build my team, but I wondered why it'd taken so long to resolve whatever issues existed. It wasn't like Calverton Industries was hurting financially.

"Any chance we can get back in the collections yet?" Eric asked.

Before I could answer, Florence jumped in. "Unfortunately not. I tried to get in there earlier today—you know, while you were off gallivanting across town," she said while looking directly at me. "And they have armed guards in front. Can you believe that? Armed guards."

"I'm sorry, Ms. Dowd. Hopefully, it'll be soon when we can go back in." I wished I knew when that would be. Interesting that she said there were armed guards. I could have used those when coming through the protest mob. Maybe they were there to make sure no more protesters arrived. Or perhaps the police had begun thinking something suspicious was at play with Big Al's death. A shiver pricked the skin along my spine.

Florence rolled her eyes. "Why can't you have your boyfr...boss make some waves?"

"What did you say?" I asked. The grit in my voice must have gotten her attention because she looked startled. It was bad enough that everyone else seemed to accuse Leo of nepotism in hiring me that I didn't appreciate her suggesting it to my face. Florence may have been borderline rude to me at best, but she wasn't going to tarnish Leo's reputation—or mine—further.

"A slip of the tongue. But can't Mr. Calverton assist us?"

Suddenly, Leo appeared in the doorway, as if Florence had summoned him like a genie. He came into the room and apologized if he'd interrupted us.

"We were catching up," I said, sounding chipper. However, I kept my gaze on Florence, as if mentally telling her to pull herself together.

"Okay, well, I stopped by to say I spoke with the police…"

"And?" Florence interrupted.

"And it's still going to be a few more days before the building is released back to us."

"Jiminy," said Florence.

"Thanks for letting us know," I said.

He nodded and left quickly. I noticed he didn't bother to ask about my newspaper interview or anything else. Maybe he was in a hurry, or maybe he didn't know, but I couldn't help feeling like he was trying to be all business. I sighed. It was my own fault. I briefly closed my eyes and tried to shake the images out of my head of what the two of us could have been if things were different somehow.

Then, I found a free spot and pulled out my laptop to do some work. Back at the Library of Congress, I used to check my email every two minutes, but I realized I hadn't looked at it once today. There were emails from Desta about my next interview and questions from Martha about what I'd found out so far. I saw a registration receipt for the festival. Nothing from Leo. I don't know what I was looking for, but clearly it wasn't there.

I felt something and looked up to see Florence staring at me. When my eyes met hers, she at least averted my gaze, but I could hear her mutter something under her breath.

"What is it now?" I asked.

"Nothing," she replied.

"It's not nothing. What's going on?"

She huffed and pulled herself up. "Look, we all know you got this job because you're dating Mr. Calverton."

"That's not true," said Eric. He turned to me and asked in a quieter voice, "Right, Juniper?"

"Of course, it's not true," I said, hoping my voice projected confidence.

"Hah. Such bad acting," Florence said. Guess my tone hadn't worked. At least with Florence being so difficult to my face, instead of behind my back, I could confront her attitude right here and now.

I gathered my resolve and stood up. "Ms. Dowd, if you have a problem with my credentials, perhaps you should take it up with the board. I have worked as an expert with the Library of Congress for several years now. I graduated at the top of my class. I've taken classes on management and administration, and I have volunteered with multiple libraries, museums, and cultural organizations, including serving on two boards. And, I'm not dating anyone, thank you very much."

Florence looked stunned. Eric gave a nod towards me. He may have been my employee, but he looked proud of my reply.

I walked over to her and said in sotto voce, "Is it going to be a problem continuing to work together? Because while I don't want to lose you, I will not have someone continually undermining me."

I didn't know what I expected Florence to do. I figured she'd argue back, maybe give a stiff upper lip and say nothing, or possibly even resign in the moment.

Instead, she started crying. Not a single tear, but the woman shuddered with sobs, dropped her arms and head onto the table.

I looked at Eric, but he shrugged and shook his head.

Carefully, I placed a hand on her shoulder. She tensed but didn't push me away. "What's going on?"

Instead of answering me, however, Florence jumped up and ran out of the room. She didn't return the rest of the afternoon.

* * *

Back at the Wildflower Inn, I found Azalea again in the kitchen with plates of blintzes radiating around her like daisy petals. The aroma was tantalizing.

Violet churned her own pretend batter in a small plastic bowl, while Clover danced around, looking for a wayward drop to gobble. When he saw me, he raced over, and I gathered him up in my arms.

"Have you been good for Auntie Azalea?" I asked. He licked my face several times in response.

"He's been great. He and Violet are best friends." Somehow, she sounded both amused and concerned.

"Can Clover stay always?" Violet asked.

Azalea turned and asked her daughter, "You mean when Auntie Juniper moves out?"

She nodded. "Auntie Juniper, you'll leave Clover with me?"

I was both touched and a bit sad. "You mean, you don't want me to stay too?"

Her eyes lit up as if she never considered the possibility. Honestly, I hadn't either. Not that there was room for me here as I couldn't constantly take a guest room from them. Well, unless we either cleaned out the attic or maybe finished the basement. Then the guest room would go back into service, while I paid rent. That might actually help provide more revenue streams to keep the Wildflower Inn going.

The idea of moving in intrigued me. I imagined waking up each morning to delicious food like this, having Clover and Violet grow up together, and helping Azalea with the payments.

Then, another thought crossed my mind. I remembered babysitting my niece. Plus, I could picture the fights Azalea that I might have, the messes Clover would make, and being constantly in the way.

If I lived here but wasn't a guest, how would that work? It wasn't like I could cook or clean well. I had no idea how to run an inn. And while it had been quiet for a couple days, would I like all the guests coming in and out at all hours? I'd be underfoot. I'm sure my sister was simply waiting for me to leave.

Azalea must have watched the array of thoughts play out across my face. Truth be told, I definitely lacked any sort of poker face.

"We could talk through the possibility," Azalea said.

To my shock, she sounded serious. I couldn't have imagined her entertaining the idea.

"I don't know," I said. "I'll think about it."

She gave a delicate but truly sweet smile. "You should."

Wanting to switch topics, I asked, "So, what have you been whipping up now?" I walked around, staring at each plate of blintzes, hopefully, ready to taste test.

"Don't go for that one," she said, pointing to one that smelled of chives.

"Why not?" I asked.

"It's my breakfast blintz. Cream cheese, chives, and a poached egg…"

"Oh, sounds delicious," I said, ready to take a bite.

"And lox. I know you don't eat fish, so I didn't want you to be surprised."

"Auntie Juniper doesn't eat fish?" Violet asked, surprised.

I knelt beside her. "Nope, I'm what's called a vegetarian."

Her eyes grew big at the large word. She attempted to say it three times before giving up. I laughed at my sweet niece.

"It means I like vegetables a lot." Granted, I also loved carbs, dairy, and sugar. If I stayed here, I would need to up my exercise routine. The decadent dishes Azalea created meant I probably wouldn't fit in Nana Z's wardrobe much longer.

Violet scrunched up her face. "Veggies? Ewww!"

"Juniper likes lots of other things, too," Azalea added. She pointed to another plate. "Like that one has a peach-plum compote. I got the peaches fresh from the farmer's market. Oh, and that one is with caramelized apples. I look forward to making it again in the fall."

My mouth watered. Part of me wanted to reach out and grab things with my bare hands and stuff them into my mouth, but I knew that wouldn't be a role model for my niece. I hadn't realized how hungry I'd been. Fortunately, Azalea handed me a plate, and I happily tried each of her experiments.

"So good, Azalea," I said in between bites.

She watched me with a smile. However, after I had gulped down more than a few blintzes, I noticed how distraught she appeared, sitting in a chair with her shoulders hunched high and her back curled over. She half-turned to face Violet, who raced across the room with Clover.

"Everything okay?" I asked.

"Yeah."

"What's up?" I didn't want to push too hard, but there was obviously something bothering her. "Is it this competition? Are you worried you might not win? Because if so, you're foolish. These are incredible. I think you could open an entire café dedicated to blintzes."

She laughed a little, and it was good to see a light glow in her eyes. "It's partially the competition. I want to make Nana Z proud, but there's something else." She pulled out her phone. "John texted me."

"Deputy Torres?" I asked.

She nodded. "He wants to go on a date. A real date."

"What did you say?"

"Nothing," she admitted.

"Does he know about your date with Rory?"

"I haven't hid anything."

Violet and Clover chased each other across the room again and into the hallway. Azalea must have been able to get a good look from where she sat because she didn't get up. As long as we heard laughter ringing, it wasn't concerning.

"You haven't hid anything. But have you been forthright?"

She sighed. "Not entirely. It'd help if I knew what I wanted."

I thought for a moment. "Look, if you're not sure about him, then maybe you should let him go."

She nodded. "Yeah, probably." Then she got up and followed the flurry of kid and dog feet stomping somewhere into the front half of the building. She didn't sound certain she'd keep him at bay. Was my sister really going to date the deputy and her husband?

Chapter Twenty-One

The next morning, I again encountered a gauntlet of protesters outside the Calverton campus. As soon as they saw me, I heard booing. Someone threw a paper airplane at me. Another one hit me in the back. Then, a third sailed by, nearly landing in my hands. I grabbed it before it reached the ground and tucked it in the pocket of my vintage seafoam green capri pants. I pushed through the group, trying not to listen to their chants or concerns.

On the other side of the mob, a couple of guards opened the gate for me to enter. They watched me meekly, as if silently apologizing for not shooing the group away. I didn't have a lot of faith in the security team here at this point, but what could I do?

When I reached the other side of the gate, I pulled out the paper airplane from my pocket. It was made of newspaper. As I unfolded it, I realized it was from the *Chesapeake Chronicle*. A shiver swept up my spine. The folded-up front page featured Luna's article on me. My hands shook as I read through the piece.

"Ah, you saw it then," said Eric, coming up behind me.

I tried to speak, but I couldn't get words out. I simply shook my head.

"It's trash. Pure and simple trash," he said.

My eyes watered, but I held it together as best as I could. "Does she always get this nasty?"

Eric shrugged. "She has her phases. But overall, the newspaper has gone downhill, and this shows it's nothing more than a gossip rag."

My sadness gave way to anger. "I hope people don't believe this." I started reading out loud from the article, "Juniper Blume is young, inexperienced, and an unwise choice to lead such a monumental project as the projected Calverton Museum. Except for a few years as a librarian, she has little background in cultural organizations, let alone directing them. Choosing her to head the effort makes no sense until you learn that she's been seen canoodling with Leo Calverton. Sources have spotted them together at the Indigo Room last month and recognized his expensive Tesla at Juniper's sister's hotel, The Wildflower Inn, on multiple occasions. Knowing that the museum is Leo's pet project, it's obvious why this untested young woman was selected, especially given the Calverton family's history of nepotism."

We walked the pathway to the building with our co-opted conference room, but outside stood Martha Dresdale. She waited on the stairs leading up to the doors, leaning against the railing with her arms crossed. Her stare could have taken down a Death Star.

"Well, if it isn't the future Mrs. Leo Calverton herself." Martha's voice dripped with condescension.

"None of this is true," I said.

"Juniper is amazing," Eric added.

Martha shook her head at him. Then she turned to me. "This was supposed to be a charm offensive, not providing more ammo to those inane protesters out there."

"It was such a strange interview," I started to explain, but Martha held up a hand in my face, effectively cutting me off. Her fingers were so close I could count the little gems on each perfectly manicured nail. While the gems sparkled like diamonds, her nails were painted a vicious shade of red.

"You better do a better job during the radio interview." She wagged a finger at me and then walked down the stairs past us.

"Doesn't she have anything better to do than harangue you?" Eric asked after she left.

I sighed. "It's important for the Calverton brand, so I guess it's important to her."

"I don't know," he replied. "It seems like she might be personally out to get you."

I held my tongue, but inside, I agreed. Martha had been nothing but difficult to me since I had arrived, and I wasn't sure why a bank executive would care. This must have seemed like a tiny project to what she normally worked on. How had I upset her so strongly?

Inside our makeshift office, Florence was nowhere to be seen. That surprised me, given that she normally arrived earlier than I did. I checked my messages, but I didn't find anything from her explaining her disappearance. I tried calling her, but my call went straight to voicemail.

"Have you heard from Florence?" I asked Eric.

He shrugged. "No, nothing."

"That's unusual."

"Maybe she's sick?"

"Maybe," I replied, but something felt off. I shook my head and tried to focus on our work. Eric updated me about the signage for the festival. As he spoke, I noticed a smile dancing across his face, like he was holding back a surprise.

"Is there something else you wanted to share?" I asked.

The smile broadened. "Yes, actually, I had an idea. I told Florence yesterday, and believe it or not, she thought I might be onto something."

"Oh?"

"We're working to put everything together for the festival, but I wondered about what happens after it ends," he said.

"And you have something in mind?"

He nodded and pulled out a map of Rose Mallow. It was a hand-drawn tourist map of the downtown area, with the boardwalk businesses and other places of interest highlighted. He'd drawn big numbers in a few places. I counted five of them.

"What if we make this a more permanent project?" he asked.

"In what way?"

He pointed at the map. "I've identified five places where we could put up permanent signs. You know, along the boardwalk, in the historic district, in front of the historical society, and so on."

"What would go on the signs?" I asked, growing more interested in his idea.

"Each would feature the history of that location, but there'd be some sort of connection to the Calvertons in the copy and photos."

I thought about his idea. It was a good one, but I thought having each sign directly connected to the Calvertons might be too on the nose. Plus, given the attitudes of the protesters, they might vandalize or even destroy the signs. "What if we include a tag at the bottom of each sign acknowledging the Calvertons' support? Let history speak for itself?"

He nodded in agreement. "That's more subtle. I like it."

I snapped my fingers. Well, at least I attempted to. I had never mastered a good snap. "Wasn't Rose Mallow a resort town over a hundred years ago?"

Eric rifled through some of his papers. "Yes, in the late 1800s and early 1900s, a steamboat used to bring people, mainly from Baltimore, to come here for vacation. A railroad ran down here as well. There were some big hotels back then."

"Anything left from then?"

He looked up at the ceiling, obviously thinking. "You know, I think there's the ruins of a hotel and spa somewhere in Redbud Park. There's that forest area to the south of us. That might be kind of cool to highlight."

I knew the spot he described. At the end of the boardwalk was Redbud Park, named for the many eastern redbud trees in the area. The park gave way to a forest all along the Chesapeake Bay. There were actually a few different ruins scattered throughout the forest. As teenagers, my sister Azalea and I loved to explore them. When she and Rory started dating, the spa ruins was one of their favorite hangout spots, away from watchful adults. I was more interested in the history of the site, wondering what had happened to the place and when it became destroyed.

"I like it," I said. "I'll talk to the board about your idea. Good work."

Eric beamed. Then, his face became more serious. "Have you made any progress looking into what happened with Big Al?"

I slumped. "I'm not sure. Probably not. Hey, did you know someone checked out all the Poe books from the library?"

"Well, that's not exactly surprising," he replied. "I mean, Poe remains pretty popular."

"Yeah, you're right. I wish there was some way to find out who had them."

Eric twisted his mouth around as if tasting something, but, being uncertain if he liked it or not. "I'll talk to Brandy. Maybe she can help."

"I ran into her earlier," I said, sounding less than confident.

"Sure, but you're not dating her."

"True. But I don't want you doing anything that would get you two in trouble. Or in trouble with her."

Eric laughed. "Don't worry. It can't hurt to ask."

"Okay, thank you."

* * *

Even by the end of the day, Florence hadn't shown up. I didn't have any phone or email messages from her either. That didn't sit right with me. I looked through the personnel files to dig out her address. I noticed her file was fairly thick as she had been working for the Calvertons for years. She had an exemplary performance report. My stomach dropped a little. No wonder she felt awful about me being here. She had been passed over for this opportunity.

Eric's file was considerably thinner. Not surprising since he had only recently started. I skimmed through it briefly, hoping it'd relax those concerns nagging me yesterday. He'd recently graduated with his master's degree in library science. This was his first full-time job in the field.

I remembered when I had started out. I'd been lucky enough to do contract work for a few private collectors. I'd enjoyed that work, getting to dig into the personal archives of an interesting person or family. I'd felt like a treasure hunter, uncovering these glimpses into the past no one else ever got to see. Honestly, those had been my favorite jobs, but few people could afford a personal librarian full-time, so eventually I sought out something more permanent.

When I started at the Library of Congress, I began at a far lower rung before working my way up to working with various rare book collections. I felt truly honored to be entrusted with their care. I smiled, thinking about how Eric seemed to exhibit that same enthusiasm.

Behind their files were some others. I assumed they were for past staff or possibly people who had interviewed for positions over the years. However, I didn't go through them, realizing I'd strayed enough down rabbit holes. I'd only gone into the personnel files to get Florence's information. Having found it, I copied it down and headed out.

* * *

Florence lived in a neighborhood called Sunnyside, filled with ranch houses from the 1960s and beyond. Although it wasn't as glamorous as the nearby historic district where the Wildflower Inn stood, the houses were well-maintained, and the yards were tidy with lots of boxwoods and pockets of colorful flowers. Kids whirled by me on bikes, and I spotted more than one lemonade stand. Florence's house was on the curve of a cul-de-sac. For all her dour attitude, her brick home had bright blue shutters and a flag in the yard that beamed "Welcome" around drawings of happy bees and butterflies.

I knocked on the door, but no one answered. I tried again with the doorbell. After a long minute, the door opened slowly. It was dark behind the door. Florence appeared, looking bedraggled. Her hair hadn't been brushed, sprouting at all different angles. Her face was pale, but her eyes were red and puffy.

"Are you okay?" I asked.

She didn't answer at first. After a long moment, she said, "I'll be back tomorrow."

"Are you sick? You should take the time you need."

"Just a cold," she replied and started to close the door. That's when I noticed something in the air. It was the same smell I'd encountered at Big Al's memorial, that memorable scent of worn leather and woodsy shelves overrun with dog-eared books. I looked around her shoulder and spotted the same large three-wick candle I'd knocked over in his house standing on a table in her foyer. It lit up a framed photograph. To my surprise, it was a photo of Florence with Big Al.

Florence followed my gaze to the candle and photo. She reached out to turn it over, but her hand stopped in mid-air. Instead, she picked it up and held it to her chest. She looked up at the sky, as if holding back tears.

"You and Al?" I asked, hoping my voice sounded more gentle than surprised.

"Might as well come in," she replied, sounding resigned. I followed her into the house. She flipped on a few lights. We went into the living room, and she motioned for me to sit on the sofa. As I looked around, I again noticed how surprisingly friendly the room appeared. She had bright prints on the walls and one with a quote in calligraphy about living a happy life. Was this really her home? Such a strange dichotomy compared to the rude and angry person I'd seen all week.

She offered me a drink, but I declined. Florence sank slowly into a canary yellow upholstered chair. "I thought I could come back to work. Throw myself into it and ignore what had happened." She paused to massage her temples. "But I couldn't. He's gone. Gone." Her voice quivered, and I thought she might cry, but she didn't.

"You were seeing him?"

She laughed bitterly. "Let's be honest and call things what they were. We had an affair. He wasn't ever going to leave Emily. I had learned to live with that a long time ago."

How long had their affair been going on? I wanted to ask, but I figured I'd let Florence lead the discussion.

She must have read my mind, because she said, "We met when I first took the job with the Calvertons. We bonded over our love of books." She smiled briefly at what I guessed was a memory. Her gaze went back to the burning candle, which we could still see from our seats. Even here, I could smell the musky scent of old books mixed with hints of vanilla and mahogany. "His family helped with the store, but they didn't share his passion for stories. He'd make up the most amazing tales. I always told him he should be a writer. I wish now he had so he would have left more behind." She pointed to the candle. "He created this candle for me. To remind me of his bookstore always. Didn't he do a good job?" Tears peppered her eyes.

I wanted to smile, but I couldn't help thinking about how angry he'd been when he learned I worked for the Calvertons. "But didn't he hate that you worked for the Calverton family?"

She lifted a shoulder and dropped it. "Not really. He could have cared less. At first, anyway."

"Something changed?"

She sighed and nodded. "He did. Months ago, maybe even a full year, he pulled away from me. He stopped calling as frequently, and our dates together became rarer. At first, I figured he'd grown tired of me. But after a while, I learned the truth."

I sat on the edge of the sofa, waiting for her to continue.

"He was dating someone else."

"Oh no," I said. I couldn't help wondering what all these women saw in him. My brief encounter with Big Al had been so unpleasant that I didn't understand the appeal. He'd been gruff and unpleasant at best. I bit back my judgments. Florence didn't need that from me now.

Florence nodded. "I should have expected it, I suppose. I mean, he'd been cheating on Emily with me for years. But somehow, I'd convinced myself I was the only one."

"Did you find out who it was?"

"I don't know."

I took a breath before asking, "What made you think he was seeing someone else?"

She lifted a shoulder and then dropped it. "You just know. He stopped being responsive. I'd see him around town, and he'd ignore me. I even saw him on the Calverton campus a few times, and he purposefully looked anywhere except at me. Something had changed. Then, I saw them once at the Indigo Room. Well, I saw him, and he wasn't with Emily. I couldn't get a good enough look at her. Some other people were in the way. I could easily see him. From the way he was dressed and his body language, I knew then why he wasn't interested in me anymore. It was all about her." She shook her head.

"I'm so sorry," I said.

"Me too."

"You said he was on the Calverton campus? Do you know why?"

"No idea except that it wasn't to see me anymore."

"But if he kept coming to the campus, why was he involved with the protests?"

Florence shrugged. "No idea. We officially broke up last month. I told him I'd had enough of the way he'd been treating me. He didn't take it well, but he still wouldn't explain what was going on. He wouldn't tell me who the mysterious woman in the Indigo Room was, just that he seemed relieved I hadn't identified her. After that, I started seeing him with the protest group. Maybe he joined them because he was angry I'd dumped him?"

That at least made some sense to me. "Okay, even if that's true, why would he have been in the library? With what looked like our missing book?"

She managed to fall back further in her chair. "I keep wondering the same thing. I don't know. I can't figure out how he'd have gotten it or why he would be there. I wanted to believe he'd come to ask for my forgiveness, but well, now I guess we'll never know."

"Oh, Florence," I said softly.

Her gaze turned stern. "Ms. Dowd."

"Ms. Dowd," I repeated, holding my hands up in surrender.

She nodded once in approval and then closed her eyes. When she opened them again, there were tears. I couldn't tell if I felt sorry for her or not. That she had been "the other woman" with Big Al for what appeared to be years was difficult to reconcile, but I understood she had been hurt several times. By Big Al, the mystery woman, and of course by me becoming boss.

"I can only imagine what you must think of me," she said, as if reading my mind.

"It's not my place to judge."

She bit her lip and said, "Would it be too much to ask you to keep this to yourself? I…" She stopped, as if trying to figure out her next words. "It hurt deeply not being able to attend his memorial. I don't think I can even safely go to the funeral. I don't think Emily knows it's me he had the affair with, but she's not stupid. I don't want to cause them more pain."

I remembered Emily accusing me of being one of Big Al's harpies. After this conversation, that made a lot more sense. I looked closer at Florence. She seemed to have aged overnight. The bags under her eyes and the lines across her face were starker. She looked on the verge of sobbing now. She radiated anguish.

"Of course. I won't tell anyone."

"Thank you, Ms. Blume."

I was stunned that she had addressed me so politely. As much as I would prefer her to simply call me Juniper, I wasn't about to push the point. This was a big deal. Maybe an iceberg had melted.

Then, another thought trickled through my brain. I stood up and said, "Ms. Dowd, why don't you take the rest of the week off? Eric and I can handle things. You deserve time to grieve."

She looked at first like she might argue with me, but then she dropped her head to her chest and simply said, "Thank you."

"I'll see myself out."

She didn't respond. I got up and headed to the door, pausing to study the candle. It surprised me that Big Al had taken up something as crafty as candle making, but I guess I had made plenty of assumptions about him. He had done a remarkable job of recreating the aroma of Boardwalk Books. I wondered what else I'd misjudged him about?

I walked out of the house and thought more about our conversation. I wanted to believe everything she had told me, but I couldn't help wondering if there were pieces left out. Had Florence really dumped him? Maybe she spun it that way, but really, he had let her go? Either way, I'd read enough stories where a heartbreak had led to murder.

Chapter Twenty-Two

The weekend went by in a flash. On Monday morning was my radio interview at Rose Mallow's only radio station WMLW-FM. The station building, like so many other businesses in the area, had seen better days. It was a small place, dark inside, with several lights out. The faded signage looked like it dated from the 1980s. Walls needed to be repainted. I sighed, thinking about the similar run-down states of the newspaper office, Boardwalk Books, and several other places I'd visited here lately. I couldn't help thinking about the difference between them and the finely manicured Calverton campus. Perhaps if the Calvertons invested in local places instead of steamrolling over it all, the protesters would be happier.

Inside, I was surprised to find Luna at a control board on a long table, flanked by a series of microphones. She wore a name badge proclaiming that she was the station manager. Who knew she was Rose Mallow's own mini-media mogul?

I noticed there weren't any cats here, though. However, like with *The Chesapeake Chronicle*, there also didn't seem to be anyone else here either. Was she the only employee of both places?

She perked up on seeing me and invited me to an open chair. "Thanks for coming out this morning, Juniper!"

I was surprised at how chipper she sounded, especially after the nasty article she'd written about me. "I wasn't expecting to see you here too."

Her shoulders danced in a small shimmy. "I also run a blog about Rose Mallow Life and a local magazine with the same name."

Basically, it's anywhere that Desta might send me for marketing in the area.

"That's great, Luna. But the piece you wrote on me…"

"Wasn't it fabulous? I felt truly inspired by your story." She clasped her hands together and bowed her head towards me.

"I wouldn't call the article fabulous. To be honest, I found it pretty hurtful."

She sighed and nodded. "Well, in late-stage capitalism, one needs to be more than authentic when it comes to selling newspapers in a dying media economy. One needs to be compelling." She waved a hand in the air as she spoke. Her nails were purple and glittery.

I didn't know how to respond to her babble. "More than authentic?"

"Telling the deeper story. Beyond the truth," she said, as if that explained anything. I didn't know how she managed to continue smiling through everything she said. Did she honestly believe the nonsense coming out of her?

"Look, I'm not going to stay here if this is another hit piece. Authentic or not authentic."

She appeared hurt. "I give you my word." She dropped her head to her chest.

Most of me wanted to leave, but I could only imagine what Leo, Desta, Martha, or the rest of the board might think if I left before the interview even started. Against my better judgment, I agreed to do the interview.

"Great. We'll start in a few minutes. The current show is wrapping up."

In the meantime, Luna showed me where to sit and how to speak into the microphone. She told me to take my time in talking and to limit my "uhs" and "ahs" if possible. She pointed out a little light that would turn green when we were in the air and a clock that showed seconds as well as hours and minutes. We only had a few left before the show started.

The light turned green, and Luna launched into an introduction for the show. "Welcome back to Rose Mallow Today on WMLW-FM. I'm your host, Luna Moray. This morning, I'm welcoming Juniper Blume, the new director at the forthcoming Calverton Museum. Welcome Juniper." She bowed at me across the table.

"Thanks for having me, Luna."

"I was a little surprised you joined us this morning after that nasty article in *The Chesapeake Chronicle*," she said. I felt whiplash from the sudden change of direction.

"Well…"

Luna interrupted me to say, "But I'm glad you did, so you can share with our listeners why you're involved with such an evil empire?" She looked at me with a brightness that didn't match the viciousness of her words. She nodded encouragingly for me to answer.

"I know that the Calverton family has been a bit, uh, controversial lately," I responded, but Luna jumped in again, interrupting my reply.

"A bit controversial? Most of the town is in an uproar about their exploitative practices. I imagine you're familiar with your company's plans to destroy Rose Mallow and replace our beautiful home with the plastic Port Chesapeake project?"

I tried not to take the bait. "I'm excited to share how Calverton has community-focused plans. Have you known that the Calvertons have invested in Rose Mallow for generations?"

"Is that all this place is to them? An investment?"

"No, of course not," I said, trying not to sound defensive. "Rose Mallow is home. For all of us."

Luna laughed. "Not you, though. You recently moved here after being up in the big ole D.C. Beltway."

"That's not true. Everyone knew my grandmother Nana Z, I mean, Zinnia Blume. I've been coming to Rose Mallow for years. I spent every summer here. And my sister Azalea…"

"Oh, the one with the big hotel for all those outsiders?" Luna asked with an eye roll.

I shook my head, even though no one could see me do so. "She has lovingly restored our grandmother's historic home into a boutique hotel, the Wildflower Inn."

"Located in that pretentious historic district, right?"

"Pretentious? I thought you wanted to preserve the charm and character of Rose Mallow. The Wildflower Inn is an excellent example of that." I hoped that Azalea wasn't listening. She couldn't be happy that I'd somehow managed to drag her hotel into this mess.

"I noticed that the Port Chesapeake plan doesn't demolish the historic district the way it does for many other areas. Could that be your influence? Or perhaps your boyfriend Leo Calverton's?" Luna asked.

"Leo Calverton is not my boyfriend!" I couldn't keep the anger out of my voice.

"Oh really? You two seem pretty chummy," she said as she leaned closer across the table.

"We are colleagues. He is my boss. That's all."

"Then tell our listeners how you ended up spearheading this new museum initiative? Have you ever started a museum before? Have you ever even run one?"

I wanted to scream, but I knew that wouldn't help anything. Instead, I took a deep breath and said slowly, "I am an expert in working with cultural organizations. I've been with the Library of Congress and other remarkable historic collections. The new museum will showcase a truly magnificent collection of material culture, reflecting the diverse history and heritage of not only Rose Mallow and southern Maryland but our connection with the rest of the world."

Luna cocked her head to the side like my dog Clover often did when I spoke. "Can you translate any of what you said?"

"I thought it was fairly clear. The Calverton family has been part of Rose Mallow for centuries. They are intrinsically connected to our town and region. During that time, many members built strong businesses, which provided countless jobs to our area. They also played an important role in supporting our community from the Little Leagues to the Scouts to scholarships and beyond. And they weren't just pillars of industry and community, but they were explorers. Generations of Calverton family members traveled the world, sometimes discovering incredible cultural treasures."

"And stealing them for their own collection?" Luna asked.

"No!" I couldn't help shouting. "They partnered with those local communities. They've founded museums and collections across the globe. Now, they're doing the same thing here with a focus on American history. Visitors will have access to a world-class museum right here in Rose Mallow."

"American history…." Luna repeated before pausing. "Like, say, Edgar Allan Poe?"

I could feel my nostrils flare, but I tried to restrain myself. "Of course. The museum and its archives will contain the works of many American masters, including Poe."

"I would be remiss if I didn't ask about your discovery of Alvin Cooley dead beside a copy of a Poe book in the Calvertons' current library building? One that isn't open to the public?" she asked with a sick sweetness in her voice.

"It was an unfortunate incident. My condolences to the Cooley family," I said. Luna looked at me, as if waiting for me to continue, but I ignored her.

"Indeed, it was unfortunate. Finding the owner of Boardwalk Books in your library. And I heard you had an altercation with him previously?"

"Altercation is a strong word. He talked to me briefly, but that was it," I replied.

She shook her head. "Haven't the police talked to you as well?"

"The police have talked to everyone who was around that day."

She leaned again across the table and said, "Aren't you someone they're investigating?"

"Investigating? Why?"

To my surprise, Luna suddenly said, "Let's take some calls from listeners. Caller, you're on the air."

"I heard that this lady you have on murdered Big Al," said a male voice. I looked around, not sure where the speaker was for the caller to slander me like this. How could I shut him off?

"I didn't murder him. I didn't even know him," I yelled.

"But you don't deny he was murdered?" asked Luna.

"I have no idea how he died. The police haven't told me."

"I heard he was poisoned," said the caller.

CHAPTER TWENTY-TWO

Luna looked at me expectantly.

"Poisoned?" I repeated. "I don't know anything about that. You'd need to talk with the police."

"Maybe the police should talk to you," said the caller.

"I didn't kill him," I replied, sounding probably more pitiful than assertive. Inside, I wanted to rip the electronics out and end this miserable interview.

"Thank you, caller. Next caller, you're on the air," said Luna.

"Is the Calverton family now bumping off anyone who disagrees with them? I always heard they were connected to the mob," said the new caller.

"Wait, now, that's not true," I replied.

"Are you with the mob?" Luna asked, as if it was a perfectly normal question.

"No, of course not."

"What about your boyfriend?" she asked.

"He's not my boyfriend!" I said, unable to hold back the bite in my voice. I gripped the side of my seat so as not to throttle her microphone.

"Next caller, you're on Rose Mallow Today!" said Luna enthusiastically. She sounded like she was enjoying the melee.

"Well, I think Juniper Blume is doing a superb job," said a familiar voice. Hearing Leo on the line, both reassured and frustrated me. I was really beginning to wish he'd never offered me this role in the first place. Then, I wouldn't have to run around constantly defending myself.

I forced a smile and said, "Thank you. It's an honor to serve Rose Mallow."

Luna looked uncertain. She looked back and forth between me and the caller. Then she studied something that popped up on a screen near her, but I couldn't make out what it said.

"I'm excited for the new Calverton Museum and to finally share this remarkable collection with the community. Juniper has the right expertise to manage this project, and I trust that she'll bring a lot of prestige to Rose Mallow."

Luna's left eyebrow arched. She must have realized who was talking. Given the glint in her eyes, I wanted to reach over and turn off the call. Or maybe crawl under the desk and unplug everything. It took everything I had not to yell out and warn Leo that this scorpion was about to strike.

"Leo Calverton, I presume?" she asked.

"Luna Moray," he replied.

"What do you have to say about the accusations against the Calverton family?" she asked, even as she studied whatever was on her small screen.

"Nothing, really. I'm pretty sure that Juniper's work will speak for itself."

She shook her head. "And what about the death…or should I say murder of Big Al Cooley?"

"That is a police matter. As far as I know, I have not heard anyone officially say his passing was anything more than an unfortunate circumstance."

"Uh-huh. Well, I'll have you know that we're interrupting this broadcast to go to a press conference with the Sheriff about the unfortunate passing of Big Al Cooley," she said with a slick smile.

I jerked up in my seat. "What?" That must have been the pop-up on her screen. It had to have been a message about the incoming press conference.

"And Ms. Blume, I believe that there's a police officer waiting for you right outside," Luna said, still into the microphone. She pointed a glittery fingernail over my shoulder. I turned and spotted Deputy John Torres standing outside the glass door of the small studio – the same deputy that Azalea may or may not have been dating.

Chapter Twenty-Three

"Deputy Torres." I walked out of the studio. Luna had switched over to the press conference. Throughout the speakers, the sheriff discussed the death of Big Al. "Shouldn't you be at that? Wherever it is?"

"Sheriff's got it. Detective Gupta's there too. They don't need me right now." We sat down on a lumpy couch in the station's tiny foyer and listened as the sheriff revealed that Big Al's death was indeed murder.

I turned, in alarm, to Deputy Torres. "He was murdered?"

He didn't look at me. Instead, he was focused on Luna, who was actively watching us through the glass door that separated the foyer from the recording studio. "Let's take a walk. I'll catch you up to speed on the press conference."

We walked outside. Nearby was a small park, and we wandered through the paths. When it seemed clear there was no one else around, he said, "We found traces of monkshood."

"*Monk's Hood?* Like in the Ellis Peters novel?" I remembered seeing Big Al's dirty fingers when I found his body.

"Well, sort of. I mean, yes, it's the same poisonous plant that inspired his mystery," he said. I was impressed that he knew Peters' work. "It's also known as Wolf's Bane, but its official Latin name is *Aconitum napellus.*"

"Wolf's Bane…'No, no, go not to Lethe, neither twist, Wolf's-bane, tight-rooted, for its poisonous wine,'" I said. "From 'Ode to Melancholy.'"

"John Keats," he replied.

"Wow, you know your literature."

He shrugged. "I was an English major."

"Turned police officer?" I asked, honestly surprised.

He gave a small, shy smile. "I didn't want to read exciting stories. I wanted to live them."

"I guess you're getting your share here."

He laughed dryly. "Yes, lately, anyway."

I felt the hackles of my neck go up. When I found the body in the cemetery, Deputy Torres had been upset about my involvement in investigating the case. He made it clear that he blamed anything that might happen to Azalea on me. When the case ended, he relaxed a bit, but I didn't get the impression we were suddenly best friends.

We wandered along the path until we found a clearing with a good-sized concrete fountain. Water bubbled and flowed. We circled around it.

"Okay, so Big Al was poisoned. From touching monkshood? Oh no, was the book poisoned? Is that how he died?" I asked, thinking and talking at the same time.

Deputy Torres shook his head. "No, no. Touching monkshood is rarely lethal. Your fingers might be impacted, but you'd really have to be exposed to a lot of the plant to die that way. Far more than it appears Mr. Cooley was. Now, ingesting monkshood is a different story."

"He ate monkshood?" I asked.

"It got inside him somehow. And it only takes a tiny amount to kill someone. I'm guessing it was in his cigar."

I remembered the dirty cigar butt on the table beside him. The memory made me shiver.

I stopped and turned on my heels to face him. "Why are you telling me all this? Why are you really here instead of at that press conference?"

He stared at his shoes. "I want to help Detective Gupta and the sheriff solve the case." I made a face indicating I didn't believe his response. He sighed and nodded. He dug one foot into the ground and twisted it a few times. "Okay, okay. I was kind of hoping that if we worked together and solved Mr. Cooley's murder, you might put in a good word to your sister."

What was this? High school? I could feel my eyes widen. "Look, Deputy

Torres…"

"John, please."

"John, I can't make up Azalea's mind for her."

He nodded eagerly, reminding me of a puppy. "I know, of course, but she hasn't been returning any of my calls."

"John, she's busy. She's got more people coming to the inn tonight, and the festival coming up, and of course, Violet." I didn't mention her date with Rory. Azalea had made it sound like he knew about their attempt at rekindling their relationship, but that was for them to discuss.

He nodded again with such enthusiasm that I thought he might hurt his neck. "That's why I didn't want to interrupt her. I'm giving her space. I figured if we worked together, you might at least mention it to her?"

I wanted to push him away, remind him how juvenile he was being, but then again, I knew I'd get more from him than from Detective Gupta. Having John help me would be an opportunity to find Big Al's killer and bring them to justice.

"I'll help you, but I can't make any promises with Azalea. We're only talking about finding a murderer."

"Understood," John replied. "Look, the detective knows you're looking into what happened. There are missing old books. There's a mysterious code. And you've been seen around town talking with people." He pointed a finger at me. "I've heard her saying, and I quote, 'Juniper's investigating. Again.' She's not happy about it."

I sighed. "The board asked me to find out what I could."

"And I can help you if you help me. So, what have you found?"

"Nothing much," I said, wondering how much I should share. I didn't want to betray either Nuri Cho or Florence Dowd. It might not be the best way to start a partnership, but given John's self-interest in impressing Azalea, I wasn't sure I could trust him with their stories. At least not yet.

"That seems unlikely."

I considered my words, as I needed to tell him something useful. "I learned something interesting about Big Al."

He waited for me to share more.

"Apparently, he only recently joined the protest, and no one knows why. Before that, he hadn't cared about what the Calvertons were up to."

John shook his head. "We know that already. We've spoken to several of the protesters about his involvement with the movement."

"Oh."

He crossed his arms and said, "Anything else?"

"Nothing helpful," I said, hoping that was true.

John made a face. "Look, you're an expert on rare books. I know the detective has talked to you before about your expertise."

I waited to see where he was going with this.

"Would you accompany me to the station?" he asked.

"Why?"

"I want you to look closer at the book and the code."

"But you said the book didn't poison him," I replied.

He shrugged. "We don't think it did, but I would advise caution with it. Even if the book didn't poison him, there is some reason he was there with it in your library. That can't be a coincidence. I don't know why, but maybe you will figure it out."

I nodded. "Whatever I can do."

✳ ✳ ✳

County forces managed Rose Mallow with a small station in town. I'd never been there before, but I'd heard the building used to be a car dealership about forty years ago. The station was quiet, presumably with most everyone else at the press station.

I cringed at the tiny closet that served as an evidence room. It was humid in there, suggesting a lack of climate control, which was not good for an old book. The place appeared clean, but I couldn't help worrying about what cleaning materials they used. I hoped that it wasn't anything harsh. Fortunately, we quickly found the book on the shelf.

"I wouldn't normally wear gloves to handle a rare book," I said to John. "Normally, clean hands are better, but with everyone talking about poison, I

142

guess it's a good thing I carry these around." I picked out a pair of purple nitrile gloves from my purse.

"You carry gloves with you?" he sounded amused.

"Yep. Tools of the trade. Even if I don't always wear them, there are other times—well, besides potentially poisonous pages—when it's helpful to have."

"Well, here, you might want this too," he said, producing two surgical masks. "Can't be too cautious."

I nodded, and we both put them on. It might be overkill, but I'd rather be too cautious than risk exposure.

I examined the *Tales* book on a tiny table in the middle of the closet room. The books in our library all contained small inserts with their information, printed onto acid-free paper, designed to do as little damage as possible to the book. Not surprisingly, that was missing. However, I did find a tiny number penciled onto the back inside cover.

"Ah ha," I said, pointing it out. "It's ours. That catalog number matches the one from our collection that's missing."

"Okay, good. I'm glad that's confirmed."

I gently examined the pages of the book, finding more traces of plant material. I wondered if my gloves were strong enough.

"Anything unusual?" John asked.

I shook my head. "More plant stuff. Maybe the monkshood, but everything else looks like it's in good...." I stopped speaking. At the back of the book, I noticed a small triangle of white hiding behind the marbleized endpaper. "There's something here."

"What?" John asked with excitement.

I gently poked at it. "Some sort of paper." I dug through my purse again and pulled out another of my favorite tools.

"What's that?"

Next to the book, I unrolled a small cloth. Inside were a series of different-sized tweezers.

"Why do you carry those around?"

I shrugged. "I guess for situations like this." He didn't appear amused by my bad joke. "But seriously, I dropped them in there at one point and forgot."

I looked through the options and chose a tiny pair. Then, I pulled at the tiny white triangle. It took a little maneuvering, but after a few minutes, I had managed to remove a small sheet of paper.

We both stared at the sheet, which was no larger than a Post-it note. Fortunately, it didn't have any of the sticky gunk on the back. Across the paper was another code. I couldn't tell if it was the same code. It had been printed on there, as if with a typewriter. I pulled out my phone to take a photo. John made a face but didn't stop me.

"What's it say?" he asked.

"I have no idea."

As I finished my sentence, we heard other voices in the station. The press conference must have ended. Quickly, we put the *Tales* book back.

"How are you going to explain finding this to the detective?"

"I'll figure something out," he replied.

"Okay, I'll work on learning more about the book, Poe, and secret messages."

"Fine, fine, but let's get you out of here."

He led me out of the evidence closet, and we scurried up to the foyer, almost knocking straight into Detective Gupta and the sheriff. According to his name badge, he was Sheriff Smith.

"What are you doing here, Ms. Blume?" Detective Gupta asked.

Before I could reply, John said, "I was telling *Ms. Blume* that she needs to stop getting involved in Mr. Cooley's investigation." His tone was cold and indifferent. I wanted to roll my eyes. Again, I felt like I was back in high school with this bad masquerade.

"Ms. Blume," the detective said with a sigh. She touched her temples and shook her head.

"Is this the same Ms. Blume as with that cemetery case last month? And that old book?" the sheriff asked.

"That's me," I said.

"Well, I heard you made things difficult for my detective and deputies. You doing that again?" he asked. Every word sounded more and more annoyed with my very existence.

"Just asking the deputy a few questions," I answered with a fake, cheery smile. I fluttered my eyes at Deputy Torres. He must have gotten the message because he took the opportunity to usher me out of the station.

"Sorry about that," he said when we were outside. "We'll stay in touch?"

"I'll let you know if I figure out the message."

He nodded and thanked me.

Chapter Twenty-Four

When I parked outside the Wildflower Inn, I was shocked to find it coated in papers. Sheets streamed across the veranda roof, littered along the lawn, and stuck up from several roof tiles. Azalea raked a pile into a corner. I reached down to grab one of the sheets. To my dismay, they were all photocopies of the *Chesapeake Chronicle* newspaper article about me.

"Oh no," I cried. "Are you all okay? Violet and Clover?"

Hearing his name, Clover sprinted to me. Violet was on the veranda with her crayons and paper. Clover danced around me, jumping up on my legs. I reached down and gave him some generous pets.

"We're fine. This must have happened while we were out on a few errands. I'm sorry, Juniper," she said.

"Don't apologize. It's all my fault." I looked around for another rake. Not seeing one, I worked on stuffing the pile of papers into an open bag. Clover attempted to help by wrestling with a sheet across the grass. Violet climbed down the stairs and grabbed a page as well. She then brought it back to her coloring stash. At least someone was getting some use of them.

Azalea arched an eyebrow. "I don't want to hear that mental leap. You didn't do this. Someone else did. Someone annoying."

"Probably one of the protesters."

"Yeah, that's my guess too. They used to be such a polite group. I'd gone down a few times before you started, and they held up signs in silent protest. Very respectful."

"What changed?"

She shrugged. "Honestly, it was probably around the time Big Al joined them. They started getting more…" She bit her lower lip and searched the skies, apparently trying to think of the right word. "More active, I guess. I don't really like their vibe anymore. Too militant for my taste."

"Really? That's interesting," I paused in between stuffing the bag. "I heard he'd only joined them very recently."

She nodded. "Yeah, I don't know what made him change his mind."

I thought I might know, but I wasn't sure I should share about Florence and Big Al, even with Azalea. Meanwhile, Clover tore up a page with his teeth. I patted him with a quiet, "Good boy."

She shook her head. "You'd think I'd have figured out how to set up my new security camera system by now, but with my assistant Keisha out of town, I haven't had the time to see about getting it put up. Plus, Rory's still recovering, so I don't want to have him climbing up there on the roof and risk him getting hurt again."

"What about Deputy Torres?"

She made a face I couldn't decipher. "I don't know. I still think I want to see how things go with Rory, so I'm not sure that'd be a great idea. I don't want to lead him on."

He would be devastated to hear that, but at least I'd asked. I wasn't Team Rory or Team John. I only cared about who or what made Azalea happy.

"We can probably take care of this ourselves," I said.

"As much as I'd like to agree with that sentiment, I don't feel comfortable with either of us climbing on the roof. Not to get the papers stuck up there or to install the security system. And unfortunately, I don't have money in the budget to pay for help right now." She sighed, but then her face suddenly lit up. "What about Leo? He can probably help us out."

"Oh, uh," I said, remembering the last time I asked for his help with Violet and Clover. I didn't want to repeat that awkward encounter. But then I looked over at Azalea's hopeful face and knew I better get on the phone.

* * *

Leo was there quickly. He surveyed the vandalism across the front yard and house. "Wow, this is even worse than I'd imagined. Let me call a couple friends, and we'll get this tackled." He turned to Azalea and added, "I'm sure we can get that security system set up too."

"Thank you," she replied. "I was waiting for Keisha to return from her camping trip with her family. I figured if she couldn't do it, her older sister could."

"Is that Desiree Douglass? I've been trying to get her to join the Calverton team for a while now. I haven't seen too many people master as many tech things as quickly as she does," he replied. Desiree owned a small electronics store along the boardwalk. She'd replaced my cell phone last summer. She and her younger sister Keisha were incredibly talented at all things technological.

Azalea nodded. "Yeah, and I think Keisha is probably going to be as good. If not better when she's out of high school."

Leo shook his head. "Wow, kids these days."

"Wait, are we suddenly old?" I asked. Leo and Azalea laughed.

"Mommy! Mommy!" Violet called out from the veranda.

"Excuse me," Azalea said. When she got up to the porch, I could hear her exclaim again. She called out to us, "This is going to take a bit."

"No worries. Take your time."

She lifted a hand and then picked up Violet under her armpits and hurried the young girl into the house. Clover barreled after them.

After Leo put in a call to his buddies, he worked on picking up sheets. I couldn't believe how many there were floating around the inn. Who had the time or equipment to make so many? My first thought was Luna, since she worked at the newspaper itself, but I couldn't understand her seeming vendetta against me.

"Thanks for coming," I said to Leo. "I mean, I know I said nothing personal, but…." I wrung my hands as I spoke.

He must have noticed because he grabbed them and held them still. "I'll always be here for you, Juniper. And for your sister."

My heart practically melted. I turned my face away as tears filled my eyes.

CHAPTER TWENTY-FOUR

"Thank you."

He let go of my hands and crooked a finger under my chin, turning it back to him. I stared deeply into his dark eyes. My chest tightened, and I thought my knees might give way. His face leaned closer to mine, and I knew he was going to kiss me. I wanted so desperately for him to do so, but the little voice in the back of my head screamed for me to stop. Another voice nearly drowned it out, telling me to go for it, but I listened to my better instincts. Before he could get any closer, I pulled away.

"Maybe I should find another job," I said in a near whisper.

"No, please don't go," he replied. I then realized he was holding my hands. It took every ounce of strength I had to let them go.

"Look at this article, though. Everyone already thinks we're dating and that my position is nepotism."

"They're wrong. You're amazing."

"And that's on top of all these people giving me a hard time for working for your family in the first place. Did you know that Harmony kicked me out of the Purple Oyster?"

"What? Isn't she your aunt?" he asked.

"Only through marriage," I replied.

"That's still family."

I shrugged. I wasn't sure it mattered. Between the protests and Big Al, I didn't know if I wanted to continue working there.

"Do you really want to quit already? In less than one week? That's not the tenacious Juniper Blume that I know. The Juniper Blume I know would never give in this easily."

I smiled at his generous assessment of my character. I'd been called headstrong more than once, so I appreciated being called tenacious. The word rang better in my head.

"I want to do something good with this job, you know? Open up the museum, share the collections, and somehow heal the rift that's formed between the Calvertons and Rose Mallow. Use history to remind everyone about how intertwined you both are. That you're still family." As I spoke, I felt a deeper conviction with each word.

"Do you have something in mind?" Leo asked.

I thought for a minute. I looked at one of the photocopies at my feet. Above my infamous article was the *Chesapeake Chronicle*'s logo, indicating that the newspaper had been in publication for more than a hundred years. I'd seen articles from several generations of the newspaper at the historical society about the Calverton family. I remembered how they told of the ways the family used to help the town.

"The Calvertons used to invest in Rose Mallow. So why aren't they doing that now? Why do they want to get rid of so many great businesses to bring in overpriced chains from the outside? Why not put their money into the people who are here now?" I asked.

Leo nodded, encouragingly. "That's a great plan."

"Plan? What's a great plan?" I asked.

"We should invest in the town." He snapped his fingers. "I've long wanted a counter-proposal to my family's Port Chesapeake development plan, and I think you gave me one."

"I did?"

He laughed. "We'll invest in the businesses here. We'll give out grants to existing places. Family-run places. The longer you've been here, the more money you'll get. We've got plenty to give them the resources they need to succeed." He was practically dancing as he spoke. The excitement was palpable. I loved the way he ran with my idea. If the Calvertons did that, then the businesses could be saved. The character and history would be preserved. I knew that would draw more people here. Maybe this former resort town could become a true destination again.

"You'll help the Wildflower Inn?" I asked.

"Of course we will. Well, I won't. You've also raised good points about nepotism. The grants will be reviewed by an independent committee. No Calvertons. Just locals helping locals."

I don't know which of us grabbed the other's hands, but we were suddenly jumping up and down, holding onto one another. Time ran slow and fast. We seemed to stop in mid-air, almost floating above the ground. He looked at me, and I couldn't stop smiling. As he leaned closer, I closed my eyes, waiting for his kiss.

Then, a car honked.

We turned, and multiple cars parked in the street in front of the Wildflower Inn. Leo's friends. Soon, they were all around us. Someone brought out a ladder, and another handed out rakes. A group of young men and women appeared, ready to help us clean up.

By the time Azalea returned with Violet in a new set of clothes, the team had already finished cleaning up. A couple were working on setting up the security system. A woman showed Azalea something about the system on a tablet. My sister nodded several times as she concentrated on how to operate the new system.

As night descended, the crew finished up. We offered them pizza, but someone said Leo had proposed a couple rounds of drinks at a nearby pub.

"You're welcome to come too, Juniper," he said to me.

"Thanks, but maybe next time," I replied. It'd been such a long day, and more than anything, I wanted to slip into bed.

He nodded, although I couldn't help noticing a glint of disappointment in his eyes. I wanted to grab him and hold him tight, but I knew better. Instead, I waved him off with his buddies. The moment with Leo may have passed, but I'd never felt so grateful.

Chapter Twenty-Five

The next morning was a buzz of activity at the Wildflower Inn. Most of the rooms had been booked ahead of the festival the upcoming weekend. Since the festival actually kicked off on Thursday and went through Monday, it extended the already long holiday weekend. Azalea was busy with breakfast for everyone. It was good to see her busy, but I could also see she was stressed without her assistant Keisha there. I knew I wouldn't be much help in the kitchen, but I realized there was another way to help. I offered to take Violet and Clover out for an hour. Azalea nodded gratefully.

We walked up the boardwalk, watching the sun rise over the Chesapeake Bay. However, about five minutes into the walk, Violet started complaining of being hungry.

"Didn't you eat before we left?" I asked.

"Need more food." She stomped her foot. It was more adorable than aggressive.

"We're almost to the shops. Maybe we can get something up here," I said as we wandered north along the boardwalk. The fancy Indigo Room restaurant was on the southern end of the boardwalk shops, but a few doors up from it was La Artesa—the panaderia Eric's mother ran. I'd never been inside since it was only open to the public in the early mornings, but we made it there before it closed.

A cheerful, hand-painted sign read the store's name in canary yellow and deep blues. Oaxacan pottery lined the windowsill. During my traveling days, I'd attended a ceramics workshop in the region, learning from a master craftsman. Although I didn't speak much Spanish, it had been incredible to explore the *barro roja* and *barro negro* clays. Nothing I created looked anything like these beautiful pieces, though.

"This place smells yummy," said Violet.

"I agree, but I don't know if dogs are allowed inside," I said to Clover. He whined a little bit as I tied his leash to a chair in front of the store. Someone sitting out there promised to keep an eye on him. "We'll be back soon. I promise."

Inside, we joined a long line of people. A couple teenagers took orders from a countertop lined with incredible-smelling pastries.

"What's that?" Violet pointed to a colorful gelatinous dessert on the counter. It was a mix of bright pinks, sunny yellows, and clear whites.

"Oh, I've had that before. It's…Nica…" I stumbled over the word.

"Nicuatole. They're one of my favorites," said a woman walking up to us. Wearing a La Artesa embroidered blouse, she appeared to be in her mid-fifties. She also looked a lot like Eric. She kneeled beside Violet and offered her a cylindrical pastry filled with some sort of cream. She looked at me to check if it was okay, and I nodded. "These are also one of my favorites, gaznate."

Violet happily took the treat. After a single bite, her face lit up. "This is the most yummiest food ever."

"I agree." The woman stood up.

"Are you Ms. Gutierrez?" I asked.

"Si. I'm Maria Gutierrez. But I don't think we know each other?"

"My name is Juniper Blume. I work with Eric at the Calverton library."

Her face darkened. "Oh yes, the library."

I wasn't sure why she was suddenly upset. There were so many possibilities. Could it be all the protests about the Calvertons? Or was she mad that Eric wasn't in the family business? Maybe she was worried about the murder of Big Al? All of those were understandable reasons to be concerned.

"You need to remind Leo Calverton to come by." She wagged a finger. "I haven't seen him in over a week." She sucked her teeth. "I have gluten-free sopapillas with agave waiting for him."

I laughed. That's why she was upset. It sounded like she'd made them special for him, since he was gluten-free and vegan. "I'll be sure to remind him."

"Good, good. I'm very proud of Eric working there. The Calvertons have been good for our business. We get a lot of orders from them."

Violet tugged on my pants leg. I looked down at her, and she whisper-shouted, "May I have another one?"

"Of course, carina," Maria said.

I don't think I'd ever seen her smile bigger.

"And one for you too?" she asked.

"Sure, that'd be lovely," I said. When she brought them over, I asked her what they cost, but she laughed at me. "Please, enjoy. Take good care of my son."

It was nice to have someone who didn't seem upset at the Calvertons. Somehow, that made the treats taste even sweeter.

* * *

When I got to the Calverton Library later that morning, Eric stopped me before I sat down in my office chair. He looked excited.

"What's going on?" I asked.

He clasped his hands together and said, "I found out who checked out all the Poe books."

"Oh?"

He leaned in closer to me, and although there was no one else in the library, he whispered, "Martha Dresdale."

"Martha?" I hadn't expected that. Why on earth would she have checked them out? She certainly didn't seem to care about the museum project except for how it impacted the image of Calverton Industries.

"I know, isn't that interesting?"

"Yeah, it is, actually," I replied. Then I remembered how she hadn't been at the party. In fact, I'd run into her on my way back to the library and archive building. Was it possible she had been coming out of it? "You know what,

Eric, I have a quick thing I need to take care of. I'll be back shortly."

"Sure thing, boss."

I hurried out of the library, practically running across the campus, but I had no idea where Martha's office might be. I didn't even know if she'd be there. I stopped on a sidewalk mid-step, nearly careening into a group of suits. "Excuse me." It came out quietly because I was still lost in my thoughts. What was I going to ask her? Did I think I'd go in and ask why she had checked out books on Edgar Allan Poe? That seemed ridiculous. And I hadn't seen her in the library building. Given the cameras around, the police would have probably noticed. I started to backtrack, figuring I was wasting my time.

Then I noticed I'd managed to find my way in front of the Calverton Bank administrative offices. Perhaps it was a stroke of luck, but I decided to take it as a sign. I didn't know what I'd find out talking to Martha, but I knew I wouldn't find out anything if I didn't. I marched inside and asked the receptionist where her office might be.

"Who are you? Do you have an appointment?" she asked.

"I'm Juniper Blume, the new director of…"

She snapped her fingers. "Oh! I know you. I read that article about you. So you and Leo Calverton, huh?" Her shoulders shimmied. "Good for you. He's hot."

"No, he's my boss," I said, knowing full well any explanation wouldn't matter. I could see the mischievous glint in her eyes, behind square-framed glasses.

"Sure, he is," she said with a wink.

I rubbed my temples. This was tiring. "Can I see Martha?"

"Oh, you can't go in right now," the young woman said.

"She's in a meeting?" I asked.

She rolled her eyes. "Sure, a meeting." She put her fingers up in air quotes.

I was surprised by her unprofessional demeanor. "Is everything okay?"

She sighed. "The bigwigs don't know it yet, but I'm quitting. Effective today. I'm tired of being berated by that nasty witch." She made a face like she'd tasted something sour. Then, she looked proud of herself.

"Good for you," I said, figuring it couldn't hurt to encourage her. "So why the air quotes on the word 'meeting'?"

The receptionist leaned across the desk and said to me sotto voce, "Anytime there's that weird odor in her office and that cheesy music playing, I know better than to go inside." She shuddered. "I made that mistake once, and I won't do it again."

"What did you see?"

She gagged and said, "Not enough clothing."

"Eww."

She nodded. "It's gross. And it's been happening more and more. I still can't clean my eyes enough."

I thought of Oedipus gouging out his eyes. Or maybe Lady Macbeth was a better analogy, trying unsuccessfully to clean off that wretched spot from her hand. "She was with someone?"

The receptionist nodded.

"And you said that odor means she is again?"

"Yep." She stuck out her tongue. "I've had enough of it here. As soon as I can tell her, I'm out of here."

"What does the odor smell like?" I asked.

She thought for a moment, twirling a pen around in her fingers. "This may sound strange, but it smells like being in an antique store. No, wait, that's not quite right."

I felt a tingle go up my spine. "Maybe a bookstore?"

She dropped the pen and snapped her fingers. "Yes, yes, that's it. But like a really old one."

That tingle crept up higher. I didn't fully understand the urge, but I suddenly knew I had to get into her office. I took off running. The receptionist called out after me, but I didn't care. I needed to find Martha's office right now.

I ran down the hallway behind the front desk, blazing past a mix of closed doors and empty conference rooms. When I came to the end of the corridor, I found Martha Dresdale's office with the door closed. Sure enough, I smelled the same scent as I had at both Big Al's house and Florence Dowd's home.

Something soft and instrumental played at a low volume. I pulled on the handle, but the door was locked.

I ran back to the front desk.

"We need to get in her office. The door's locked."

"I told you she wasn't to be bothered. She must have started locking the door after that time," she said, rolling her eyes.

"It's important. Do you have a key?"

"Why? What's the matter?" She asked while rummaging through a drawer. She produced a set of keys. "Do I need to call security?"

"I don't know," I replied, but a nasty feeling crept into my stomach.

The receptionist led the way down the hallway, and I followed her. She fiddled through the set of keys as she went, stopping on one of the steps outside of Martha's office. Then she handed the keys to me. "I really don't want to see them like that again. I'm only doing this because of you."

I nodded and opened the door. Inside her office, the same big handmade candle I'd seen in the other houses sat lit on her desk. Music played from an old CD player in the corner.

Martha lay collapsed across the tabletop. Just out of reach was another leather-bound book. I couldn't see it closely, but I had a suspicion it was another one of our missing Edgar Allan Poe books.

Behind me, the receptionist screamed.

Chapter Twenty-Six

This time, both Detective Gupta and Deputy Torres showed up, finding me slumped on the ground in one of the empty conference rooms along the same hallway. Deputy Torres checked on me first, while the detective went to speak with the receptionist.

"You doing okay?" he asked.

"Not really," I replied truthfully. "Before going in there, I thought Martha might actually have been Big Al's killer."

"Why?"

I sighed and stared out the bank of windows on one side of the conference room. Nestled deep inside the campus, it felt like I had been transported to a European castle, given the rock-strewn buildings, tall oak trees, thick shrubs, and winding paths. Almost. I'd looked up the history of the campus. It was barely historic, having been created in the 1960s in this pseudo-retro style. It was as real as the nearby abandoned Bayside Amusement park. At least the Wildflower Inn was authentic. I'd had enough of fake things.

"I didn't tell you everything," I said slowly. His eyebrows shot up. "There was more I'd found out about Big Al."

"Like what?" he asked. His voice was fairly steady, but I detected a concerned undertone.

"I should probably tell Detective Gupta this, too."

"You can tell her again during your interview with her," he replied. I wanted to protest that I was talking to him, but I knew the drill. I'd need to repeat what I'd seen and learned several times. "But why don't you start by talking to me."

I nodded. "Big Al had been cheating on his wife," I said. Deputy Torres immediately pulled out a pad of paper and started taking notes.

"With whom?"

I debated not telling him about Florence, but what was the use in holding back? It would all come out sooner or later. I explained about his long affair with my employee, the candles he'd made smelling of the bookstore, and how I believed Martha was the woman he had recently started seeing.

Deputy Torres shook his head. "Wait, if he was seeing Martha, then why did he join the protest?"

I shrugged. It was something I'd been wondering, too.

"And if they were dating, why did you think she might have killed him?"

"Well, I don't know why, but it was more that I found it strange to have run into her near the library building. She hadn't been at the welcoming party with the other board members. Either way, it looks like I was wrong."

"Possibly," he said.

"What do you mean by 'possibly'?"

"I'm not sure, but maybe she did kill Big Al. And then maybe someone else killed her?" At least Deputy Torres was more forthcoming with his thoughts than Detective Gupta. I appreciated that.

"Someone who knew enough to light that candle and put on some music. They knew that it would keep the receptionist away. Oh no, I hope that doesn't mean there are multiple murderers." My stomach reeled, considering the possibility.

"Wait, wait, I didn't say that there was. We have a lot more to investigate. Is there anything else you didn't share with me before?" His stare bore into me. I shifted my weight from foot to foot, deciding if I should drop my other bombshell about the weird bookshelf in Boardwalk Books. But I didn't see how that could be relevant.

I was saved from answering by Detective Gupta. Unlike Torres in his uniform, Gupta wore another polished suit. Today's was a deep ultramarine blue with a silk cream-colored blouse underneath. As always, she wore bright gold jewelry, which glistened under the conference room lights. I didn't know how she worked so much while wearing heels—today's being taupe—but she seemed tireless.

"Ah, Miss Blume, why am I not surprised to find you here?" She smiled as she shook her head. "But actually, I'm glad you're the one who found her."

"You are?" Deputy Torres and I said at the same time.

"It looks like we found another one of your missing books."

"I thought so," I replied, having noted the old book on Martha's desk.

"We're not sure if it has poison on it, but sticking out was at least part of yet another encrypted message. Having any luck deciphering the first one?" she asked. I looked at Deputy Torres, wondering if the detective knew I had seen the second note as well. This time, he maintained a poker face, so I didn't bring it up.

"Nothing yet."

"We'll get you a copy of this one to study too. And there's one more we found from the other book." She snapped her fingers, and a junior deputy appeared. After whispering into his ear, he disappeared from the room. I was relieved that I didn't have to hide knowing about the other note. That made three of them. All were encrypted.

I don't know how long we spent discussing what I'd seen. I revealed to Detective Gupta what I'd shared with Deputy Torres about Florence and Martha. Unlike Torres, Gupta remained stone-faced as I spoke.

"That's everything?" she asked.

"Well…." I bit my lip. I debated not telling them about Nuri and Boardwalk Books, but even if I wanted to protect Nuri's confidence, I needed to come clean about everything I'd found out. Even if I wasn't sure how it was relevant, it wasn't my job to decide what was and what wasn't. If I had shared my suspicions before, maybe Martha would somehow still be alive.

"Well, what?" Deputy Torres asked. Detective Gupta looked at him in surprise. "Sorry, I didn't mean to interrupt your investigation." He said in apology to her. She turned back to me and rolled her hand like a circle in the air, urging me to continue.

"This is a little weird, but there's a locked hidden shelf in Boardwalk Books."

"Mr. Cooley's store?" the detective confirmed, even though we both knew it was the same place.

"Right. I stopped by there and ran into my old friend Nuri Cho."

"Old friend? How do you know her?"

"We were in college together. Well, graduate school. Studying to be librarians. We were actually roommates for a time."

"You said that you ran into her. Did you not know she was here in Rose Mallow?"

"I had no idea she was here. I haven't seen her in years. Ever since…" I stopped before saying more, but it was too late.

"Ever since what?" she prodded.

I knew it'd come out sooner or later. "Ever since Nuri left school. I don't know why she left, especially when we were so close to finishing our degrees. I didn't see her again until I came into the store."

"How long ago did she leave school?"

"Around five years ago."

"Okay, so what did you find in the store?" she asked.

"There's a shelf behind the front desk. It's under Plexiglass and locked. Nuri doesn't have a key. Most of the time, it'd been hidden under fabric and other things," I said.

"What's on the shelf?"

"Really rare books. Museum quality ones. Probably first editions." I remembered how those books stood in stark contrast to the rest of the store, which was mainly dog-eared paperbacks. All the books were special, but these were different. They were valuable.

"Like by Edgar Allan Poe?"

"I didn't see anything by him there that day, but yes, similar to that," I said. "But Nuri never saw them sell or Big Al even open the case. Sometimes, though, a book would somehow disappear."

"Disappear?" Deputy Torres repeated. Again, Detective Gupta looked at him. She briefly arched an eyebrow before her face turned cold again. He held up his hands in apology. She turned to me to continue.

"She said it was like a magic trick. She never saw anyone open it or take anything out, but occasionally, it'd go away, and something else would appear later on."

"Why didn't you say anything before?" Deputy Torres asked. Detective Gupta rolled her eyes behind him, but she didn't knock him. I knew he was really asking me directly why I didn't tell him any of this earlier.

"Well, I…"

Suddenly, the junior deputy reappeared. He handed me a manila folder. Inside was a copy of the note they'd found. I examined the document while everyone watched me closely.

"I don't want to get your hopes up," I said. "I'm a librarian, not a code breaker."

Detective Gupta smiled. "We know, but sometimes, you recognize resources we don't. I figure it can't hurt to have you looking."

As she finished, I knew who I had to see next. I did have access to a resource they probably wouldn't have thought about.

Chapter Twenty-Seven

I shouldn't have been surprised that the historical society was already closed for the day. Being staffed by volunteers, it kept odd hours. I tried searching for Harold's home address using my phone but didn't get anything helpful. I didn't want to return to the Calverton campus after the second murder, so instead, I turned to my most trustworthy resource: the local library.

"Hey there!" Brandy waved from her spot at the Information Desk, so I strode over. I did need some information after all. Judging by her friendly smile, I figured she was no longer upset over our Poe chat. That was a relief. "I heard it was a chaotic day. You doing okay?"

I shrugged. "As fine as anyone can be. What about Eric? I sent him home after finding Martha, and he seemed pretty torn up."

Brandy sighed. "Yeah, two deaths like this are taking a toll on him." She leaned over the desk and whispered, "I think he's worried that the police will think he did it."

"What? Why would they think that?" I hadn't expected her to say that. I hadn't known Eric long, but he genuinely seemed like a sweet-hearted person. His mother certainly was, too.

She looked left and right before speaking, "Remember what I said about his background?" I thought back to our discussion in her parents' florist shop about Eric being from Mexico originally.

"Oh, you think that his status might be in trouble?" I asked, lowering my volume as well.

She nodded, looking glum. "I mean, I don't, but he does. It breaks my heart to see him so upset." Then she set her jaw, looked me straight in the eyes, and said, "But I won't let that happen. I won't let anything happen to him." The fierceness of her words threw me, but I appreciated the sentiment. I was glad he had Brandy in his corner. People tended to underestimate librarians, but I knew we were capable of more than anyone expected.

"I promise, I'm going to find out what's going on."

Someone came behind me to the desk, so I moved aside while Brandy pointed them to the graphic novels. Then she turned back to me. "Eric also asked me who had checked out the Poe books, which I figured was your asking." Instead of looking alarmed, she leaned over, appearing conspiratorial.

"Guilty. It actually led me to suspect Martha."

"No kidding? How did you get from one to the other?" she asked.

"Well, I know it was a stretch, but it seemed surprising to me that she would have done so right after the missing Poe book turned up. Then I remembered that she wasn't with everyone else when Big Al must have been in the Calverton library. I still don't have all the pieces, but I had gone to her office to find out more," I replied, leaving out the part about the candle and her potential affair with Big Al.

"So then, why are you back here?" she asked.

"Honestly?"

She nodded, looking enthusiastic.

"I need to find the address of Harold Graham," I said. "Can you help me?"

"Well, sure, but who is that?"

"Oh, right, Eric was here when Florence and I went to the historical society," I said, remembering. "He's an older gentleman who volunteers there."

She was already digging into the computer. As she typed, she asked, "So, why do you need to speak to him?"

"Oh, because…" I almost revealed his background and help in breaking the codes we'd found in the Poe books, but I stopped myself in time, which was impressive. I couldn't help thinking about the old WWII poster that warned Americans about how "Loose lips sink ships!" meaning that anyone could be a spy. I almost laughed at the idea of Brandy being one. She watched me with earnestness and interest. Still, I didn't think that either Detective Gupta or Deputy Torres would appreciate me sharing the codes with her. "I wanted to ask him something about the town's history."

"And you need his home address to do that?" she asked, looking uncertain.

"I also wanted to bring him some of my sister's honey cake," I added, amazed at how quickly the lie formed on my lips.

"That sounds sweet. Literally," she said with a laugh. Brandy paused, typing. "Weird, I don't see him in the usual database. He's kind of like a ghost."

"That's strange."

She nodded and tapped a finger to her lips. "But I wonder…." She got up and roamed around the library. I followed close behind. "Most of the town's historical resources are at the historical society, but we still have some in our research section." We wandered the shelves in the very back of the library. She stopped mid-shelf and looked at the leather-bound books, seeming to count them with her fingers. I looked over and smiled, recognizing what she was searching for.

"City directories!" I cried.

"Exactly," she said. "You said he's older and with the historical society, so I figured he's been in the area for a while and might be in some of the last volumes. We even have a couple of Yellow and White Pages, too, if we need to go more recent, but really, these have held up better."

In a time before phones, places would put out annual directories of their area's residents, including their address and occupation. I'd used them many times before to do research.

We found Harold's address in the first volume we searched, which happened to be the latest city directory the library owned, dating back nearly fifty years ago.

"Nice work."

Brandy did a little curtsy. "All in a day's job for a librarian."

"That's right," I replied with a laugh. "But yes, thank you."

"Hey, you figure out who is making life hard for my Eric, and I'll do anything that I can to support you," she said, holding up her fingers like a

Girl Scout.

"I promise. I'm sure I'll be back soon."

* * *

Before I headed to Harold's house, I stopped by Boardwalk Books to check in on Nuri. She was at the checkout counter. Today, she was sporting all black along with a spiked collar. Her eyeliner was thick and long, giving her cat's eyes. Her gaze locked on me as soon as I entered the small store, and it wasn't friendly. More like a death stare.

"I take it the police visited again?" I asked her.

She folded her arms against her chest, and she sized me up. Eventually, she nodded and said, "I'd asked you not to tell them about the mystery shelf. Not until I did."

"I'm sorry, Nur, but there was another murder."

She slumped a bit, her expression relaxing, and she shook her head. "I know." Her arms fell to her sides. "Honestly, I'm more mad at myself than you."

"No, don't be."

"I should have told them already." She wiped her eyes. Her dark eyeliner smudged. "I keep wondering if I could have prevented that woman's death."

"Did you know her? Ever see her here?"

She shrugged. "I don't think so, but I'm not certain."

I looked behind her shoulders. The mystery shelf appeared to be gone. She followed my gaze and nodded. "Yeah, the police took the whole thing away."

"Did they say anything about it?"

"Nothing. Just waved around a search warrant."

"Did they take anything else?"

Nuri nodded. "Yeah, lots of files and a candle from Big Al's office. That was weird."

Maybe not too weird, given the candle in Martha's office, but I didn't know what was my place to share.

"Oh, wait!" She slunk below the counter. I heard boxes moving and a few things rattling about. When she popped up again, she had a piece of paper in her hand. "I found this." She pushed the paper across the table. Even before I saw it, I knew what it was likely to be. Sure enough, it was another encoded message. Was that four now?

"Is this the original?"

"No, I found it the other day on the floor back here, almost entirely hidden by stuff, and made a photocopy. The police took the one I found. I heard you might have found something similar?" she asked.

"How did you hear that?" I didn't like that my investigating was getting around. Not that I'd been as subtle as I would have liked. Deputy Torres had made that clear.

"This is a small town, Juniper. Word spreads."

I sighed. It was true. "Can I take a photo of it?"

"This copy's for you."

"Thanks."

"I'm not holding anything else back anymore. I don't want anyone else to die, Juniper. Honestly, I'm scared. I'm debating whether or not to keep Boardwalk Books open."

I put my hands out across the counter. She grabbed them in hers and gripped fiercely. "We'll figure this out, Nuri. I promise." I released her hand briefly and held it up. "A rogue's swear?"

Her face lightened quickly. We had come up with the complex handshake during library school, thinking we were being so cool. "Rogue's swear."

Chapter Twenty-Eight

I stopped by the Wildflower Inn before heading out to Harold's house. After giving Clover a quick walk and both of us some dinner, I headed out in KG beyond the outskirts of town. According to my GPS, Harold lived in a more rural area to the west.

As I drove out of town, a black car appeared behind me. It never honked, but it rode up close on KG's tail. I sped up a few times, but I didn't want to miss my turn-off. The car kept my speed and continued to ride on my bottom. I looked into my rear-view mirror, but I couldn't see the driver as the windows were tinted. Then I noticed that the front plates were obscured, so I couldn't read the number.

As we kept speeding along the back road, my heart began thumping faster in my chest. I tried sticking my hand out to wave the car around, but it didn't go past me. There was no one else out here. I looked for places to pull over or turn around, but the sides of the road were tall fields.

The car came closer. In the rear-view mirror, it looked like we were connected, but they didn't bump KG's back end. My hands gripped the steering wheel for dear life, as everything felt shaky. My breathing was hard and fast, close to hyperventilating.

Then, the bump jolted me. It surged through my entire being. The black car was more powerful than KG, so it didn't take much to get me swerving along the road. I panicked that we'd go skidding into the fields. However, before I could go crashing off the road, I managed to straighten out. As I did, the black car blew past me, racing ahead until it disappeared, honking manically.

Thoroughly freaked out, I slowed down, nearly stopping on the tiny excuse of a shoulder. Eventually, I found a driveway and pulled over, catching my breath. I considered calling the police, but I wasn't sure what to tell them. I didn't know the make or model of the car, and I couldn't even read the license plate. Telling them a black car almost ran me off the road wasn't particularly specific. The most that might happen was that it'd be reported and stuck in a file somewhere. Besides, I didn't even know that the car was targeting me so much that I had been in the wrong place at the wrong time for this obnoxious driver. What I did know was that coming out here was more of a trek than I'd expected, so I better go check on Harold while I was already out this far.

* * *

Before long, I was off the main roads and onto single-lane streets, until even those gave way to dirt paths. I debated continuing, but there were enough tire tracks in the dust for me to feel confident others drove this way, too. As I continued, the sun began setting, and dusk coated everything in a hazy orange hue.

Eventually, I found the address. Harold's driveway was long and tree-lined. It led to what once was a great palatial building, but now, the white paint was faded and cracked, several upper-level windows were boarded up, and ivy climbed up the pillars of the portico. I could still tell that the Greek revival structure must have been a tremendous home once upon a time. I guessed it was antebellum, predating the Civil War. I wondered if it'd always been in Harold's family.

I pulled KG into the round driveway in front of the grant portico. I climbed a small flight of steps to knock on the oversized doors. Nothing happened. I spotted a doorbell and tried it, hearing the melody reverberate inside. After a minute, he still hadn't come to the door. I tried spying inside to see if there were lights on, but the curtains to the first-floor windows were drawn tight.

As I was about to give up, I heard something. Curious, I crossed around the building. While most of the grounds were overgrown, I spotted a well-cared-for garden plot in the back. In the middle was Harold, examining a squash blossom. He was whistling and singing to the plant, which must have been what I heard upfront.

I coughed a few times until he looked up and, although obviously surprised, waved brightly at me to come over.

"What brings you out here, Miss Blume? Especially so late?" he asked. While at the historical society, Harold sported nice khakis and a button-up shirt, but here he was in dirt-stained overalls with a ripped white shirt underneath. His face was flushed, probably from being out in the sun for a long time.

"You, actually."

He arched an eyebrow at that. "Well, why don't we find a nice spot to sit down and catch up on. I was getting close to breaking for the day as is, now that the sun's setting. Would you care for some iced tea, lemonade, or a mix?"

"Can't resist a good Arnold Palmer." Even as it grew slightly darker, it remained hot and humid. A mix of iced tea and lemonade sounded welcome.

He smiled and led me to the back porch, where I sat on an iron patio chair with an old cushion that didn't provide much cushioning. "Let me go wash up a quick bit, and I'll be back shortly."

As he wandered inside, I checked out the kitchen through a screen door. It was a small place with countertops and appliances screaming that mid-century modern vestige I adored. While I ached to examine these historic pieces closer, I could tell that they were well-loved. Baskets of fresh vegetables and fruit were heaped high on the light pink counter space, as limited as the space was. Today's kitchens could probably fit two or three of these inside, but I suspected there was enough space to get many delicious meals done. A cutting board was half off the counter, hovering over the farmer's sink, right beside a small gas stovetop and oven in a cheery but faded pastel blue. A small center table was covered in a floral-patterned tablecloth. The whole room resembled a time capsule.

Harold returned with a pitcher of iced tea and lemonade and a couple glasses. He sat them down on a nearby iron table. It was fascinating to me what things in this place were kept immaculate – like his vegetable garden and the kitchen—and which he'd stopped bothering with, like the exterior of the house, the high grass surrounding it, and this patio furniture. I suspected that Harold lived here alone and didn't get much help caring for the place. My heart sank slightly at the thought.

"Hope you like your drinks on the sweet side. I've always had a strong sweet tooth. Ever since I was a little boy," he said.

I tried the drink. It was fabulous, but he wasn't kidding. I felt like I'd sucked on a Pixie Stix. I wouldn't be able to down the whole thing, but I could enjoy it in little sips.

"This is quite the place."

He nodded. "Yes, it sure is. Call this the Echo Glen Mansion. Not sure why. It's been in my family for generations. I actually had a field school last year from a nearby university doing archaeology there." He pointed in a general direction, but it was hard to distinguish with the high grass. Eventually, the field gave way to forest, so I assumed it was around there.

"Did they find anything?"

"Yep. Good students. They think they may have found some of the old buildings where enslaved people lived. Not proud of my family owning other people. It's a dark part of our history, but I refuse to ignore it. I'd rather lean into it, shine a light on the truth."

"Maybe that's why you like Poe so much," I said, wondering how he'd respond to the reference.

He nodded slowly. "You know you might be right. Or maybe it's because of Poe that I understand the darker side of humanity, including my own family's."

I pulled out photocopies of the encoded messages. He practically jumped into the air upon seeing them. "Are these…oh wow…may I make copies of them?"

"Please. I'm hoping you'll have more luck decoding them than I have."

"I heard about that woman at Calverton dying. Nasty stuff. I assume this is connected to her passing, too?" he asked.

"Unfortunately, it appears so."

He held each sheet close to his face and studied them carefully. "You know, I have another, uh, codebreaking friend in the area. From back in my days in the service. I think between the two of us, we'll get it figured out."

"Can your friend be trusted?"

A mischievous smile played on Harold's lips. "With this? Yes, definitely."

"Good luck. Let me know if you figure anything out."

"Thanks, Miss Blume."

"Please call me Juniper," I said.

"Of course, Juniper. I can't tell you how good it feels to be doing something useful like this again. I suspect we'll get it decoded quicker than you imagine."

"Thank you."

Chapter Twenty-Nine

The next morning, my phone's buzzing woke me up. I'd missed three calls from Harold. Each voicemail sounded progressively more and more excited. "I think we're onto something," he said in the first message. "Oh, dear, I didn't look at the time. I'll call you in the morning." A few hours later, he left another message, saying, "I know it's after three in the morning, but I really believe we're on the right track here." He paused before saying, "I'll tell you more tomorrow. Well, today, but later on." His last voicemail was, "Call me as soon as you get this."

I tried calling him a couple times, but it kept going straight to voicemail. Maybe he'd fallen asleep after a long night of decoding. Not sure what to do next, I gave Clover a long walk. When I returned an hour later, I tried Harold again but still didn't get an answer. I didn't know if the number was his landline or if he had a cell phone, so I hoped he was away from the phone.

Yet, something felt strange, given how often he'd called me overnight. A gnawing feeling sat uneasily in my stomach. Remembering how that same feeling led to me finding Martha, I decided not to ignore it any longer. Instead, I texted Leo and Eric that I'd be a bit late and jumped into KG to investigate.

I drove back out to Harold's house. There was more traffic this time but no sign of the annoying black car. The more I'd thought about it, the more I figured I'd been the unwitting victim of a rando's road rage, probably irritated that I'd been in his way on an otherwise empty back road. I'd certainly experienced my share of frustrated drivers in D.C. and around its notoriously grid-locked Beltway. Everyone was in a rush to get somewhere.

Truth be told, even I'd become ridiculously upset when dealing with slow drivers. I regretted the time I'd used my horn to express my frustration when the driver was likely new to the area. Not my proudest moment.

I parked at the same spot in the circle drive as I had last night. As before, no one answered my knocks or ringing of the doorbell.

"Probably in the garden," I said to myself as I wandered around back. However, he wasn't there. The back screen door to the kitchen was wide open, so I poked my head in and called out, "Hello!"

No one responded.

"Lots of people leave their doors unlocked out here," I reassured myself, trying not to worry. Peering into the kitchen, I spotted the sheets I'd given him last night atop the table with the floral-patterned tablecloth. Maybe he had finished decoding them? I told myself he had undoubtedly taken a nap.

"He wouldn't mind if I took a peek," I said to no one. "I won't go anywhere else."

The room felt as if someone had stepped out for a moment. Next to the sheets were two coffee cups. One was still half full, although the coffee had cooled off. The other was polished off. I suspected they had been for him and his old service buddy.

I examined the papers. Harold had written all over them. Another set of handwriting was obvious, too. That must have been his friend. I pictured them working here through the night, reliving probably some amazing memories. I didn't want to disturb their efforts, so I snapped a few photos with my phone.

That's when I noticed an odd smell. Like rotten eggs. Or sulfur. I realized that the sickening feeling in my stomach wasn't solely from anxiety but from something else entirely. Something far too real of a threat. I turned around and heard a hissing noise coming from the range. All the gas burners were on, but the flames were yellow, not blue.

I'd had a gas stove in my townhouse in D.C., so I knew this wasn't right. I tried turning off the burners, but two of the knobs wouldn't budge. Their flames kept going strong. I didn't know where the gas turnoff was.

This was trouble. I didn't know how much gas was already in the house, and if the burners wouldn't shut off, it could ignite at any moment.

I screamed at the top of my lungs, hoping that if Harold was somewhere inside, he'd hear me and get out. More than that, I sent out a silent prayer that he wasn't here.

Part of me wanted to race through the house, making sure he got off safely, but I knew I was running against time here, and I didn't have any clue how much I had left. The house was too big, and I needed to escape. Now.

I ran outside and around the house to KG. Once inside, I hit the gas pedal hard and coaxed my little roadster to hit its highest speeds. We zoomed down the long driveway, putting several hundred yards between us and the gas leak. I wanted to call 911, but I couldn't risk taking my hands off or possibly slowing down. We needed to get as far away from the house as possible.

An enormous boom rattled behind me.

I gazed into KG's rearview mirror. An explosion rocked Harold's house. A bright orange fireball erupted. Dirt and debris flew high into the air.

Thinking I was far enough away now, I skidded to a stop and looked out the back window. My heart thumped in my chest at the sight. The beautiful old mansion I'd left was engulfed in a thick fog of smoke, billowing high into the air. As parts of the smoke faded, windows into the damage appeared, revealing the place to be in shambles.

"Harold!" I jumped out of KG and ran back towards the mess. I probably made it a hundred feet before realizing what an idiotic decision I'd made. I'd acted on instinct. Most people ran from trouble, but I had headed straight towards it, driven by adrenaline and anxiety for my friend. Ahead of me was nothing but fire and rubble. I couldn't do anything to help. My knees wavered, and I leaned against a tree on the side of the driveway.

I fell to the ground and dug out my cell phone, still nestled in my back pants pocket. I called 911. Then, I called Detective Gupta and texted Deputy Torres. At least, that's what I must have done. The next bit of time was blurry. I couldn't slow the thunderous clap of my heart beating a violent tattoo in my chest, and my breathing came fast and furious, almost to the point of hyperventilating. All I could think about was Harold. He had been helping me out, and now he might be dead. Tears clouded my eyes as I worried about what I'd dragged him into.

It seemed like an eternity before the parade of emergency vehicles appeared. Soon, there was a caravan of fire trucks, police cars, and ambulances zipping up the long driveway. Most sped by me, but an ambulance pulled over, followed by a silvery sedan. As a couple of EMTs checked me out, Detective Gupta and Deputy Torres walked over.

"What happened?" Detective Gupta asked.

"Harold. Is he inside?" Even as the EMTs took my pulse and shined a thin penlight in my eyes, I couldn't focus on anything else.

"Who is that? Is that the person who lives here?"

I nodded slowly.

"Detective, she's in shock," an EMT said. "We should get her to the hospital."

"No! Find Harold." I felt a desperate tug deep inside me. I grabbed the EMT's arms and practically shook him, repeating, "Find Harold. Make sure he's okay."

Deputy Torres was on the phone. He turned to the detective and said in a loud whisper, "Oh no, the big guy's coming. So's the media."

The detective shook her head. "Juniper, we'll see you at the hospital."

"No, no hospital." I knew I was upset, but I couldn't be strapped down in a hospital room now. I needed to find Harold and what he'd found out. Then I remembered what was on my phone. I pushed away the EMT who'd been examining me. I flipped through my photos and pulled up the ones I'd taken of the papers moments before I'd realized the danger I'd been in.

"What's that?" the detective asked, kneeling beside me.

I didn't answer. I looked closer at the photos, making them large enough to actually see what he'd written. His handwriting was difficult to decipher, but I could make out some words. As I read, I pieced together the rest.

"Oh my goodness," I said in a near whisper.

"What?"

"It's all about the books."

"What is?"

"Everything," I replied.

Chapter Thirty

A few hours later, I'd recovered most of my senses. I was at the police station with Detective Gupta and Deputy Torres. They'd printed out my photos. Thanks to the work that Harold and his buddy had accomplished, we now knew the code for the secret messages. There were still a few gaps, but the message was evident.

The messages were between Annabel Lee and C. Auguste Dupin—characters straight out of Edgar Allan Poe's stories. While Harold and his buddy had written question marks next to the two names, I had a strong hunch about their identities.

"Annabel Lee has to be Martha Dresdale," I said.

"Does that mean C. Auguste Dupin is Alvin Cooley?" Detective Gupta asked.

"If I'm right, then Martha had been stealing rare books from the Calvertons' collections," I replied. "She'd then give them to Big Al to sell, dictating the prices. They were less than market value at an auction, but each still brought in thousands of dollars for both of them, assuming they split the proceeds in half."

"That makes sense. Then those were the books he kept along his secret bookshelf?" she wondered.

I nodded as it seemed likely. We were still left with a lot of questions, though.

"Okay, so if Mr. Cooley was selling books that Ms. Dresdale stole from the Calvertons, who was he selling them to?" asked Deputy Torres.

Detective Gupta shrugged. Her face was tight and grim.

"Do you think he sold them to one person or more than one?" I asked. "Were they connected to Big Al and Martha's murders?"

Deputy Torres looked as stumped as I felt. None of us had an answer. No one had found Harold or his friend yet, either. I hoped that he was okay.

"There's someone else involved," said the detective. I was shocked to hear her offer her thoughts but bit my tongue, hoping she'd continue. She turned to me and said, "I didn't get the impression that Ms. Dresdale was a book expert."

"If she was, she hid it well," I replied, remembering the times she'd scoffed at the library project. Either she had been lying, or…I snapped my fingers. "Someone else knew which books to steal."

"Exactly," Detective Gupta replied.

"Oh no," I said, as I realized there must have been someone on the inside. Either Florence or Eric. It had to be one of them feeding information to Martha Dresdale. My heart sank at the idea that either could be a murderer. Eric had been so lovely since I met him. I didn't want to believe his enthusiasm had been anything but earnest. I couldn't accept that he could do these monstrous acts.

As much as Florence had rubbed me the wrong way, I didn't want to believe she could be capable of such evil. Still, between the two, she made more sense than Eric. She'd been involved with the collections for longer, she had more expertise, and most of all, she had more motivation to kill the others, especially her ex-boyfriend and if the candle clue was right, his latest girlfriend.

"We need to look into Florence Dowd. Maybe she had been the third person in the scam. And maybe things went bad when Big Al broke up with her to start dating Martha."

"Deputy?" The detective said.

Deputy Torres nodded. "On it."

"Wait," I said. "Could I talk to her first?" We'd developed something of a rapport during my visit. I hoped that might continue. "I may learn more."

"No," said the detective at the same time the deputy replied, "Good idea." She turned to look at him, and he shrugged.

"She could probably get more details out of her than we could," he said.

Detective Gupta considered this. She tapped a bright pink nail against her lips. "Just this one afternoon. That's it."

"Sure."

"And if she's not at the library, I don't want you tracking her down."

I hemmed and hawed, since I didn't expect her to be there. "I already went to her house once."

"But that's when you didn't think she was a murder suspect."

"True, but—"

"Uh uh. No buts. If she's not at the library, you call me. If she is at the library, you call me. If you're right, then she's already killed two people. I don't think it'd take much for her to kill again."

"We'll be on call," Deputy Torres added.

"Okay," I said.

"And we'll notify Calverton security," the detective added.

"Not yet," I argued. If Leo caught wind of this, he would probably send me in with a full-fledged security detail. But I needed her to think I was alone if I was going to get any information from her. "I don't want her to suspect anything is up."

"Fine. But, Juniper, to be clear, I don't like this idea," Detective Gupta added.

To be honest, neither did I, but I felt I owed it to Florence. More than that, I owed it to Harold. I had forgotten the seemingly bad blood between the two of them. I didn't know what had happened, but it had been obvious when we went to the historical society that they didn't like each other. Was the issue something deep enough that Florence would have been behind the explosion at his house? I debated saying something to the detective, but I figured if I offered that concern, they really wouldn't let me talk with her. For once, I kept my mouth shut.

* * *

I found Florence in the conference room where we'd made our temporary office. I decided to go with a casual route first. "I thought I gave you the rest of the week off, Ms. Dowd."

She sighed and shook her head before gesturing to her laptop and the large stack of files in front of her on the long conference table. "Imagining the work piling up here…" She shuddered. I had the sense that she couldn't take being home alone but wouldn't admit to it. "Someone had to take care of things. With you off caravanning across town and Eric being who knows where…"

"Eric's not here?" I asked, surprised.

Florence tsked. "I don't know why they hired him. He's too new and obviously lacks a strong work ethic if he's not here now. And it's not like he has much of a library background."

I was about to defend him when I paused on her last statement. "What do you mean he doesn't have much of a library background? I thought he came well qualified," I said, although honestly, I'd barely looked at his resume when I rifled through the files the other day. I remembered seeing he had a master's in library science. Not that I'd examined Florence's deeply either. Good job, I thought, really not knowing your only two employees.

"I've had to show him how to do even the most basic things. He might as well have been a first-year intern, for goodness sake," she replied. "What are they teaching in school these days? Anything? Probably some New Agey stuff that isn't remotely helpful for collections stewardship." She started thumbing through a file and looking at her computer screen.

What had Brandy said about Eric? She had been worried because he had been born in Mexico. I really needed to learn more about my staff. But then again, it'd been less than a week, and we'd faced two deaths together, so maybe I knew what was important. Still, a thought nagged at the back of my head.

However, I couldn't focus on that yet. I needed to see what I could get out of Florence before the authorities descended. It seemed the small amount of relationship we'd created at her house was still intact. At least enough that she'd keep complaining about whatever bothered her. I didn't get the sense she had any animosity towards me right now. She seemed more pitiful than anything else. Was she that good of an actress, or could it be that she wasn't the one who had killed Martha Dresdale and Big Al Cooley?

"So, Ms. Dowd, I assume you heard about Mar…Ms. Dresdale's death?" I asked, adjusting for her preference for formal names.

She looked up from her file and computer, appearing simply sad. "It certainly was a tragedy." She pursed her lips before saying, "May I be honest with you?"

"Always."

"I never really understood that woman." She didn't sound upset, only confused. "What on earth was this big, important banking person doing running around our library? I mean, it'd be one thing if she was a collector or had even studied history or English in her past, but from what I've read about her, she's always been about money, money, money. I didn't get why she was interested in our project."

"Did you get along with her?"

She shrugged. "I guess as well as anyone. I met her a couple times, but for the most part, she was fairly dismissive of me, even when she knew I was interested in, well, the director position. I tried not to take it personally, but it was strange, given how much she focused on other aspects of the library."

"Like what?"

Florence breathed deeply. "Well, she didn't seem to care at all about the collections. Honestly, I think she thought this place was a waste of space."

"But she cared about something else?"

She nodded. "Two things." She held up a finger. "Putting Eric into the collections tech position." She held up a second finger. "And you being hired."

"I'm sorry, what?"

"I didn't understand it either, but she was very keen on both of those."

"That's interesting." I had always assumed that Leo had simply placed me in this position, so why was Martha involved? Maybe I'd misunderstood the hiring process.

I wished I was back in the library so I could dig through the personnel files. Maybe there were copies on my computer's shared drive. I pulled out my own laptop and set about searching. As I did, I kept an eye on Florence, but she continued with her work. She didn't seem upset that I was there.

Using my researcher skills, I located the folders for the collections technician position, including copies of all the applicant resumes and cover letters. I had expected there to be hundreds of applications for a position like this, but there was only one application package. It was from Eric. He wrote a glowing cover letter about wanting to work here and how his work in public libraries would make him an excellent candidate.

"Wait, what?" I hadn't meant to say that aloud, but I was confused. Eric had been clear that this job was his first professional position. As far as I knew, he'd never worked in any library. I opened his resume. To my surprise, he listed extensive experience in not only Rose Mallow's public library, but internships with several other archives and libraries, as well. According to this, he had a Masters in Library Science too. I wish I had paid more attention when I'd looked through the files the other day, but this was distinctively different from what I'd seen there.

"Something the matter?" Florence asked.

"No, nothing," I replied. Thankfully, she didn't probe more. Curious, I thought about who did work in a public library: Eric's girlfriend, Brandy Rivers. I found her resume on a social media site. To my surprise, her resume was identical to his. I tried to find his profile online, but came up empty.

I searched through the website of the school they had both supposedly gone to for their library degrees. There was a recent article spotlighting Brandy as an alum and featuring a program she'd launched at the library. I couldn't find anything about Eric.

What did this mean? Had Eric used her resume to get in? My stomach sank. Maybe he had lied about other things as well?

Thinking about what Brandy had told me about his family, I searched online for a Gutierrez that worked at the National Institute of Health. Was that a lie, too? However, it didn't take me long to find a man I presumed was Eric's father, given his name. There was even a page dedicated to him with a photo. He looked like Eric. Like Brandy had said, he was an esteemed doctor who had published extensively about studying plants for pharmaceutical purposes. When I scanned the list, I gasped loudly. There were multiple articles about using monkshood. The same plant that had been used to kill Big Al Cooley.

"Okay, really, what's going on?" Florence asked. "You look like you've seen a ghost."

My mind spun. Had Eric killed Big Al and maybe Martha Dresdale? Had he been the third person in the book-selling ring? I rubbed my temples, fighting back a migraine.

However, I couldn't rule out Florence. Maybe she was a good actress? If she'd known that Big Al was cheating on her with Martha, she may have still been the one to kill her. And she might have gone to great lengths to stop Harold from decoding her secret messages, especially given their history—whatever it was.

"Ms. Dowd, may I ask you something?" I asked, practically repeating how our conversation started.

"Of course."

"Why do you and Harold Graham not like each other?"

She made a sour face. "You want to know about *that*?"

"Yes, please."

"You are a strange woman, Ms. Blume," she replied with a head shake. "He and I have been rivals for years. Probably decades at this point."

"Rivals?" I repeated.

She nodded. "Every year at the Rose Mallow Labor Day Festival, Harold always beats me with his eggplants. I don't know how he does it, but I cannot get my eggplants to grow to be as big as his. I'm ashamed to admit this, but one year, I accused him of cheating."

"How do you cheat at that?"

Her face sunk into her chest. "By buying them from someone else."

I was shocked. Who on earth would believe that Harold could be anything but an honorable person?

"It was foolish, and he's never forgiven me for my humiliating jealousy." She looked truly sad. "I really should apologize."

"And that's it?"

She looked confused. "Yes, that's it."

"You didn't blow up his house?" The words gushed from my mouth before I could stop them.

"I'm sorry, but what did you say?" She stood up. Her gaze turned stern.

The headache danced harder. "I guess you haven't heard yet about this morning."

"Heard what?"

"Harold's house blew up."

"It what?" She looked genuinely shocked. "Is he okay?" She placed a hand over her heart.

"I don't know. He's missing."

"Oh no, that can't be. We're supposed to have a rematch this weekend at the Festival. I was going to finally apologize. Is his garden okay?"

"I have no idea," I replied.

She sat back down in her chair, obviously taken aback by the news. "I…I…." Tears formed in her eyes. "I don't want to win by default. I want to beat him. Fair and square." Somehow, I knew this was how she expressed her sympathy.

"I know, Ms. Dowd. We'll find him. I'm sure of that." Although, sadly, I was very much not certain of what I said.

She nodded before her head paused mid-nod. She looked up and stared at me with a cold expression. "Wait a moment…"

"What?"

"Did you ask if *I* blew up his house?"

"Well, what I meant was…"

She stood up. "Do you really think that I could do such a horrific thing?" She turned her head sideways and seemed to be thinking. "Your other questions…. Your investigation…"

Oh no. My stomach dropped, and my head pounded. I had a suspicion she was figuring out what I'd been up to during our conversation.

"Do you think I would have hurt Al? And Ms. Dresdale, too? Do you truly believe I'm a murderer?" Somehow, Florence managed to look deeply wounded and profoundly strong at the same time.

I said no, but I didn't believe my own voice. I wanted to explain, but how could I? What could I say to her to justify thinking she might be a murderer? And how could I tell her that my findings in the personnel files may have cleared her by revealing Eric's lies? Instead, I slumped into my seat, resigned to whatever she'd say next. I deserved her wrath.

"I know it's normal to give two weeks' notice," Florence said in a surprisingly even tone, "But I hope you'll understand that my leaving is immediate. I will send a letter, but I will not conduct an exit interview." As she spoke, her even tone gave way, erupting into a bitter sadness that stung me to my core.

"I'm sorry, Florence," I said in a near whisper.

"Ms. Dowd," she replied.

"I knew it was one of you two, but I didn't know which."

"One of us two? You mean Eric or me? You think that child could have killed someone?"

I cupped my hand against my cheek. "I don't know what to think. Someone killed Big Al and Martha. Someone blew up Harold's house. And it all has to do with books being stolen from our library."

"How do I know it's not you?" she said with a sneer.

"I guess you don't. It wasn't, for the record."

She shook her head. "All I know is that ever since you've arrived, it's been complete and utter chaos. And if I thought I had been humiliated before you started, well, you've managed to take that to a whole new level now, Ms. Blume."

With that, she stood up and waltzed out of the conference room, leaving me alone with our files. I wanted to race after her and fix my mess, but there was a far more immediate concern to attend to. If Eric really was the murderer, I needed to find him and what he was up to as soon as possible.

Chapter Thirty-One

After telling the police it wasn't Florence, I set out to find Eric. I didn't want to believe he could be involved, but I needed to learn more.

Since he wasn't answering his phone, I headed to the library to see if Brandy could give me any updates. Plus, I needed to let her know what he had been up to. I didn't want to scare her with what I suspected about Eric, but I knew it was important to keep her safe.

However, she wasn't at the library. A clerk told me she was out at Redbud Park, setting up for the booth for the Rose Mallow Labor Day Festival.

I drove down to the park, but the lot was full of trucks and vans of the vendors setting up for the festival. Instead, I parked on the street up near the Wildflower Inn and ran down the boardwalk behind the hotel all the way south to where it ended in the park. I'm not much of a runner, especially in my dress shoes, but I sprinted as much as I could. Halfway down the boardwalk, I lost the shoes and carried them over my right shoulder.

Next to me, the sun glistened along the Chesapeake Bay. On a humid day like this one, I could barely make out the other side of the shore, making it easy to pretend this was the ocean. However, except for a small beach down in the park, there was no beach between the boardwalk and the water. The waves gently crashed against the rocks below me.

At the end of the boardwalk, a thick ribbon closed off entry into the park. Someone had attached a handwritten sign saying, "VENDORS ONLY." I put back on my shoes and ducked under the ribbon, when I collided with a large woman holding a clipboard.

"Excuse me," she said. "And you are?"

"Oh, I'm with the Calverton Museum," I said, wondering if I should have mentioned the public library instead.

She consulted her clipboard. "About time you arrived. Someone showed up with your materials hours ago, and they've been sitting there."

"My materials…." I immediately thought of Desta. She must have gotten all the marketing materials already taken care of. Even though we'd spent all week getting the exhibit squared away, I had actually forgotten about setting up and staffing the booth with everything happening.

The woman gave me a lanyard with my official pass to the festival. I decided to stop by my booth to see what I was dealing with before finding Brandy.

The vendor area was in a large meadow. Besides the vendors, there was a small stage where a band was setting up and an area for the food and craft competition. Beyond the meadow to the west was a shallow hillside lined on top with food trucks. I could also spot amusement park rides and games getting ready behind them. They had several acres before it ended in the parking lot.

To the east of the park was a small sandy beach and the Chesapeake Bay. To the north was the boardwalk and residential areas. To the south was a large forest with trails leading every which way. I had explored the forest often as a teenager, but it'd been years since I'd gone through it. That was where the old spa ruins existed, and Eric and I wanted to create interpretive signs for them. I hoped I was wrong and that he wasn't behind Big Al and Martha's murders. All I could picture was his beaming smile. I tried to block the emotions swelling within me, locking them up as deep as I could.

Our table was near the front of the festival. I was shocked to find the vast number of cardboard storage boxes sitting around my solitary 6' table with two chairs. Even with a cursory glance, I guessed there were at least 20 on top and below the table. There was a large, thin, zippered cloth bag. Maybe that was a pop-up tent? Or signage? I wasn't sure. All I knew was that I didn't have time now to go through any of it.

I weaved through the vendor stations, searching for the library. Most places were fully prepped. Perfectly ironed tablecloths covered their tables, announcing their organizations. I spotted some local businesses, the Rose Mallow Artist's Guild, the friends of the Fire Station, a couple marinas, and several more. However, I couldn't locate the library station.

Finally, as I was about to give up, I found Brandy with her table in the very back row of the festival, before it gave way to the food trucks. She had brought a library cart lined with boxes and materials and was positioning everything atop the bright tablecloth.

"Did you need a hand?" I asked as I walked up.

"Oh, you startled me," Brandy replied. "No, I think I'm about ready. Then I'm going to help my parents' stand."

"For Flower Power?"

She nodded and wiped her brow. "Yeah, it's been a long day already. I helped them haul over a lot of bouquets and fall floral arrangements. Still a little early for pumpkins."

"Does your own family grow your own plants?"

She smiled proudly. "My parents have a farm more inland. Been in the family for generations. We've got about a hundred acres out there. Grow all sorts of things."

"So impressive," I said.

"Once I finish here and with them, I'm treating myself to some funnel cake and lemonade." She gestured towards the food trucks with her chin.

"Are you doing this all by yourself? Is Eric here?" I asked.

She blinked a few times and replied, "Why would he be here?"

"He didn't come to work today. I thought maybe he was giving you a hand."

Brandy shook her head. "Uh, no. I haven't seen him."

"So, he's not sick or anything either?"

She shrugged. "Not that I'm aware of."

I wondered how far to go with my questions, but I figured I wouldn't learn much holding back. "Brandy, how long have you been with Eric?"

"Maybe four months. Why?"

"Well, uh…this is awkward, but I think he might have used your resume to get his job at Calverton," I said.

"What are you talking about?" she asked.

"Did you also apply to work with us?"

"I don't understand…"

I pulled out my phone and opened a copy of Eric's resume. Then I handed it to Brandy. She read it, looking more and more confused as she did.

"Wait, what…" She started to speak a few more times but paused each time. "But this is…"

"It's your resume. Isn't it?" I asked. "Eric copied your resume to get the job at Calverton, didn't he?" She was still staring at the screen, so I gently took my phone back from her.

"I have to go," Brandy said as she began walking away.

"Wait, Brandy, talk to me. It's important." I called out, but she turned away from me. I followed after her, but she began running. I was about to lose my shoes again to chase after her when someone called my name.

I turned and found Azalea smiling wildly at me. Her eyes were wide with thick shadows beneath them, and her hair was unkempt, frizzing in different directions. "Juniper, Juniper! It's a miracle!"

"Wait, Azalea, I need to—"

She pushed a fork into my mouth. After I stopped almost choking, I chewed and swallowed the amazingly scrumptious bite of blintz.

"That's divine, Azalea," I said.

She grinned and nodded furiously. "I know, right. It's *it*. The one. You know what I mean?"

"It tastes like Nana Z's."

Tears welled in her eyes, but I could tell they were happy ones. I suspected she looked so disheveled because she'd been up all hours of the night and day working on perfecting her blintzes. "It really does. I got it. My blintzes are finally perfect."

"But I need to…"

She interrupted me to say, "I know the judging isn't until tomorrow, but I wanted to get everything set up and ready early. Get the lay of the land. And then I saw you, and I knew you would appreciate this."

"I do, but I have to—"

"I don't care if I win or lose, Juniper. I feel like she's here. In this dish." The tears changed to sad ones, pouring down her cheeks. "I think she'd be proud of this one, right?"

"Oh, honey, of course she would be. She'd be proud of anything you did." I tried to hug her, but as she was carrying the big dish of blintzes, all I could really manage were a few awkward taps on her shoulders. Azalea began crying more.

"I know, I know. I'm just so relieved."

"Are you going to be okay?" I asked.

She bit her lip and nodded. I didn't want to leave my sister, but I needed to find Brandy and maybe locate Eric. I felt torn. But watching her be so raggedy and emotional, I realized that she needed me first.

"Where are you going? I'll give you a hand," I said.

"Oh, you don't need to do that. I'm sure you're busy," she said in an unconvincing voice.

"Never too busy for you."

Tears formed in the corners of her eyes again. My normally level-headed sister never cried this much. She must have been exhausted.

"Thank you, Juniper."

I spent the next half hour helping Azalea find where she was going and getting set up. Since I'd already lost so much time, I then trekked back to the upcoming museum's station. I pulled open the boxes, checking out all the amazing materials that Desta and her team had created. They had turned Eric and Florence's research into gorgeous pop-up displays. They were well-designed timelines showcasing how the Calverton history intertwined with Rose Mallow's. They'd included high-resolution scans of the historic images my staff had found. I was surprised by how touched I was. Both teams had worked so quickly to create something incredible. I only wished that one of them hadn't been a murderer.

After about an hour, I headed to the parking lot area, deciding it might be a quicker way home. To my surprise, I spotted Brandy next to a black car, talking on her phone. She faced the woods, so she didn't see me.

As I walked to her, someone came up behind me and whispered in my ear,

"Don't go any further. Slowly back away." I felt something pressing hard in my back.

Chapter Thirty-Two

A hand clamped over my mouth, muffling my scream. In my fear, I bit the hand. It flew off me as the person yelled, "Oww!" The hard thing in my back fell away.

I spun around. I wished I could sweep kick or some other cool martial arts move, but instead, I swung wildly with my fists.

"Juniper! Stop! Please! It's me!"

"Eric?"

He waved the hand I'd bitten, obviously trying to relieve the pain. Looking at him, I realized that the hard thing was the corner of his messenger bag, not anything worse. It must have lined up perfectly with my back when he covered my mouth.

"We need to get out of here," he said.

"Why did you attack me?"

"Attack you? I think you got me much better. But please, hurry. Let's go."

"Why would I go anywhere with you? You surprised me and flung a hand over my mouth. That's why I fought back. I didn't know it was you." And I might have attacked even if I had known it was him, since I suspected he was the killer.

"Please come. It's for your safety," he said. I realized he wasn't even looking at me, but off in the distance. I followed his gaze and saw it trained on Brandy.

"What's going on?" I asked. When Brandy shifted, Eric dropped behind a parked car. Out of impulse, I joined him. We crouched behind the car and stared through the windows to see her turn back.

"Is that her car?" I whispered to him. I peeked up enough to see she was leaning against a black sedan. I couldn't be positive, but it reminded me of the one that had nearly run me off the road going to Harold's house. However, black sedans were common, so this could simply be my brain leaping to conclusions.

Eric nodded. "Yes, it's hers. She got it recently." He gestured for me to follow him. Out of curiosity, I did. We crouch-walked between the cars until we got to a large white van. Eric peered out around the corner to see if Brandy was watching. She must not have been because he came back and started talking.

"You can't trust Brandy," he said.

A shiver ran up my spine. I wasn't sure that I could trust him. "But you copied her resume to get this job," I replied. I didn't want to outright accuse him of murdering Big Al and Martha. What if he then targeted me? Then again, we were hiding beside a generic white van. It wasn't exactly the safest place for me.

He sighed. "It was her idea."

"What?"

"Brandy wanted me to get the job, so she applied on my behalf. She promised that she'd make sure that anyone checking into it wouldn't find out about my lack of expertise."

"How did she arrange that?"

"I guess using her librarian skills? I don't know. I'd been helping in my mom's bakery, but she was so excited when she saw this position advertised. She told me I couldn't pass it up," he replied.

I rubbed my forehead. "Are you saying Brandy is involved with... everything?"

He nodded slowly. "I found this in our apartment." He opened the front pocket of his messenger bag to pull out a pair of thick gloves. Then he opened the main pocket to bring out another Poe book.

"Another one of ours?" I asked.

"Yeah. When I tried asking Brandy how she got it, she claimed not to know anything. But I didn't believe her. I think she took it on one of her visits to see me," Eric replied. I reached out for the book, but he pushed my hands away. "You'll need gloves."

"Oh, that's typically not true, you know about gloves and old books. It's a big misconception. I mean, yes, you're right. I should since my hands haven't been cleaned—"

"Juniper!" Eric whisper-yelled.

"Sorry, sorry," I said, waving an apology in the air. This wasn't the time to get into the esoteric logistics of how to handle old books.

"It's not that. Look, I'm not sure, but I think the book might be poisoned," he said.

I dropped my hands down quickly. "Monkshood?"

"How did you know?" he asked.

"The other two books were stolen. They both had traces of monkshood. And it appears that Big Al and Martha both died from it."

He dropped the book back into his messenger bag. "From touching it?"

"I think ingesting it. Or maybe being injected. I think the monkshood was included in the book for an extra measure?" I thought about what Deputy Torres had told me. "Look, we should take that to the police."

"No way," Eric replied.

"Why not?"

"Because they'll think I did it. I know they're asking around. They already bothered my mother at the panaderia. And they know my dad did pharmaceutical research on monkshood. And if you figured out my resume is fake, well, they probably will too if they haven't already." His eyes watered. I worried he might start crying. "But you believe me, right? You know I didn't hurt anyone?"

I wasn't so sure, but I nodded. Eric let out a deep breath, and his shoulders relaxed.

"So, uh, are you the one who called the radio station?" If he couldn't go about the normal channels directly, maybe he tried an indirect route to express his worries?

A small smile appeared. "Since I didn't think I could go to the police, I wanted to find some way to let them—and you—know about what's going on."

"So, how did Brandy get the poison?" However, as soon as I spoke, I had the answer. "Her parents' flower shop."

"They have several acres on a farm west of here. I know they grow a lot of flowers out there. I don't know if they grow monkshood there. Not exactly something that would be included in a florist's store," he said with a shrug.

"Where is it?"

"I've only been there once. But if you go down Route 42 for maybe ten miles, you'll see a sign for their Flower Power farm."

We looked around the big van again. Brandy was gone, and so was her black car.

"We should go after her," I said.

"I don't know that it's a good idea," Eric replied.

"You didn't want to go to the police, though."

"Yeah, but I'm worried that if she finds out I'm onto her she might go after me or my family," he said. I nodded. That, unfortunately, made sense. "You should take this." He thrust the messenger bag towards me.

"Where are you going?" I asked.

"I can't tell you that. The book will be safer with you." He continued to press the bag into my arms. I gave in and took it from him. "Don't tell the police, please. If you do, I don't think you'll be any safer than I am."

With that, he headed away. I initially went after him, but in the maze of the parking lot, he disappeared quickly.

Chapter Thirty-Three

I felt like I was carrying a bomb. Even though I had my gloves, I didn't feel safe getting any closer to the book. I knew I should take it to Detective Gupta and Deputy Torres, but if Eric was right, I didn't want to put him in more danger. Besides, I didn't have any proof that Brandy really was behind anything. Instead, I decided to take the book back to the Calverton Estate and see if Leo could help me.

I spotted Florence working in our makeshift office. "I thought you'd be gone."

She sighed dramatically and said, "This collection is more important than any one of us. I've been the only one taking care of it for years. I can't abandon it now."

"I am very sorry. About everything."

She looked like she didn't believe me.

"If you love this collection as much as I know you do, then you'll care more about keeping it safe than anything else, right?"

"Well, yes, of course."

"Then I need to ask you something."

"Okay?" She sounded uncertain, but she didn't push me away.

"Ms. Dowd, what do you know about Brandy Rivers?"

Her left eyebrow arched. "The librarian? Mr. Guiterrez's girlfriend?"

"Yes, the same."

"Not much."

"I see. Was she ever around before Eric started?"

"Possibly, but I'm not certain," she said.

"Possibly? Was she ever here without Eric?"

She looked up at the ceiling, obviously thinking. "I think so. It appears that Mr. Guiterrez frequently forgot things, so she'd bring them in on his behalf." I thought about the first time I met her when she brought him his lunch. "But sometimes he wasn't here. I didn't think much about it." However, I could see something sparking in her eyes now.

"Let me know if you think of anything else."

"Oh, I see," Florence said suddenly, shaking her head. "She's the next one on your list, isn't she? Is that all you do, Ms. Blume, is go through every single person as a potential murder suspect?"

Her accusation stung, so I replied with more than a tinge of anger, "Well, two people have died, and the police haven't found out who has done it yet. Besides, Eric found one of our lost Poe books in the apartment he shares with Brandy."

She perked up at that. "Did he now?"

I picked up the messenger bag. "But it might have been poisoned. I'm going to take it to Leo to have it examined."

"How do you know it wasn't Eric?"

"Well, I…" To be fair, I didn't know it wasn't him. Maybe he'd lied to me to cover up his tracks. I couldn't be sure. I really hoped the book would provide some answers.

"Which are you, Ms. Blume? A librarian or an investigator?"

"Are they really all that different?" I asked.

She jutted out her chin in a little nod, as if that somehow explained everything.

* * *

I headed to find Leo. His office was a couple buildings over. As I walked there, someone called out my name. I turned to spot one of the other Foundation board members. He'd been the greasy member who had slipped his arm around my waist at the introductory lunch. I held back a shiver.

"Where are you headed?" he asked.

"Going to Leo."

"Ah well, I can save you some time. He's already gone for the day. Said goodbye to him less than twenty minutes ago."

"Thanks," I said without meaning it. Instead, I turned to head back.

"Wait, Juniper."

"Yes?"

"Leo and I discussed your idea for helping the community. You know, I'm also the president of the Rose Mallow Chamber of Commerce," he said. I hadn't known that. Honestly, I wasn't even sure what his name was. "I think it's a great idea. Might really turn things around."

I also wasn't sure which idea he was describing, but I didn't want to look doubly foolish.

"Do you think it might change the minds of some of the protesters?" I asked.

He scratched his bearded chin and then nodded. "It really could. Honestly, being a local business owner myself, I understand where the protesters are coming from. Things are hard these days. It's very easy to look at the Calverton family as the problem, but it's more complex than that."

I had to agree there. Between online shopping and being so far from any major city, I imagined there were a lot of reasons times were difficult for local businesses. I'd seen my sister's inn go through times when no one was staying and other weeks when things sold out. It wasn't consistent enough.

"But the whole Port Chesapeake idea would wipe out all the shops," I said.

"Right, so I hope we can convince the family to change course. Move in your direction of investing in the community itself."

Okay, so at least now I knew what idea of mine he was referencing. It made me feel good that Leo was actively championing it. I hoped that it'd be a real option in response to steamrolling the whole town and rebuilding the luxurious but inauthentic Port Chesapeake.

"That would be phenomenal. May I ask what your business is?" I at least felt less silly asking that than his name. I could always look it up later. Librarian research skills for the win.

"Oh, you don't know?"

Well, so much for not feeling silly.

"I apologize. I've been taking in a lot of information lately, so it's hard to keep everything straight."

He laughed. "Yes, I can only imagine. Well, let's start fresh." He held out a hand to me. As much as I didn't want to, I shook it vigorously. "I'm Teddy Rivers. Owner of Flower Power. I think you've met my daughter Brandy?"

I couldn't keep the look of surprise off my face, but I tried to cover it quickly with a smile. "Oh yes, of course." I noticed he was still gripping my hand. "She's been a great help."

"That's good. I know you've had such a trying week."

I shrugged and wished he'd let go of my hand. Was it my imagination or was he gripping it even tighter?

"Such a pity to lose Big Al and Martha. We've been neighbors to Boardwalk Books for years."

"Were you close?" I asked with a small gulp in my voice.

"More or less. Can I be honest with you, Juniper?" He came closer to me, practically spitting on my cheek.

"Sure..."

He shook his head. "I can't say I'm sorry Big Al is gone. That man took advantage of anything—and anyone—he could."

"What do you mean?"

He suddenly dropped my hand and backed off. "Oh, nothing, nothing. I've said too much as is. I'll let Brandy know you said hello." With that, he gave me a wink and sauntered off.

With Leo out, I wasn't sure what to do with my potentially poisoned parcel. I worried where it might be most safe. I didn't want to take it back to the Wildflower Inn, as I worried that Clover or Violet might somehow find it and get sick. I considered taking it to the police, but I remained concerned that Eric was right and would be endangered if it went to them.

In the end, I decided to keep the book with me. Although not the most comfortable, I spent the night in the conference room. I let Azalea know I was working late, and she promised to take care of Clover.

Chapter Thirty-Four

I arrived the next morning at the Rose Mallow Labor Day Festival early, but Florence was already there. She'd set up the pop up displays Desta's marketing team had created, put out the tablecloths, and even arranged all the swag to give out.

"This looks really good," I said, admiring her handiwork.

Florence beamed with pride. "It does, doesn't it? Honestly, I didn't think we could create all this in less than a week, especially with everything that's happened, but we did."

"I'm grateful for all of your work, Ms. Dowd," I said.

She nodded appreciatively and started hiding the boxes and display containers for the materials. It seemed she had calmed down about me. I would accept any sort of uneasy truce we could navigate. I was about to help her when Harold appeared unexpectedly.

"Harold!" I ran over to him and wrapped him in a hug. "I was so worried about you."

He laughed a little. "I'm sorry to have had you fret. But trust me, I still have enough skills left in me to evade trouble."

"Yeah, but that wasn't trouble. Your house exploded."

He shrugged. "It's unfortunate, but I'm alright at least." I suspected he had stronger feelings than what he was revealing to me.

"Where were you? It looks like you're unhurt."

"Right as rain. I had taken some of the decoding work over to my old intelligence buddy. Fell asleep on the couch. When I heard what happened to the house, I stayed put. At least until the dust settled. Metaphorical and literal."

"I'm not sure the metaphorical dust has settled. Unless…did they catch who did that to your place?" I asked.

He sighed. "Not yet. I used to have a camera system set up, but it hasn't worked in probably a decade. My buddy Dor was always telling me to get it upgraded, but I never got around to it. Taking care of that big old house was a lot. I didn't want to give it up though. Been in the family for generations. And I love the garden." His eyes looked misty, and he dabbed briefly at their corners.

"Is Dor your intelligence friend?"

"For decades. Most of my life, really," he replied.

"That's good. Did you make any headway on decoding the rest of the message?"

He instantly perked up. "We made good progress actually—"

"Excuse me," Florence interrupted.

"Ms. Dowd," Harold said.

"Mr. Graham," Florence replied. Then she dropped the formal tense and cried out, "Oh, Harold! I'm relieved you're okay." She engulfed him in a big hug.

He wrapped his arms around her in return. "I couldn't let you win the eggplant contest without a decent fight."

They both laughed.

"I need Ms. Blume. She has important things to do right now," Florence said, stiffening back up.

"More important than this? Juniper isn't just saving history. She's saving lives." He pulled out an envelope and handed it to me. I knew it must contain the rest of the decoded messages. I hoped that it'd finally reveal the truth of who was behind the stolen books and murders. Was it Brandy or Eric? Or someone else?

However, before I could look inside, a group of protesters swarmed our booth. I couldn't tell how many people there were. Maybe fifteen? I spotted several of the same signs I'd seen at the Calverton gates protests.

"Hey, hey! No no! Calvertons gotta go!" protesters chanted.

I tried to usher Florence and Harold out of the melee, but the group wouldn't let us leave. No one touched us, but they formed a tight circle around our table, so we couldn't easily get out. I wondered where the security was. Or the police.

"You're here for Calverton. You need to explain them!" said a man with a goatee.

"Yeah, explain yourself!" a woman added while shaking her fist.

"No, I…" I couldn't figure out what to say.

Someone else laughed. "You're as clever as you were on the radio."

"And the newspaper!" Several chuckled, and one pretended to fly a paper airplane through the air. Although I doubted anyone would admit it, I figured I'd found the culprits behind the papering of the Wildflower Inn.

"Oh, come on," I replied, but too many people were laughing. I wanted to shrink down to the size of a mouse and burrow my way out of there.

"Come on, you Calverton con!"

"Yeah, Calverton con!"

"At least let them go," I said, nodding towards Florence and Harold, but the mob wasn't interested in listening to my pathetic pleas. Suddenly, I felt a hand grab mine. I nearly shouted and threw my arm back in defense, only to find it was Leo. He'd broken through the group. He smiled at me in a reassuring way.

"You should tell them your idea," he said.

"My idea?" I asked. I thought about my conversation with Teddy Rivers yesterday. I figured that must have been what he was alluding to. "Now?"

He nodded.

I gulped but figured it was my best shot. I climbed up on the table. The protesters calmed down slightly, watching me with curious intensity. To my surprise, Leo climbed up beside me. Florence and Harold stood behind us with the table, keeping them away from the protesters.

"What's going on?" the goatee guy asked.

"Look, we've heard you. Loud and clear. Look at these signs," I gestured towards the displays. "They show how intricately connected the Calverton family has been to Rose Mallow. For generations. Like so many of your families and your businesses. You make this town great. It's time to renew that commitment. I'm here with Leo Calverton to announce that the Calvertons are going to invest in you. In us."

"How?" someone asked.

Leo said, "We're going to give out grants to the businesses of Rose Mallow. All the businesses. We're planning a meeting for a few weeks from now to discuss the details, and I hope all of you will join us."

"We'll make sure all of your concerns are heard and addressed," I added.

Leo nodded. "But for right now, please, enjoy the festival."

After our announcement, people relaxed. Some lingered to ask questions, but most headed away, curious but no longer furious.

"You okay?" I asked Florence and Harold, who came out from behind the table.

"Is that true?" Harold asked. "Are the Calvertons really going to invest in the community?"

Leo nodded. "I'm going to make sure it happens. I've long wanted to provide an alternative option to the Port Chesapeake concept, and Juniper provided a vision. I've laid out the costs to the family and how this will be a cheaper and more sustainable path forward."

"That's incredible," said Florence.

"All thanks to Juniper," he said, turning to look at me. I could feel my cheeks burn red.

"No, no," I said, but he took my hands and shook his head.

"Don't be so modest," Harold said.

I couldn't easily turn off being uncomfortable, but at least it was for something positive, not for murder and mayhem. "Thank you."

* * *

The first morning of the festival was a big hit. For being September, the weather was surprisingly mild. I couldn't believe how many people came by over the course of the day. We were a popular booth, and to my amazement, most who came by didn't complain about the Calvertons but wanted to know when the museum would open or to find out more about this grant program they'd heard others discuss.

I took a lunch break in the early afternoon after Florence. After scouring the different food trucks for vegetarian options, I spotted a stand from the Purple Oyster. It was packed with people. I wasn't sure that Harmony would want to see me after kicking me out of her café, so I walked by it.

"Juniper?"

I turned and saw Harmony. She waved me over. She made a couple comments to her staff and then stepped out from behind the stand.

"Yes?" I asked with caution.

She wiggled her shoulders before saying, "I'm sorry about the other day. I shouldn't have taken my irritation at the Calvertons out on you."

"Thank you, Harmony. That means a lot to me."

"Azalea told me about this grant program they're offering and how you helped make that happen. I'm going to apply."

"That's good. I hope everyone in town does."

"I also heard what a hard week this has been on you." She sighed. "And you're family. I should have been there for you instead of being the first to knock on you." Earlier in the summer, we'd learned that Harmony was the aunt of Azalea's estranged husband, Rory. He was staying with her while he recovered and as he and Azalea figured things out. She opened her arms, and I happily hugged her. "How about one of my amazing summer salads? On the house?"

"That would be amazing," I replied.

She snapped her fingers. "And, of course, one of my scones?"

"Yes, please!" I loved her scones. "Thank you, Harmony. I've missed you."

"I've missed you too."

* * *

All the picnic tables were full, so I found a clear spot on the grass near the woods. As I ate, I finally looked through the decoded messages that Harold gave me. They comprised more communications between Martha and Big

Al about fencing the Poe book. This time, there was a third name: Berenice. Yet another Poe character. I wondered who this might be.

I didn't suspect Florence anymore, and the previous names corresponded to the gender of the true identity. Did that mean Eric was not involved? If so, then who was?

I finished eating and stood up to throw away my trash. After that, I took a slow stroll before heading back to the table. On the hilltop, I found a quiet spot where I gazed down at the festival spread out before me. It was hard to understand why someone would want to hurt this beautiful town.

"Don't turn around," said a voice behind me.

Chapter Thirty-Five

Again, I felt a hard piece of metal in my back. The voice was definitely not Eric's. I recognized it immediately. It was Teddy Rivers, Brandy's dad.

"Give me your cell phone and that paper." He pushed the metal harder into me. It felt like a gun, but I didn't want to find out for certain. I held both above my head, and he took them from me.

"Why are you doing this?"

"Let's take a walk. Over there."

"In the woods?" I could see plenty of people wandering along the trails. I didn't want anyone to get hurt.

"To start with. There are a few special trails deep inside we can take."

"Please don't hurt anyone."

"I won't if you cooperate. And I've left a present at your booth if you don't."

"A present?" I repeated.

"The kind you don't want to open," he said.

I gulped and let him direct me through the woods. The path would have been pleasant if not for the looming threat. I focused on naming which trees I recognized: oaks, magnolias, tulip poplars, dogwoods. Anything to keep the anxiety from creeping up my throat. We passed other people, and I kept a big smile on my face, not revealing the danger all of us were in. If Teddy had killed Big Al and Martha, he could kill anyone, and as much as I didn't want to die, I really didn't want to see anyone else get hurt.

We headed deeper into the forest. I noticed fewer people around. Lofty pines and redwoods towered overhead, shading the sun. Eventually, he nudged me to head to the left. At first, I didn't think there was a trail, but after we passed a few trees, I realized we were following a narrow footpath. No one else was on it, and it didn't take long until the sounds of the festival receded deeply into the background, muffled by the thick forest.

"Where are we going?" I asked.

"We've got a little way to go," he replied. "Did you know this used to be my family's land? The Rivers have been here as long as the Calvertons have been. But you don't see any booths for us out there. No one is celebrating us." There was a thick sludge of disgust in his voice. I thought about something Brandy had said in the library about how her family had been here for as long as the Calvertons. I hadn't realized that she meant such a deep-seated animosity, going back generations.

He paused. I stopped, too, unsure what would happen next.

"Do you see that there?"

I followed his pointing finger. Squinting, I made out something between the thick brush. It looked like a wall, but I couldn't be certain. "Yes. What is it?"

"That's my family home. Well, what's left of it."

We headed closer. The trees thinned out, and I made out the ruins of a building. There wasn't much left standing except for parts of the stone exterior wall. The interior walls had collapsed, and thin, long sticks poked out at random intervals. It was hard to distinguish between rocks and debris from the ruins' remnants. Ivy had nearly engulfed everything.

"Over there was a garden," he said. We walked around the outskirts to where an open meadow lay. "It was here in these woods that I learned about plants. My mother kept the most beautiful garden. She had an impressive green thumb. Her flowers attracted everything from bees to birds to bats."

I pictured the gorgeous garden back at the Wildflower Inn. I knew how special gardens could be. My thumbs were very much not green, but they were still a place where I felt at peace. I wondered if I'd ever see them again? Catching myself, I pushed the thought away. Not helpful. I needed to figure out what he was up to, and then maybe I could find out how to stop him.

"I imagine it was lovely," I said, hoping I sounded more encouraging than scared.

He smiled. "She could grow something out of the worst soil. Not only flowers, but her vegetables too. I didn't appreciate them as a kid." His laugh was hard. "But I do now. I grew up with a literal farm-to-table in my own home. I was truly fortunate."

"She sounds special."

"She was indeed. I see bits of her in Brandy. But probably more of my father."

"Did he love to garden too?" I wanted to keep him talking.

"Pop? Not a chance. He thought our flower shop was a silly woman's exercise. He always told me to see the bigger picture."

I thought about asking what he saw of his father in Brandy, but since he didn't seem to like his dad, I wasn't sure it was a safe line of questioning. He continued on his own.

"Pop taught me the cycle of life. He pointed it out right here in the garden," Teddy said. "Our cat Moxie loved the garden too. She killed many birds. And then, one day, a fox from the woods killed Moxie." He kicked a spot in the dirt, revealing a small stone with a tiny painting of a cat. I figured this was Moxie's grave.

"I'm sorry."

"Cycle of life. Kill or be killed. Just like Pop said."

I didn't try arguing.

"Same thing with the Calvertons and Rivers. Except we were the ones killed. The Calvertons won. Every time. They have that big estate, all these riches, and all we have left is our small shop—one that they intend to destroy along with the rest of the town."

"What about the grants?" I asked. Maybe he hadn't heard the news? But that didn't make sense, since he was on the Foundation board. He must have known.

He laughed loudly. "You believe that charade? I don't believe for a minute that they're going to do anything that supports anyone but themselves."

"What do you mean?"

Teddy shrugged. "They'll find a way. Once they get their tenterhooks in you, they latch on and never let go. Like vultures. You'll see. They'll use that money to make more money for themselves. Nothing about these people is altruistic."

"How did the Calvertons hurt your family?" I asked, hoping I wasn't making things worse.

He sat on the remnants of a wall. Now, I could easily see the gun, which caught a ray of sunlight through the tree canopy. He kept it trained on me.

"How didn't they?" His laugh was dry and bitter. "You saw on your own timeline for those ridiculous signs. Nothing ever happened in Rose Mallow without them. Once upon a time, the Rivers had land, a big farm, and were a budding agricultural powerhouse. We experimented with different crops, different hybrids…anything you can imagine. We were going to revolutionize the agricultural industry the way the Calvertons had done to the financial and real estate industries."

"What happened?"

"Same thing that happens to most businesses in this town. They owned the bank, and they stopped giving us money. We responded by playing with politics. A couple ancestors were on various town and county councils, but we couldn't compare to the growing juggernaut of the Calvertons. Even if it wasn't their name on the ballot, it was their people. Suddenly, we lost our lands. Called it 'eminent domain.'" He did air quotes around the phrase. "Convinced the town to turn this into a park several decades ago. Made it sound all nice and generous. But in reality, they didn't want to compete with another company."

"And now?"

"You've seen our tiny store. Flower Power was my mother's project. It is a tiny remnant of the great farm business my family once ran. We have a small patch of land left outside town. Crumbs we were allowed to keep," he said with disgust.

"Then why are you on the Foundation board?"

He cocked his head to the side and eyed me curiously. "Oh, come on, everyone knows to keep your friends close and your enemies far, far closer. But they're so arrogant; they had no idea how I felt. They seriously thought

I wanted to help them. Hah. Who do you think secretly organized the protests? Made sure that they could continue? Even right up at our gates with our security people. There are benefits to working from the inside. Surely, you understand that."

I had no idea what he meant. Did people think I was involved with the museum for some ulterior motive?

He looked around the ruins of his family's home. "Being on the inside meant I could be a true snake in the grass. People don't even realize how many things around us are incredibly toxic. You see that plant over there?" He pointed with his gun. I followed his gaze to see what looked like an ordinary shrub. "That's giant hogweed. Quite toxic. And right there, that's jimson weed. Also toxic. Same with that spotted water hemlock over there. Everything around us can kill you."

"You poisoned Big Al and Martha? Through their books?" I asked.

He shuddered. "I didn't poison the books. Just the people. Put it in Al's cigar and Martha's drink. The books were overkill." He shook his head.

"No, it wasn't," said another voice. Out of the trees appeared Brandy. I hoped that she had come to save me, but the hard glint in her eyes destroyed my optimism. "It's important to have a backup plan, Dad."

He waved away her response. "You shouldn't have bothered adding all that, Brandy. Their deaths would have looked natural if you had left the books alone. No one would have suspected anything without your meddling."

Brandy's face reverted to that of an obstinate teenager. "You're wrong. No one was going to believe that their deaths were natural. I figured adding monkshood to the books would make it look like Eric did it."

"You set up your own boyfriend?" I asked in disbelief.

She shook her head, as if she couldn't believe I asked that. "We needed someone to take the fall. I didn't have enough time to set everything up against him properly because of *you*." She spit out the last word.

I wasn't sure what to do, being so hidden out back here. Where we were was remote. I couldn't hear anything from the festival, and I hadn't seen anyone else. At least I could buy more time by keeping them talking. Maybe I'd finally figure out a plan. Fortunately, they both seemed to enjoy hearing their own voices. I gathered that they were dying to reveal what they'd done.

"How did it all work?" I asked.

"My daughter, the mastermind," Teddy said with a sweep of the hand. I wasn't sure if he was sincere or sarcastic.

Brandy turned to me and said, "He still doesn't get it. While he was all worried about the Port Chesapeake nonsense, I made real money."

"By stealing the books?" I asked.

"Hah." His father's voice sounded like a verbal eye-roll.

Brandy ignored him. "It was a team effort with Big Al and Martha. We stole the books from the Calvertons, and then Big Al would fence them through his bookstore for profit. I'd get the books to him through a secret shelf connecting Flower Power to Broadway Books. Or the buyers could pick them up from our shop. Lots of options," she explained.

"I told you that shelf was a waste of time," Teddy said.

"You didn't mind the money I gave you. I didn't even share all of it with you. I kept a pot for myself. To get out of this hick town."

He didn't reply.

"But something went wrong?" I asked.

"Originally, I was going to work at the Calverton library to identify the best books to steal," said Brandy, "But Martha thought it'd be better if I stayed at the public library and got Eric to take my place. We'd be more spread out that way. She figured it'd make it harder to pin down any of us. And if things were figured out, Eric would get in trouble, not us."

"But that's not what happened, was it, darling?" Teddy said.

Her shoulders slumped. "I realized they were cutting me out. Martha and Big Al figured that since Eric didn't actually know any library stuff, he'd be super easy to manipulate. Then they decided they could keep all the profits for themselves. I discovered the coded messages they left for each other."

Brandy must have been Berenice. The third Poe character, after Marsha as Annabel Lee and Big Al as C. Auguste Dupin.

"So they had to go," Teddy added. "Enough with people cutting out the Rivers."

Brandy nodded. "And unfortunately, now we need to kill you too, Juniper.

I'm sorry. I was excited about another librarian coming to town, but I should have known better. That research desire runs too deep."

"We can force her to eat some of those poisonous mushrooms over there," her dad said. "It'll look like an accidental death."

"But that'll be far too slow," Brandy complained.

"Not if we lace it with a little something extra," he said.

"We can't trust it. Use your gun. Why bring it otherwise?"

"Then it won't look accidental! You can't seem to understand that," he yelled.

"We'll bury her back here. Alongside your precious Moxie. No one will find her. No one ever comes here." Her tone suggested she didn't want to be back here either.

"This is our home. You have no pride in being a Rivers."

Brandy rolled her eyes.

Teddy turned to me. "This is why she became a librarian instead of joining the family business. She's never cared about us or this place."

"He's right. I wanted the money to get out of this tiny, backwaters town, away from all these small-time crooks," she said in a voice laced with thick sarcasm.

"Who are you calling backwaters? Small-time?" Teddy got up close to Brandy. They kept arguing.

For a moment, I was mesmerized. I'd never argued with my dad this way. Then again, he wasn't a murderer. I shook my head. They continued yelling at each other.

"I don't care about your stupid cycle of life story."

"Why don't you show some respect?"

"Because you don't deserve any!"

I took advantage of the distraction and crept away. I moved slowly, scared that a single twig breaking underneath would release them from their angry hold upon one another. Backing up, I felt for the ruin wall with my hands, and slid a leg over. Then another. Keeping my gaze as steady as I could manage on them, they seemed unaware, entranced by their anger. Past the wall, I moved faster, daring to peek over my shoulder.

Once I got to the edge of the woods, I found the narrow trail we'd come in on, turned, and started running for my life.

"Hey! Get back here!"

The gun fired, but the bullet hit a tree nearby.

Chapter Thirty-Six

I didn't look back. How did we come in? Everything looked the same. I sped up, unsure if I was on the right path. I zigged and zagged, taking whichever forks I could find.

I didn't hear them now, but they could have become quiet, listening to me twist and turn through the maze of trees. I kept running, looking for any signs that I was heading back to the festival.

We used to come into these woods often when I was a teenager spending summers in Rose Mallow. My sister Azalea particularly loved to come here with Rory to get away from everyone. I didn't have a boyfriend back then, but being the younger sister, I tagged along with her. We'd spend hours getting lost here. Or, to be honest, they tried getting me lost so they could spend more time together alone. Fortunately, they never truly succeeded.

I knew that there were hundreds of acres here. Maybe more? On the north end, the forest bordered Redbud Park where the festival was happening. On the east was the Chesapeake Bay. The woods climbed in elevation. While Rose Mallow was barely above sea level, the ground here scaled upwards, and it soon became a cliff edge to the water. I wasn't sure what was to the south of here. Another town? A dead end? I couldn't remember.

I mapped as much of the forest as I could from my memories. It'd been so many years ago, but I dug into what I could, hoping I'd tap into some deep muscle memory.

It didn't work. I was lost.

Panic bubbled in my stomach. Could I actually get lost here? If they found me—killed me!—would my body ever be discovered? Stay focused. Count the trees. I wiped my hands across my face and pushed onwards. No matter the fear trembling inside, I couldn't give in. The danger of being caught was even worse. I needed to find help.

The path dead-ended. If it had even been one. But I didn't stop. I dug deeper into the forest, climbing through ferns and vines and hopping over tree roots. Spiderwebs broke across my face. I smacked them away and kept going, but my pace was too slow. Snail-like.

Footsteps crunched behind me. I didn't dare look back, but I could hear them gaining. My whole body tensed. I clenched my fists and readied myself for a fight.

A hand reached out.

I instinctively swung at it.

I missed.

"Shhh!"

It was Eric. I grabbed onto him, about to cry, but he shook his head and held up a finger to silence me. I nodded. He motioned for me to follow him.

We continued through the thick brush of the woods. I listened for Teddy and Brandy, knowing they were likely not far behind. Fortunately, Eric appeared to know where he was going. I took hope in that and clung tightly.

He led me to a dry ravine, overrun with plants. Buried beneath the layers of English ivy and kudzu was a large den of a hole. Not big enough to be called a cave, but it could fit a person. Two seemed iffy, but beggars can't be choosers. I crawled in, and he followed behind. It was tight with both of us inside. I realized I was crouched atop a sleeping bag. This must have been where he was hiding.

"Where is she?" Teddy yelled somewhere above us.

"This way!" Brandy called out. I held my breath, hoping that they wouldn't spot us down here. I heard them lumbering off into the distance.

I tried gesturing to Eric to call the police on his cell phone, but he shook his head.

"After I figured out what Brandy was up to," he whispered to me, "I knew I was next on the hit list. I had already found a tracking device she left in my messenger bag."

"The same bag you gave me?"

"I got rid of it," he assured me, but I didn't feel comforted. "So when I went into hiding, I left my cell phone behind. I didn't want to risk her finding me before I came up with a plan."

"You should have gone to the police." I wish I had, too.

His head dropped. "I saw how you reacted when I tried explaining everything to you. It'd have been worse with the police. At least you couldn't lock me up. Deport my mother."

"You're worried they'd do that?"

"I don't know. Maybe. Yes." He nodded. "I was born here, and my dad has a green card, but my mom…well…let's say her story is a little different."

"Oh, Eric." I put my arms around him. He accepted my hug. Brandy must have lied about his being born in Mexico, but unfortunately, it sounded like his mother's situation was less certain.

"I didn't want to jeopardize her status."

"She must be worried sick about you," I said.

He dropped his head. "I left a note in the bakery. I hope she'll understand."

"I'm sure she will."

"Thanks."

"So you came here to create a plan?" I asked. "What is it?"

He opened his mouth, paused, and then closed it again. "I don't have one yet."

"Look, if we go to the police, I'll vouch for you. Leo will vouch for you. He'll make sure your mom is safe," I said.

"You really think so?"

I nodded eagerly. "Assuming you know how to get back to the festival?"

"Yes, I can get us there, but it's a trek. Not easy. I'm amazed you found me."

"Found you?" I repeated. "Thank goodness you found me! I was completely lost."

"With all the research I've done the last few days, I spent a lot of time looking at area maps. Did you know this area used to be Brandy's family's home?"

"Actually, I did."

"Of course you did," he replied with a small laugh. It was good to see him smile. "Encyclopedia Blume."

"Not the first time I've heard that one." I didn't add that I'd only now learned the background behind the woods that day. I'd take whatever win I could at the moment. "But can you lead me back?"

"Alright," he replied with a sigh.

"It has to be better than staying here indefinitely."

"True. Okay, I'll follow your lead, boss," he said. "Well, assuming you are still my boss. Now that you know the truth, I assumed you'd have fired me."

"No, Eric. We'll work that all out later. But no, I won't fire you," I promised him.

A bigger smile crept across his face. We snuck out of the hiding hole and headed back through the woods. I had no idea how far we were from the festival. Out here, I couldn't hear anything coming from them.

We hiked through the dense forest. Everything looked the same to me, left or right, up and down, but Eric obviously knew where he was going. As long as I stayed with him, I felt safe that we would find our way home.

Then, I saw the Chesapeake Bay dazzle through the trees.

"We're really high up," I said. We'd gone even further south than I had realized.

"Yeah, the woods go up a lot. Or maybe it's just the beach drops. Not sure. But that is Chesapeake Cliffs." He led me to a thin trail that followed the edge of the woods. Looking down, the cliffs dropped at least a hundred feet down. There was a narrow sandy beach scattered with large rocks and then the sparkling blue waters of the Chesapeake Bay.

I'd forgotten about Chesapeake Cliffs. We used to go there when I was a little kid. My family used to visit the beach all the way down there to search for tiny shark teeth. I saw some families below, but we were too far away to get their attention.

"There you are!" Brandy appeared with her dad behind us. "And with Eric, too. Oh good. Come on, sweetheart, why don't you come over to me?"

"Eric, run!" I yelled and pushed him along the trail.

CHAPTER THIRTY-SIX

"But what about—"

"Run!" I shouted.

He took off into the woods. Teddy followed him, leaving Brandy with me.

"Oh, this is too perfect," she said, brandishing the gun. Although I was terrified to see it, I was relieved that her father didn't have the gun with him. I prayed Eric would make it back safely.

"You don't have to do this, Brandy."

"You're right. I don't have to do anything. You just have to trip. Fall off that cliff behind you. And if the fall doesn't kill you, then the rocks along the shoreline below will."

I looked behind me. The edge was perilously close. She was right. I wouldn't survive this fall. I stared at the oblivious people below. There was one family with a kid making a sandcastle. The child scooped a shovel into the sand and then dropped it slowly into his bucket. The kid's actions gave me an idea.

I crouched down, feigning being sick to my stomach.

"Oh gross," Brandy said. "Are you going to throw up? You must have a weak stomach."

I pretended to brace myself against the ground, but really, I scooped up the dusty dirt and several stones from along the edge. Then I stood, turned, and flung the mess at Brandy. It hit her in the eyes. She screamed and wiped at her face, dropping the gun.

I sank low to grab the gun. Brandy pawed at her face. I picked the gun up and pointed it at her. "Get walking."

She spat out some of the dirt that must have gotten into her mouth. "You're not going to shoot me."

I cocked the gun. This world-traveling librarian had studied many things. Fortunately, one thing I explored was gun usage and safety. After the antics earlier in the summer, I'd even gone to a local range a few times to practice, although neither Azalea nor I wanted any guns inside the Wildflower Inn. I'd also taken some self-defense classes, but they hadn't exactly prepared me for being between a cliff edge and an untamed forest.

"Want to test out that theory?" I asked Brandy.

She scrunched her upper lip. Her eyes darted between me and the weapon in my hand. I figured she was deciding if I was bluffing. I hoped we wouldn't find out, as I didn't have a backup plan.

A rush of wind blew up behind me, almost knocking us both over, but we steadied ourselves. A 'whoop whoop' noise grew so loud, I had to cover my ears, barely maintaining my hold on the weapon.

Chapter Thirty-Seven

A police helicopter appeared. It flew above us before lowering down, nearly coming level with the edge of the cliff.

Out popped Deputy John Torres. He surveyed the situation, appearing surprised to see me holding a gun leveled at Brandy.

"Juniper's going to kill me!" Brandy cried.

"Yeah, right," he replied.

"But she has a gun!"

Realizing I was still standing ready to go, I lowered the weapon. Deputy Torres nodded, putting a hand out to show I should give it to him. I reached out, but as I did, Brandy looked like she was going to make a break for the woods. Fortunately, he also spotted her pivot, so the deputy ran at her and knocked her into the brush.

"Brandy Rivers, you're under arrest for the murder of Alvin Cooley and Martha Dresdale." His voice continued droning on as he handcuffed her.

Finally safe, I put the gun down on the ground.

"Bring it in the chopper," he said.

We all climbed inside. I went first, followed by the Deputy who sat between Brandy and me. He gave me earphones to muffle the sound. After putting them on, I realized that the earphones also allowed us to speak to each other.

"You doing okay, Juniper?"

I could hear Leo's voice, but I didn't see him at first. Then he waved from the front passenger seat. I wanted to fling my arms around him, but we were already ascending into the air and heading away from the cliff edge.

"Wait!" I shouted. Although we all wore the headphones, it was still loud, and we each yelled into our microphones.

"What?" asked Detective Gupta. She was the one flying! Was there anything she couldn't do?

"Brandy's dad is chasing Eric Gutierrez. Save him!"

Deputy Torres gave me a thumbs-up. "Already nabbed him."

"Who do you think told us where to go?" the detective asked.

I sighed, relieved. It was finally over.

* * *

Detective Gupta flew the helicopter back to the festival, where she landed on an empty patch near the parking lot. Back on solid ground, everyone—including even some protesters—cheered when Detective Gupta and Deputy Torres escorted Brandy into a waiting police car to join her father.

I spent the next hour sitting at a picnic table, explaining what had happened to the police. When I finally finished, Leo joined me, giving me a big hug. Eric joined us after he finished his interviews. So did Florence and Harold, along with another older woman that I didn't recognize. However, before I could talk to anyone, Azalea raced up to me.

"Oh, Juniper, are you okay?" She nearly picked me up with the strength of her hug. Fairly impressive, given how petite the two of us were.

"I'm going to be fine now that Brandy and her father have been caught."

I pulled Eric and Florence aside. "I'm so sorry to you both for ever thinking you could have been involved."

"But who would have expected that Ms. Rivers could do something so… unlibrarian-like?" Florence Dowd replied. Her lip curled in disgust.

"I had no idea until the other day," added Eric. Florence patted him on the arm with genuine concern.

"None of us did," she said.

"Except for you, Juniper. Excellent detective work yet again," Harold said, walking up to us.

"Indeed. I heard you also helped crack another case earlier this summer?" asked the older woman beside him. "She would have been a valuable asset in our department, don't you think, Harold?"

"That's for sure, Dor," he replied.

I looked up in surprise. This was his old intelligence friend Dor. I hadn't expected his contact to be a woman. I didn't want to think I was so sexist, but I figured, with their age, that it would have been unlikely to have been a woman working in whichever security agency they had been involved with.

Dor. That name also struck me as familiar, although I wasn't sure where. I noticed Dor was watching me. A lopsided smile perched on her face, as if she was egging me on, hoping I'd figure it out. I snapped my fingers.

"Dor. Any chance that's short for Dorothea?" I asked.

"Oh, she is good, isn't she?" Dor said to Harold.

"Told you so." He winked at me.

"Dorothea..." Florence muttered. "Wait, you don't mean..."

"Dorothea Calverton. The same woman whose name graces our library building," I said. Dor took a small bow.

"Ms. Calverton," said Florence with a stutter. "I...I want to say thank you." She looked awestruck.

"And thank you, Ms. Dowd. I know how much you, Mr. Gutierrez, and Ms. Blume have done for my family's collection. I'm grateful for your hard work. I've been away for a long time, but now that I'm back, I plan to come in and review everything. While I trusted Leo to manage things in my absence, that Foundation board—not so much."

That was an understatement. Given that the Foundation board chair had been stealing from the collection and another member had murdered her, things needed to be reevaluated. I needed to evaluate my situation. Honestly, I wasn't sure how much I wanted to be part of the process or not. My week working for the Calvertons had been difficult for me. I wondered if it would get better under her leadership.

"Grandma gets things done," Leo said.

"Wait, this is your grandmother?" I asked.

"Well, yeah. She's pretty special." Leo looped an arm around Dor. Now that I saw them side by side, the two looked a lot alike. Although Dor's hair was no longer the dark black of Leo's, they had matching green eyes, long noses, and the same lopsided smile.

"How did you not tell me before?"

He looked at Dor with a face that said it was her fault. "Grandma told me to keep her name out of it. She didn't even like that her name was on the building."

"So gauche," she chimed in with a laugh.

"Dor was the black sheep of the family," added Harold. "She never went for putting her name out there and having all the publicity."

"Probably why I went into undercover work," she said.

"You worked undercover?" I asked.

"Harold and I did for years. But don't ask for details. That's still classified." She put a hand on his shoulder, and the two laughed heartily.

"So, what happens now?" asked Eric. "Does the library reopen? Do I still have a job?" He took the words out of my mouth, but I wasn't sure of the answers. I looked at Leo and Dor. They faced each other, as if consulting telepathically.

Leo nodded and turned back to us, saying, "There's a lot to recover from this week. The collection still needs to be cared for, but I suspect the plans for the museum may be on hold while we figure out everything."

Dor looked at Eric and said, "It's my name on the building, and the collections still belong to my family. Of which I'm the oldest. Pretty sure that makes me the matriarch."

"No one would fight that," Leo added.

"I'm pretty sure what I say goes, especially since it's my money funding everything. And that means you three have jobs as long as you want them. Mr. Gutierrez, we'll get you whatever training you want—assuming you want it."

"Yes, ma'am!"

Dor shook her head. "Oh no, none of that now. Please call me Dor. That goes for you too, Ms. Dowd."

"Okay…Dor." Florence made a face like she'd sucked on a lemon. I still didn't know why she was so prickly about formal titles, but I appreciated her willingness to bend for Dor.

"And as for you, Ms. Blume…." Dor eyed me up and down. "I have a few things I'd like to discuss with you. Privately." I followed her towards the edge of the woods. "I've seen your newspaper article and listened to you on the radio."

"Oh dear," I said.

She laughed. "Yes, probably not your finest hour. But I know that you're a good librarian and an even better researcher. Look at what you uncovered this week." She shook her head, but I could tell she was impressed. "I want to make you an offer."

"What kind of offer?" I asked.

"Well, you can continue leading the collections on the Calverton campus if you'd like. Or, if you'd prefer, you can handle my personal collection."

"Your personal collection? Is it not on the campus?" I asked.

She gave me a mysterious smile. "Not all of it. Not my most important pieces. What you saw in the collection are things my family has brought back from all over the world. Like the Poe books. But what I have is more private."

My face burned red with excitement. "You mean like your family's personal archives?"

She nodded. "Yes, exactly. I have our diaries, photos, scrapbooks, and other documents. It goes back generations. And, of course, I have my personal collection of books that I didn't want to put into the library. At least not yet. I still have some good years left in me."

"Wow," was all I could muster.

"So instead of working for Calverton Industries, you'd be working for me. And me alone," she said. "Although I'll warn you that a few people have called me 'prickly.'" She laughed, but I wasn't sure if that was a genuine concern or not.

Then, another thought dawned on me. "Wait, just you. Not for Leo?"

A bigger smile charted across her face. "Correct. Just me."

I looked back to the picnic tables. Leo stole glances our way. If he wasn't my boss anymore, then that meant we could try dating each other. My heart raced faster in my chest. Then again, what would it mean if I worked for his grandma and we broke up?

"I'm not sure. I mean…your grandson…" I stumbled over my words.

Dor leaned closer to me. "I love Leo more than life itself, but how do I say this? If you break his heart, he can handle himself. He's a grown-up. And I assume you are, too?"

I nodded. She winked at me.

"Well, what do you think? Will you be my personal librarian? I'll more than match your current pay, but you'd be working in my house, not at the campus."

I sighed. My whole body relaxed at the idea of not having to return there. I thought that after working at the Library of Congress that I had been used to dealing with big bureaucratic institutions, but I'd never encountered such a volatile mix of protesters, small-town politics, and murdering board members. Plus, getting an increase in pay meant I could help Azalea more with the Wildflower Inn.

"Will it leave the collections on the campus in jeopardy?" Regardless of my personal feelings, I didn't want to leave a vacuum in leadership there.

"Oh, I think that Ms. Dowd might do a good job managing them. Don't you? And now that I'm back, I think we can get some more people working for her."

Florence may have been a stickler, but she loved the collections. I trusted she would see them cared for properly.

"I'm interested," I said.

"Great. We'll get together soon to go over the details. You deserve a couple days to rest after all this turmoil."

I appreciated her offer. "If you don't mind, I'd like to tell Leo."

"Go right ahead," Dor said.

With that, I waltzed back over to the group, went right up to Leo, and planted an enormous kiss on his lips. He tensed up in surprise but then relaxed into it. He took me in his arms and swooped me around into a swoon for a deeper kiss. I heard the others cheering us on.

Chapter Thirty-Eight

fter the festival booths closed late in the afternoon, the food trucks, carnival games, and music kept going. After sending everyone home, I stuck around to finish closing our booth and also to learn the winners of the foods and crafts competition. As I worked on filling a box back up, I heard a voice.

"Oh, Juniper! I've been manning the cat rescue booth, but I meant to find you."

I turned to find Luna. She carried a cat in her arms. "This is Thistle." If I wasn't mistaken, Thistle was one of the rescues I'd seen in the newspaper office. The cat wore a little handkerchief around her neck, saying, "Foster Failure." As much as I didn't enjoy seeing Luna, I was happy to see Thistle had found a forever home.

"What do you want?" I meant the question to sound innocuous, but it came out with more venom. Luna's treatment of me in both the newspaper and radio had been unfair.

"I came to apologize." She found an empty seat. Thistle climbed on her lap. I sat down beside them in the second chair.

"Is that so?"

"I haven't been completely honest with you."

"Oh?"

She sighed dramatically. "Florence Dowd is my best friend." Luna had to be at least twenty years younger than Florence. I also couldn't imagine anyone as opposite a person from Florence as Luna. However, this case had taught me that people were often not as they seemed. I shouldn't make snap judgments. "She's been my neighbor for a long time, and we've also been playing tennis together for probably five years now. She's like my big sister."

"I didn't know that."

"She had complained a lot about you becoming the director of the upcoming museum. She said you were too young, too close to Leo Calverton, and…well, a few other things I won't repeat."

"Is that why you cast me in such a negative light in the press?" I asked.

She nodded. "Florence was really depressed. She'd gone through some sort of big breakup, and then you came in, and it really soured her. I felt so awful for her. I guess it soured me, too."

She hadn't seemed to know that Big Al was behind the breakup, but I didn't think it was appropriate for me to share that, even if Luna was Florence's best friend.

"I'm super empathetic, and her being down and out really put me on edge. I shouldn't have treated you that way. You didn't deserve it."

"I appreciate that. Although honestly…." I breathed deeply. "I deserved it."

Luna arched an eyebrow, almost as if she expected I was tricking her.

"You weren't wrong, Luna. Taking on this project put me in over my head. I've never run a museum before, let alone started a new one. I didn't know what I was doing. And I didn't know how corrupt the Calverton Foundation board was. So, I'm bowing out. I'm returning to what I know and love best – being a librarian."

Her eyes grew big. "Wait, you're ditching the Calvertons?"

I opened my mouth to say something, but then I shut it. I didn't think Dor would want it getting out everywhere that I was her new personal librarian.

"What are you going to put out in the paper about Brandy and her dad?" I asked instead.

Luna lit up. "A special section devoted to the murders. And don't worry, this time, you'll be cast as the hero."

I put up my hands. "Oh, please. I'd rather not be cast as anything."

"But you've only been in Rose Mallow since the start of the summer, and you've already solved…" She counted on her fingers. "Three. Three murders! You're a modern-day Nancy Drew."

"I'm just a librarian."

"Just a librarian." Luna shook her head in disbelief. Thistle pawed at her hands for attention. I leaned over and gave her some generous pets. "I'd love to do an official interview with you. Both for the paper and on the radio again." She leaned closer to me. Her smile widened.

"Thank you, but no thank you," I replied.

"Well, let me know when you're ready to change your mind. I promise this time will be better. For real." She winked before standing up and walking away.

Call me unrealistic, but I believed her.

Chapter Thirty-Nine

After winning the blue ribbon for her blintzes, Azalea celebrated by taking Violet, Clover, and me for ice cream. We wandered along the boardwalk, enjoying a soft breeze off the Chesapeake Bay. As I finished up my cone, I noticed we had ended up in front of Boardwalk Books. It was still open, and I spotted Nuri working at the counter.

"Are you okay if we stop here for a minute?" I asked.

"I love this store. I'm glad it's been able to stay open. I'm going to check out the used cookbooks," Azalea said.

"I want a book," said Violet.

"Sure thing, sweetheart. I bet we can find something for you."

"Oh, but is it dog-friendly?" I asked, looking at Clover. He ran up to me and danced upright, bouncing against my shins.

"Of course we are," said Nuri, coming to the door. She held out a dog biscuit. Suddenly, she was Clover's newest best friend.

"How are you doing?" I asked.

She shrugged. "Could be better, but honestly, it could be a lot worse. You already know that the police took away the mysterious shelf that connected Boardwalk Books to Flower Power. I told them everything I knew and gave them the security camera footage, too. But they said I could keep most of the store open. We can't mess with that part over there yet." She motioned through the doorway to the taped-off area behind the counter.

I followed Nuri inside. Today, she continued her punk rock vibe with a vintage shirt for another band I didn't recognize and a weathered leather vest. I wasn't sure how she wasn't hot in this thick September heat, but she didn't seem to mind. She had also changed the rings. Each finger showed off one letter or symbol on a thick gold ring. One hand spelled out NURI, followed by a heart. The other read BOOKS.

"How's Big Al's family?" I asked.

"As good as one can be, given the circumstances. They don't want to keep the store now that he's gone, so I'm buying it from them."

"You are?" My voice was half excited and half nervous for her.

She nodded. "Yeah, and then I'm going to expand. I'll knock down that wall and move into the space next door." She motioned towards the wall between Boardwalk Books and Flower Power.

"You're going to buy Flower Power?"

"Thinking about it. With Teddy and Brandy arrested, the family wants to get rid of the store. Although I'd probably continue to stock some flowers, too," Nuri replied.

"That makes sense. Good for you." I was glad for her ambition and enthusiasm. Part of me wanted to ask her more about what had happened between her leaving library school so suddenly and ending up here, but I figured that could wait until another day.

"Thank you. I plan to apply for one of those grants the Calverton family is promising," she said.

"Yeah, so do I," said Azalea, walking up with an armload of books. "The buzz is that they will really make a difference for all of us. It sounds like it will help me keep the Wildflower Inn."

"How did you get so many books so fast?" I didn't think we'd talked all that long.

She shrugged. "I couldn't decide on which cookbook so I'm getting all of them."

"Great!" said Nuri. I looked forward to trying Azalea's delicious attempts.

Like mother, like daughter, as Violet followed up with almost as large of a stack of books. Clover followed from behind. The stack towered over her uneasily, but she navigated the bookstore with ease. She dropped them on the floor in front of the counter. Amazingly, they remained stacked neatly in place.

"All of those?" Azalea asked.

"All of those," repeated Violet.

We all laughed.

"Did you need some help with that?"

We turned to see Rory in the doorway.

"Rory!" Azalea nearly flew to him. He welcomed her with open arms. Her embrace must have caused him some pain, given the grimaces on his face, but he held on to her tightly.

"I heard you won the blue ribbon for your blintzes. I'm so proud of you," he said. "I'm sorry I couldn't make it. I was in a weekend session of physical therapy. But every day, I'm getting stronger."

"I know you are. I'm so proud of you, too." She fell into his arms, and he closed his eyes, holding her.

"Daddy! Daddy!" Violet pulled at his pant legs.

"Hey there, kiddo." He kneeled beside her and ruffled her hair.

"We got ice cream," she said.

"You did? Was it good?" he asked.

She thought about the question and then replied, "So so. I'm still hungry."

"Still hungry?" Azalea and Rory said at the same time. Everyone laughed.

"I wanna go to the Purple Oyster," Violet said.

"Of course you do," replied Azalea, shaking her head.

"Well, she is a growing kid," Rory replied. "We could all go."

"Go ahead," I said. "Clover and I will catch up with you later. Take your time. Grab one of her amazing doggie biscuits for him."

Azalea smiled and nodded. "Nuri, can I come back for the cookbooks?"

I waved her away. "I'll get them and bring them back to the Wildflower. Have a good time."

"Thanks, Juniper." She grabbed Rory's left hand and Violet's right hand, and they walked out of the bookstore together. It made my heart nearly burst to see their family coming back together. There was so much love flowing through them. I almost felt sorry for Deputy Torres. He obviously cared deeply about my sister, but it seemed unlikely that was going to go anywhere now. I remained Team Azalea, and if that meant her getting back together with Rory, I couldn't imagine a happier ending for them.

Nuri and I exchanged a look. She was smiling ear to ear. "I look forward to finding a love like that one day," she said.

"I'm sure you'll find the perfect woman," I replied.

"Yeah, I hope so. How are things going with you and Leo?"

I shrugged and tried to appear nonchalant. "I guess I will find out now."

"Oh, don't smile so coyly. You're excited, aren't you?"

"Well, yeah." I could feel my cheeks burning red. Nuri simply laughed.

After paying for the cookbooks, I headed back to the Wildflower Inn, eager to find out more about dating Leo and what treasures his grandmother had in her private collection. The thought of cataloging diaries, photo albums, scrapbooks, and letters made my rare librarian heart sing. Not only was Rose Mallow starting to really feel like home, but I believed that I might have finally found my place here.

* * *

Leo worked quickly. Within a few weeks, there was a call for grants to help local businesses. Azalea applied for a significant grant for the Wildflower Inn. The Port Chesapeake project vanished. While I heard the protests stopped, community sentiment remained tense. Even Azalea remained cautious about the Calvertons, reminding me that Trojan horses came in all shapes and sizes.

Fortunately, Azalea didn't mind that Leo came over to the Wildflower Inn frequently. Since he was about to head off to another archaeological dig, he spent as much time with us as possible. He also promised me that he was looking into Eric's mother's immigration status and would make sure she was taken care of. He reassured me that Eric would keep his job.

Leo and I also met up at his grandmother's place, where I quickly fell into the rhythm of my new job. Digging into her family's personal papers was a much better match for my interests than managing an enormous start-up museum with the potential for over a hundred staff. I still cringed at the thought. It was the right job for someone, but not for me.

Harold hung out at Dor's home regularly as well. Since his home was a lost cause, he moved into a condo near the town center. Fortunately, Dor offered him a plot to continue gardening since he had promised Florence a rematch at next year's festival.

I talked to Dor about doing some oral histories of her life and family. She promised to think about it but warned that much of her life remained confidential. If you ask me, I think she liked the aura of mysteriousness that came with being a retired spy. Or whatever her actual job was. Neither she nor Harold would reveal much.

From time to time, I also helped Nuri out at Broadway Books. She, too, applied for one of the Calverton Foundation grants, hoping it would allow her to take over the former Flower Power space. I couldn't wait to see her store expand. Other local places sought funds, too, including La Artesa and the Purple Oyster Coffee Shop. I felt a sense of pride in knowing that I had a hand in Rose Mallow's revitalization. I thought about Teddy Rivers' warning that the grants may come with strings attached, but hopefully, that would prove false.

Florence and Eric continued their work with the library. Florence was named the new executive director, and I heard she soon had a solid staff working with her. Before long, historical markers sprung up across the town, sharing the area's history and features. While a few of the signs mentioned the Calvertons, most focused on the stories of the people who lived and worked in this beautiful place. There was even one recognizing the Rivers' land that became the park and woods. My former colleagues had done a great job celebrating the town's heritage. I couldn't wait to see what would happen next with the museum project.

Although I had only moved here a few months earlier, I couldn't believe that I had ever wanted to be anywhere but Rose Mallow. Interestingly, the town's namesake flower is also known as Swamp Hibiscus. That this brightly colored beauty can flourish even in the most unexpected of places gave me hope to do the same.

Acknowledgements

Thank you to the so many people who made *The Tell-Tale Homicide* possible, including my agent Cindy Bullard of Birch Literary, Shawn Reilly Simmons of Level Best Books, my beta readers Cathy Wiley, Rosalie Spielman, Nancy G., Ann N., and QNPoohBear, along with the rest of my street team, the Silver Sleuths, my writing group including Cathy Wiley, Rosalie Spielman, Marcia Talley, Debbi Mack, Becky Hutchinson, and Mary-Ellen Hughes, the Sisters in Crime Chesapeake Chapter (especially the Zoom writing group), Kristen Harbeson, my mom, and my family, especially my husband Matt and our kid Nate.

Thank you to everyone reading! I'm grateful to all of you, especially those who have left reviews, asked their local library and bookstore for my books, follow me on social media, subscribe to my newsletter, and participate in the Silver Sleuths team. You all are amazing! If you haven't signed up yet, you can do so at www.daphnesilver.com. When you join the newsletter, you'll also get the free short story "A Midsummer's Night Scheme."

A Note from the Author

Being a bit of a Poe-natic myself, it was fun to add in tidbits about Edgar Allan Poe. He had deep roots in Maryland, as his great-grandfather moved to Baltimore in 1755. Poe, however, didn't live in Baltimore until 1832. While here, he wrote some of his earliest stories, including "MS. Found in a Bottle" and "Berenice." It was also in Baltimore where he married his younger first cousin Virginia Clemm in 1835. Her tragic early death from tuberculosis is thought to serve as the inspiration for his poem "Annabel Lee." Today, the home he lived in has become the Edgar Allan Poe House and Museum.

In 1849, Poe showed up unexpectedly in Baltimore, semiconscious in Fell's Point on Election Day. Dressed in strange clothes, he was found in a gutter outside a tavern serving as a polling site. He never fully regained consciousness to explain what happened to him, and unfortunately, he died on October 7th. There continue to be over a dozen theories purporting to explain his unusual death. You can visit his (and Virginia's) grave at Westminster Hall in Baltimore.

Curious to learn about the art and science of deciphering codes? The National Cryptologic Museum is also in Maryland, run by the National Security Administration. Housed in the former Colony Seven Motel, many people suspect that the building used to be ground zero for spies. You can also pop into Washington, D.C. to visit the International Spy Museum for more about spy history.

Part of my research into poisons included a tour of the Stabler-Leadbetter Apothecary Museum in Alexandria, Virginia. Although the museum houses a significant collection of herbal and medicinal remedies, many of these drugs become toxic if used improperly. As the Swiss physician Paracelsus said in 1538, "All things are poison, and nothing is without poison; the dosage alone makes it so a thing is not a poison."

An unexpected research rabbit hole for this story was exploring radio call signs. It turned out to be hard naming Rose Mallow's radio station because of the rules surrounding them. I learned how starting in 1921, stations east of the Mississippi River start with "W" while those to the west begin with "K." Believe it or not, I have another local museum recommendation! The small but mighty National Capital Radio and Television Museum is in Bowie, Maryland, not far from D.C.

Finally, I loosely based the Rose Mallow Festival on the Labor Day Festival in Greenbelt, Maryland, where I live. Begun in 1955, this is our biggest city festival each year, including rides, vendors, parades, shows, a used book sale, and competitions. While I'm not sure that anyone has ever submitted blintzes before, I believe it'd be a wonderful addition.

Recipes are found on my website at
www.daphnesilver.com/recipes.

Join My Newsletter

Join my newsletter list at www.daphnesilver.com to get the free short story, A MIDSUMMER'S NIGHT SCHEME! A rum runner's mansion, a 1623 copy of Shakespeare's "First Folio," and a performance of a *Midsummer's Night Dream* set in a speakeasy… what more could a history loving librarian want? Juniper Blume had simply planned a fun night out with her sister Azalea. She certainly didn't expect to stumble upon a rare books' puzzle in a classic locked room style mystery. Will she figure out the truth before the final curtain drops?

About the Author

Daphne Silver is the Agatha Award-winning author of the Rare Books Cozy Mystery series. She's worked more than twenty years in museums and symphonies and has the great fortune of being married to a librarian. When she's not writing, she's drawing and painting. She lives in Maryland with her family. Although she's not much of a baker, she won't ever turn down a sweet lokshen kugel.

SOCIAL MEDIA HANDLES:
  www.facebook.com/daphnesilverbooks
  www.instagram.com/daphnesilverbooks

AUTHOR WEBSITE:
  www.daphnesilver.com

Also by Daphne Silver

As Daphne Silver:

Crime and Parchment (Level Best Books, 2023)

As Lauren R. Silberman:

The Jewish Community of Baltimore (Arcadia Publishing, 2007)

Wicked Baltimore: Charm City Sin and Scandal (History Press, 2011)

Wild Women of Maryland: Grit and Gumption in the Free State (History Press, 2015)

Chesapeake Crimes: Storm Warning (2016)

Fish or Cut Bait: A Guppy Anthology (2015) (as Lauren Moffett)